Blue As Blue Jeans

Fran Stewart

Blue As Blue Jeans

ISBN: 978-0-9749876-7-5 (13)
0-9749876-7-0 (10)

This is a work of fiction. Any resemblance to any person living or dead is purely coincidental.

This book was printed in the United States of America.

Doggie in the Window Publications
PO Box 1565
Duluth GA 30096
www.DoggieintheWindow.biz

Praise for Fran Stewart's Biscuit McKee Mystery Series:

"Stewart's Martinsville has such richness to it."
—Steven Macon, reviewing for The KitchenSink Journal
www.KitchenSinkJournal.com

"Delightfully told and cleverly plotted"
—Jean C. Keating, author of *Paw Prints through the Years*
www.AstraPublishers.com

"Warm, friendly . . . kept me in suspense"
—Wanda Brown, Management Consultant, Director of The Enneagram Institute of Georgia

"Even poets, those lachrymose wearers of black, will find Fran Stewart's work a lively and engaging distraction from Peering Morosely Into The Mists. Get a latte and relax. Stewart endears."
—Steve Shields, author of *Daimonion Sonata*
www.StevenOwenShields.com

"Outstanding talent"
—Rick Prigmore, author of *The Joy of Living*

Praise for *Yellow as Legal Pads*

(Winner of the "IPPY" - Independent Publishers Book Award)

"Ms. Stewart weaves a carefully crafted, intricate murder mystery of betrayal and mistaken identity here. And, unlike many 'cat mysteries,' this writer acknowledges that a cat is not a cute human in feline skin. Her cat is warm and loving in a most cat-like manner. Most impressive is her deft handling of what could be a very complicated chronology. She handles all with skill, and she'll keep you turning pages to the very last word. Give it a try if you love murder mysteries, cats, or seeing a writer at the top of her game."
— Brian Jay Corrigan, author of *The Poet of Loch Ness*
www.brianjaycorrigan.com

Books by Fran Stewart

The Biscuit McKee Mystery Series:

Orange as Marmalade

Yellow as Legal Pads,

Green as a Garden Hose

Blue as Blue Jeans

Indigo as an Iris

Poetry:

Resolution

For Children:

As Orange As Marmalade/
Es Naranja Como Mermelada
(a bilingual book)

Non-Fiction:

From The Tip of My Pen: a manual for writers

Dedication:

to Darlene Carter
you know why

and
in memory of my parents
who, like all parents,
did the best they knew how to do

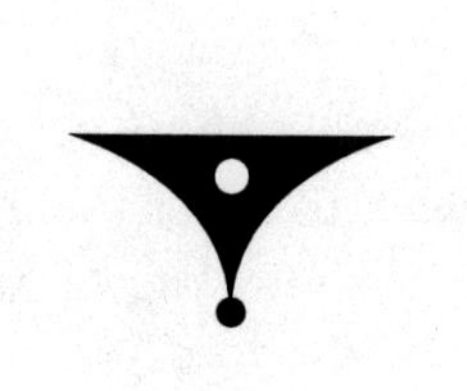

My Gratitude List

Cowan's Book Nook in Ellijay, **Humpus Bumpus Books** in Cumming, **The Singin' Bean Coffee House & Eatery** in Lawrenceville, and **Quigley's Rare Books** in Dahlonega. Melinda & Barry, Paul, Cindy & Patty, and Tom all believed in me, and carried my books here in Georgia when nobody else was paying any attention whatsoever. I will be eternally grateful, and as long as I have breath in my body, I will keep encouraging people to support independent bookstores.

My niece and good friend, Erica D. Jensen, who taught me after all these years how to make good brownies.

The folks at Docielo (www.dolcielo.com) who make even better brownies than I do (and that's saying a lot).

My editor, Nanette Littlestone, who this time did not make me eliminate a character. Hooray! She did make me change a few of them, but *Blue* is a better book as a result. One comment after my first draft was, "Does this woman have *no* redeeming qualities whatsoever?"

Rodale's All-New Encyclopedia of Organic Gardening © 1992. At least, it was all-new then, but I'm still using it and appreciating it after more than a decade.

And, finally, my heartfelt thanks to the amazingly patient and incredibly helpful folks at Doggie in the Window Publications.

From my house beside a creek
on the back side of Hog Mountain, Georgia,
Fran Stewart
June 2006

Preface

Mark Twain's daughter reflected, years after her parents had died, "Mama loved religion, but Papa loved cats." Indeed, in the opening paragraphs of his *Pudd'nhead Wilson,* Twain wrote that a home may be perfectly acceptable and proper, but without a well-petted and pampered cat, "how can it prove title?" The cat is the only domestic animal denied a mention in the Bible, and it seems that, until recently, writers (despite their personal affinity for the feline) have tended to avoid giving the cat a place in literature.

While horses and dogs have enjoyed the literary spotlight in classic works such as *Black Beauty* and *Old Yeller,* to name but two, the much-maligned cat has been relegated to playing the heavy against a legion of tricky cartoon mice and birds. Though it is true that Poe wrote "The Black Cat," anyone familiar with it knows how very little that story deals with its title character (a creature that serves the literary function of an alarm bell). It is therefore with pleasure that we can welcome the fourth installment of Fran Stewart's "rainbow" mystery series featuring the wholly feline Marmalade and her human companion, Biscuit McKee.

Unlike so many cat stories that turn cats into cutesy sleuths, the Biscuit McKee Mystery Series allows Marmalade to be a cat. Anyone who truly knows cats will appreciate Marmalade—McKee's wholly independent, sincerely loving, completely feline, empathic partner in life and crime.

There is one other element to these "rainbow" mysteries that will delight the fan of literary excursion. While each book has its own sense of completion, and the reader will find a satisfying resolution to each installment, there seems to be something else at work below the surface. Very much like the *Harry Potter* series, Biscuit McKee appears to be solving one mystery after another in what is actually a much larger puzzle—one that only begins to emerge by reading all of the books. Therefore, if you are new to this series, do please enjoy your trip to Martinsville in *Blue as Blue Jeans,* but don't stop here. Go back and see what happened in *Orange as Marmalade, Yellow as Legal Pads,* and *Green as a Garden Hose.* Then, with the rest of us, wait in anticipation for the rest of the rainbow to reveal its colors.

Brian J. Corrigan
Award-winning author of *The Poet of Loch Ness*
and Professor of Renaissance Literature
North Georgia State College
www.brianjaycorrigan.com

The People of Martinsville

Some of us are not people

Biscuit McKee, librarian in Martinsville, Georgia
her 2nd husband - **Bob** Sheffield, the town cop
I call him Softfoot
her sister - **Glaze** McKee
Smellsweet
her son - **Scott** Brandy
her daughter - **Sally**
Sally's husband – **Jason** Atkinson
her cat - **Marmalade**
Excuse me? Widelap is my human
her **Mom** - Ivy Martelson McKee, a potter
her grandparents - **Grandma** & **Grandpa** Martelson

Ariel Montgomery, student & deli employee

Annie McGill, owner of *Heal Thyself* health store

Auntie Blue - Biscuit's aunt

Clara Martin, self-styled First Lady of Martinsville

Doodle-Doo - Maggie Pontiac's rooster

Easton Hastings, a redhead
her sister - **Louise** Hastings Cronin
her father - **Rupert**

Elizabeth Hoskins, former owner of 213 Beechnut Lane
her son - **Lyle**

Glenda Harvey - Biscuit's friend from childhood

Henry Pursey, minister of The Old Church

Ida & Ralph Peterson, grocers

Madeleine Ames, writer of thrillers
her brother - **Father John** Ames, priest at St. Theresa's

Matthew Olsen - Biscuit's next-door neighbor

Melissa Tarkington, owner of *Azalea House Bed & Breakfast*

Melody Cummings, town clerk

Myrtle Hoskins Snelling, reporter

Nathan Young, family physician

Paul Welsh - Biscuit's neighbor across the street

The three "Petunias" (library volunteers)
Esther Anderson
Sadie Russell Masters (& her husband - Wallis)
Rebecca Jo Sheffield, Bob's mother

Radio Ralph Towers, announcer for WRRT

Reebok Garner, a cheerful young man

Roger Johnson, sign-keeper/would-be musician, garbage collector

Sam Hastings, **Bobby** Sheffield & **Tommy** Parkman (in 1955)

Sharon Armitage, hairdresser
her husband - **Carl**, kenaf farmer & gas station owner
her manicurist - **Pumpkin**

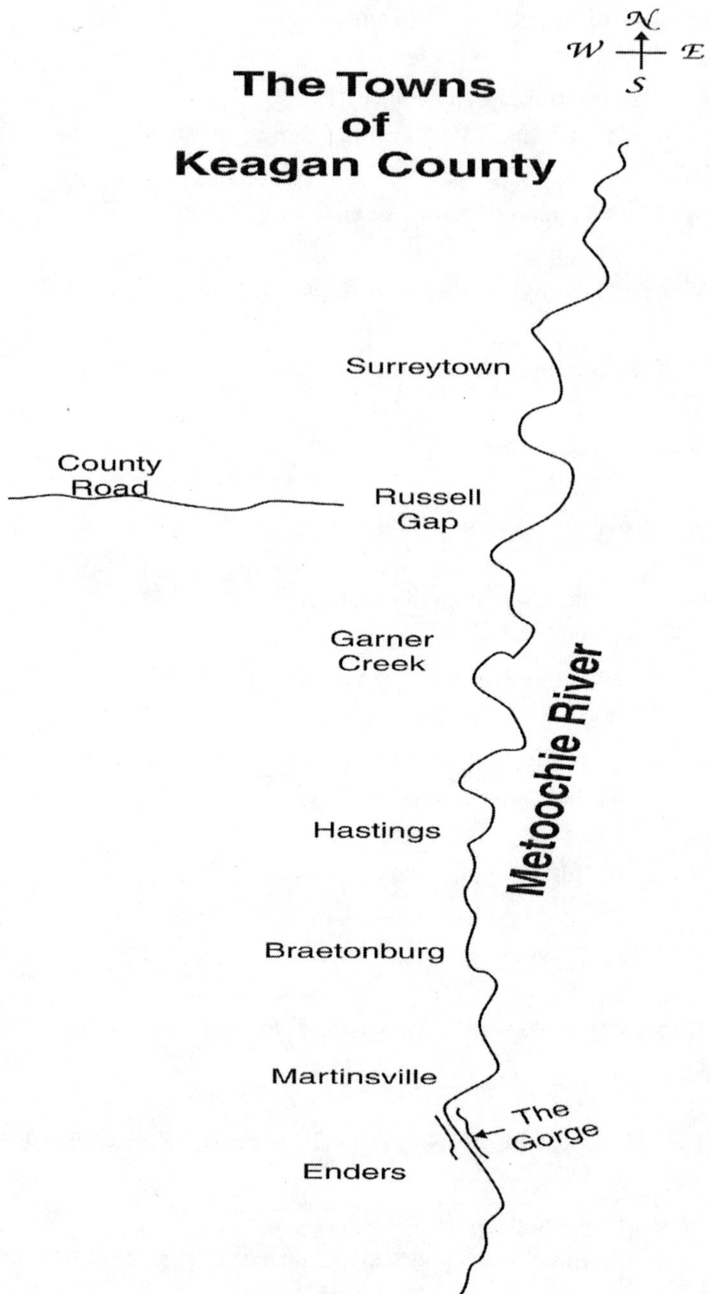
N
W
E
S
The Towns
of
Keagan County
Surreytown
County
Road
Russell
Gap
Garner
Creek
Metoochie River
Hastings
Braetonburg
Martinsville
The
Gorge
Enders

Part I
Discovery

Chapter 1

Friday, November 1, 1996

THREE WEEKS OF almost constant downpour was ridiculous. I liked rain, normally. This was abnormal. Three or four days in a row was the usual max for northeastern Georgia, and the river that paralleled First Street could handle that amount of water. Those two and a half extra weeks, though, had swollen the little Metoochie River into a treacherous invader, ready, if it even once breached the upper reaches of the town park, to inundate the businesses perched in their long row like bedraggled sparrows on a telephone line. The owners, sparrow-like themselves, fluttered and fumed and conferred. Wooden barriers, some thought. Sandbags, others decided. And now there was a dead body, tangled in the remains of the once-sturdy town dock.

Three weeks ago, the placid wide pool that was a town gathering place in the summer had been a quiet place, never visited by boaters because of the enormous rocks at each end that blocked river traffic of any sort from both directions. Usually the Metoochie passed between the boulders on the south end and meandered through a narrow gap into the Gorge, as we called it around here. Now, though, the storm-fed torrents had swept the town's thirty-foot-long redwood dock downstream a hundred yards or so and jammed one end of it into the gap between two of the larger boulders. The boulders no longer broke up the water's flow, no longer stopped river traffic. The rocks were still there, of course, but now a goodly depth of water coursed above them.

For the past week, kayakers gloried in the new speed of this rampaging river. The more timid ones, although I couldn't imagine anyone timid venturing into a kayak, paddled into the shore and heaved their boats up what was left of the beach onto First Street. The others, which meant most of them, kept going, plunging into the gauntlet between the overbearing cliffs lining the Gorge. Even above the roar of the storm, shoppers on First Street could hear their bellows of challenge, of delight, of terror as their small craft were buffeted by the treacherous currents that had never been seen before on the Metoochie.

The rest of us, particularly those who lived, as Bob and I did, higher on the hillside between the river and the surrounding cliffs, could hunker down inside with a hot cup of tea and a purring cat, . . .

My name is Marmalade.

. . . but Bob was the town cop.

He is Softfoot.

Carl Armitage, who owned the gas station and the town movie theater, called Bob with the news that one of the kayakers had found a body wrapped in the wreckage of the dock. I could tell Bob wanted to stay inside. Cops can't always choose what they want, though. Poor Nathan, the town doctor, would have to be out there, too, inspecting the body to determine the cause of death.

I call him Goodhands.

Bob kissed me somewhat absentmindedly, which didn't surprise me at all, considering where he was headed. It was to his credit that he remembered to kiss me at all. We'd already been married six months. My first husband, dead these last six years, had quit remembering the goodbye kisses after only two or three months. I loved Sol, but Bob was a much more attentive husband, even when he was headed out to look at a dead body.

I pulled the collar of his raincoat a bit higher. Rainwater down the neck is no fun at all, particularly this rainwater. The first two weeks, the rain had been Georgia-warm, but as the storms continued, those balmy gentle showers turned to a nasty wind-driven deluge that left fingers icy and faces chapped. I thoroughly enjoyed my job, but right then I was delighted that my library was closed for repair work.

It is better here, Widelap. I do not want to get my feet wet.

I'm the librarian here in the little town of Martinsville, Georgia, tucked so far away in a dead-end valley that tourists never find us. I married Bob Sheffield, the town cop, six months ago. My mother is a potter who named her two daughters Bisque and Glaze. In grade school my friends started calling me Biscuit and the nickname stuck. When I married Sol Brandy, my first husband, I'd kept my maiden name. Biscuit Brandy was more than I could bear. And then, after I was engaged to Bob, I was doodling on a piece of scrap paper one day and saw what my new monogram would look like if I became Biscuit Sheffield. So I kept McKee. I never mentioned that to Bob, by the way.

When I took on the job as librarian here I inherited Marmalade, the orange and white library cat.

What do you mean? You inherited me? I adopted you.

She solved the mouse problem at the library and kept me company there and at home. She has the loudest purr I've ever heard.

And you still do not listen to me.

The library had been in existence only a year and a half, and already it needed some repair work on the reference shelves. But that meant I could stay indoors and Marmalade could take a vacation from mouse patrol for the day.

I closed the heavy front door behind Bob, watched him trudge down the sidewalk, past the remains of what had been a flower bed yesterday morning. Practically nobody in Martinsville had a garage. The old houses weren't built that way. We sure could have used one, though. Bob would be soaked before he made it to the curb. I returned to the kitchen where Marmalade purred loudly on the chair I had recently abandoned. The remains of breakfast littered the little round table that nestled into the nook of the bay window. Maybe just one more cup of tea, I thought. I cleared off the more revolting of the dirty dishes–dead scrambled egg is disgusting once it dries on a plate–rinsed them and set them in a pan of hot soapy water. The phone rang as I poured my tea.

"Hey, Biscuit, this is Myrtle. How you folks doing there?" Myrtle Hoskins Snelling, our town's very own reporter for the *Keagan County Record*, was seventy years old, but that never slowed her down.

I am doing well, thank you.

I thought about answering truthfully. The rain had slowed me down. I felt creaky and slightly grumpy. But she hadn't meant how are you *really* doing. It was just something Georgia folks say to start a conversation. "Fine, Myrtle," I answered as Marmalade purred beside me. "And you?"

"Fine." She could have had shingles, and she still would have said *fine*. "What's this about a dead body?"

It hadn't taken her long. "Who called you?" I asked.

"Clara Martin."

The self-appointed town crier. I should have known. Her husband, Hubbard Martin, was the chair of the town council, a position that had stayed in the Martin family ever since the town was founded in 1745. Clara's self-appointed title was the First Lady of Martinsville. You could hear the capital letters ringing. Humph. Big fish in a little pond, if you asked me. I put thoughts of Clara aside and turned my attention back to Myrtle.

"We don't know anything yet," I told her. "Carl called Bob a few minutes ago. Some kayaker found a body near the town dock."

"Nonsense," Myrtle snorted. "The dock got washed away last week in this dratted rain."

"Well, what's left of it is stuck near the entrance to the Gorge, and the body was tangled in there. Somebody must have fallen in the river and drowned. Bob's gone to look."

"All right," she sighed. "I guess I'll get out my raincoat and my bumbershoot."

"Myrtle, stay home. Your umbrella won't last long in these winds." I could hear them howling outside the kitchen window. The woods that bordered on our back yard looked like they were staggering home after an all-night binge. Myrtle would be lucky if she could even stand up in such a ferocious gale.

"Duty calls," she proclaimed. The dial tone punctuated her declaration.

I replaced the phone in its cradle. "I like that woman, but I think she's mildly nuts," I said in the general direction of Marmalade.

She pats me nicely when she greets me.

Marmalade purred back at me. Her sweet little rumble sounded almost like an answer . . .

Mouse droppings!

. . . and when she snorted, I could imagine her arguing with me. I scooped her up and settled down with my tea to watch the sheets of water lash the windows.

What a terrible month October had been. Oh, maybe not right at first. But it certainly wasn't a month I ever wanted to live over again. And then, to end with a drowning like this. Well, it was just awful, that was all. My Grandma Martelson always used to tell me to be like an iris, tough enough to stand anything. So, I thought as I sipped my tea, I guess I could stand October. Now that it was over and done with. It really started on the last day of September, though. That was the day I called my sister, Glaze.

Chapter 2

September 30, 1996

THREE YEARS AGO, when Grandma Martelson's dementia had reached the point where my mother just couldn't handle her anymore, we'd had a family gathering–Auntie Blue (christened Beulah, but nobody called her that) joined in by phone from Colorado, where she was living at the time–and decided to put Grandma in the Happy Days Nursing Home where Grandpa was already living. He'd been there ever since his stroke. When he recovered enough to be put onto the assisted-living floor, he regularly terrorized the nursing staff by pinching their fannies and groping them when they were helping him in and out of his wheelchair. If he'd had an ounce of good humor, they probably would have put up with the situation, but as it was, all the female nurses refused to deal with him, and he now was in the sole care of the two male orderlies and the one male nurse in the facility.

Fortunately Grandma was in a separate room. The women all lived on the third floor. The men on the second. She hardly ever knew what day it was or where she was, or who we were. But there were moments of lucidity when she would come back from a rambling story she'd been telling. The story would start with her as an adult on the farm in Georgia and in a sentence or two would become the tale of a trip she took to Memphis when she was a young girl, the farthest she ever traveled from her home in the Metoochie River Valley. Then she'd look up at us as we sat there trying to make sense of her ramblings and she'd say, "I don't know what I'm talking about, do I?"

"Well, Grandma," I'd tell her, "maybe you do, but I sure can't figure it out!" Then we'd both laugh until she faded out again and forgot what was so funny.

Every few weeks, my mom and I would meet at the nursing home and load my grandparents into both our cars–each one in a front seat–to take them to the old house in Braetonburg where I grew up, just three blocks down the road from the huge farm house they'd lived in all their married life. We'd serve them lunch with Grandma sitting in the wing chair in the living room and Grandpa in his wheelchair, both of them swathed in big white towels to catch the inevitable dribbles. We'd try to carry on a conversation, but sometimes it was enough just to let them look around the living room. Or let Grandma walk slowly out to the flower beds in the front yard.

Then we'd put them back in the two cars and take them home to Happy Days.

I WAS ALWAYS in and out of my grandma's kitchen from the time I could walk. She was a stern woman, but I loved her. I had the feeling, though, that there were private parts of her life that she would never share. Sometimes I'd drop by the farmhouse and she'd be down on her knees in her iris patch–the one I'd helped her plant when I was a kid–weeding and humming under her breath. She loved those flowers. "They're tough," she used to tell me. "Tough enough to stand anything. Anything." She'd look at me as if gauging whether or not I'd absorbed her message, but I was never quite sure what the underlying message was.

Once I asked my mom about it, and she said that Grandma

had had a rough life. Heck, I *knew* that. Farm wives always had rough lives.

Glaze and I used to head for the cookie jar every time we went into the farmhouse. I have no idea how Grandma managed to do all that baking, what with her other chores, but somehow the old yellow crock with pink and purple daisies painted on the side of it, was always full. Oatmeal cookies. Sugar cookies. Simple old-fashioned treats, but ones that Glaze and I treasured. I can't recall a time that I didn't want to go to Grandma's house, but Glaze gave up going when she was about six and I was maybe eleven. Even the promise of her favorite sugar cookies couldn't lure her there. We finally owned a TV set, and all she wanted to do was sit and watch it after school, even though there was only one channel. So I'd go see Grandma by myself.

GRANDPA WAS SO frail now and his health so tenuous, nobody could figure out how he went on living. I secretly thought he was too ornery to die, but I didn't voice that opinion nowadays. I had complained to my mom about his attitude once, when I was in my teens. "Don't be too quick to judge," she told me. "You don't know the whole story."

"I may not know the *whole* story, Mom, but that's only because you haven't told me. He's been cranky as long as I can remember and he's always bragging about those stupid practical jokes he plays on people. But when I tried to tease him once, he didn't like it at all. Why is he so mean?"

"Your grandpa has . . . some . . ." She groped for her words, swimming through a murky pool, looking for an invisible ladder up to the air. "He has always had some . . . challenges," she finished, rather lamely, I thought.

As I remembered that lopsided conversation, I picked up the phone and called my sister, Glaze. She was forty-four years old, living in Philadelphia until she could either find another job or decide to move back to this area.

"Do you think Grandpa's crazy," I asked her without preamble, "or am I the only one who thinks so?"

"Biscuit, you get the prize for starting phone calls in the most astonishing ways."

She was right. Not long ago I'd called her asking about her several suicide attempts way back when. Glaze is bipolar. Fortunately it's controlled with medication now, and she's been through a healthy regimen of therapy, too. But she used to be a mess.

"Well," I persisted, "do you?"

"I don't talk about him," she said with a heavy dose of finality in her voice.

"All I need to know is what you think about him."

"I don't," she said.

"You don't what?"

"I don't think of him." She ground out the words like a food processor mashing rutabaga. "Ever."

I couldn't leave well enough alone. "Why not?" I asked.

"Don't you *ever* mention that man in my presence again," she snarled. I found myself backing up across my own kitchen, as if I could distance myself from her venom.

Somewhere I had an early photograph of my grandfather, taken in the 1920's or '30's. He was standing next to his mule at the edge of his field up on the plateau above Braetonburg. A tall, heavy-set man, with a bulbous nose and bland blue eyes, although, of course, the photo was black and white, yellowish now with age. His right hand rested on the mule's neck. Clumps of Georgia clay stuck to his heavy work shoes. His neck was almost nonexistent. He looked strong, like a football player or a boxer. It always surprised me to see the strength and volume of him in that photo, because all my memory of Grandpa, and the reality of him that I saw regularly at Happy Days, was stooped, scrawny, wrinkled, brown-spotted, and snide.

There was just a dial tone to keep me company. Glaze had hung up on me. I decided not to call her back.

Part II
October

Chapter 3

Tuesday, October 1st

I COULD SEE half of Bob's reflection in the bathroom mirror. He was straightening his tie, or so I supposed from the movement of one shoulder and elbow. He gave it a final tug and asked, "Do you have Father Ames' phone number?"

I brushed ineffectively at the stray wisps of hair that tickled my face. Most of those wisps were a mousy gray. I wasn't feeling up to par, and my image showed it. "Yeah," I droned. "It's in my address book. I left it on the bureau." We traded places so I could brush my hair into a semblance of order.

He rummaged around and came up with the little book, covered in a navy blue fabric. "I'm going to call him right after breakfast," he said. He was out of my line of sight, but I could hear him thumb through the pages. "It's not here," he complained.

"Sure it is. You're just not looking in the right place."

"I'm looking under A for Ames."

"Like I said, that's not the right place. I list everybody by their first name."

"That's not the way it's done, Woman." He sounded awfully peremptory for seven o'clock in the morning.

I walked out of the bathroom and leaned against the bureau. Why is it people always prop themselves up on available furniture? "That's the way I do it," I told him.

He kept rummaging. "It's still not here," he grumbled. "I'm looking in the J's for John."

"That's because I never call him John. I call him Father Ames."

Bob rolled his eyes at me and thumbed his way backwards through several pages. "So, I look under F for Father?"

"No." It was obvious to me. "You look under P."

"P? For crying out loud, Woman, why on earth is it under P?"

"For priest," I said. It made perfect sense. I took the book out of his grasp, looked up the number, wrote it down for him, and tucked the little piece of paper in his shirt pocket. I stood on tiptoe and kissed the end of his nose. Then I carried the address book downstairs and put it back in the top drawer of the desk where it belonged. I liked being methodical.

LATER THAT MORNING, I walked from my bedroom into what I called my sewing room so I could look out the front window. I loved this old house. It was a bit drafty, but the wide porch that wrapped around the front and sides shaded the rooms during the summer's heat and gave us a place to sit outside during rainstorms. The gray wood and green shutters gave the house a dignified air, and the various dormers and eyebrow windows near the roofline made for an interesting architectural mishmash.

The yard needed more flower beds so we wouldn't have to mow so much grass. But the existing flowers beds, a controlled riot of violent red Crocosmia and orange dahlias, native asters and some late-blooming peonies, were certainly prolific. They were one of the things I'd loved about the house when I first saw it. Even with all the rain, the profusion of flowers and massed greenery was impressive. Elizabeth Hoskins, the prior owner, certainly had a green thumb. Now all I had to do was keep them up, and everyone would think I was a master gardener. Not that I was any sort of slouch when it came to gardening. No, I could spout botanical names with the best of them, but I had to admit I'd never had Elizabeth's flair for landscaping.

She told me long before we bought the house that Lyle, her son, had double dug every single flower bed. That was years ago, before they even called it double digging. It simply meant that he'd dug wide, deep trenches where the flowers would go, then mixed the dirt with lots of manure and turned it back into the trenches. No wonder Lyle hadn't wanted the house. He probably remembered only the back-breaking work.

Each year, as the dirt from those double-dug trenches settled, Elizabeth would add compost around all the plants. Gradually the beds built up into mounds covered with flowers, shrubs, ornamental grasses, and small trees. That was way more work than I wanted to do, even if I could talk Bob into digging the trenches for me. Still, it *did* result in dirt so soft and fluffy you could turn it with a spoon.

I had only one bone to pick with Elizabeth. She'd planted a flowering dogwood in the full sun of the front yard. It was twenty feet tall or so, but it didn't have that ethereal quality of shade-grown dogwoods tucked back into the edge of the forests that line so many of the roads in this county. I always felt faintly sorry for it, struggling to get along in a sunny yard, when all it probably wanted was to shelter underneath a nice Katsura Tree or a Zelkova. Oh well, it was still alive. It just wasn't happy. Still, it cast a light enough shade itself that the flowers and shrubs around it were thriving.

The back yard was even more lush than the front. The big vegetable garden that filled a goodly portion near the house overflowed with produce, interspersed with flowers of all sorts. Elizabeth believed in the concept of combining plants for natural pest control. All I'd ever done was plant marigolds everywhere around my garden in Braetonburg, but Elizabeth put onions in the same rows with the carrots and planted radishes with the cucumbers and let catnip ramble around the eggplant.

I like the catnip.

Maybe that was why Marmalade tended to hang out in the eggplant patch whenever I was in the garden. Everything was so robust, you'd think Elizabeth had the best fertilizer source in the world, but she swore she never used fertilizer. Even the trees in the woodsy area at the center of the block were huge and lush. Maybe it was because of the creek that ran down the hill from Maggie's spring-fed pond up in the next block. Still, Matthew Olsen next door shared the same creek, but he didn't have such lavish growth in his yard. Just a couple of small trees and a few dreary little azaleas. Well, Elizabeth must simply have had what my mom always called "The Touch"—that quality of caring attention that made anything flourish.

Of course, I'd helped by building my own three-bin compost pile right after I moved in. Compost was a wonderful addition to any garden to keep the soil all loamy and rich. Elizabeth used the pile method, but I thought bins were tidier.

I turned away from the window. Only a true gardener could wax this enthusiastic about a compost bin. It was a bit disturbing, though, to look out at all the weeds taking advantage of that rich earth. When my knee was injured in June, I'd fallen way behind on my garden chores, and weeds grew faster than teenage boys. The weeds were still winning. I was beginning to feel royally sorry for myself when the phone rang. "Who do you think it is?" I asked Marmalade. I limped into the bedroom. My knee always seemed to bother me more whenever I thought about it.

It is Smellsweet.

Marmy meowed at me as I reached for the phone. "Hello," I managed to say just before the message machine picked up.

"You've reached the home of Biscuit and Bob," my voice yapped. I could hear someone saying hello? hello? beneath the noise of the message. "Wait a minute," I advised the mouthpiece. "It'll be through in a second." I watched the Joe Pye Weeds at the back fence. Even in the rain, they were growing like Jack's beanstalk every day. By the time I'd listened to me telling the world to leave a message and I'd call them right back, I figured the person on the other end, whoever it was, would probably have hung up. But after the beep my sister's voice chirped up.

"Biscuit?" she said.

I guess she'd decided to forgive me for whatever I'd said yesterday to tick her off. "Hey, Sis! What's up?"

"Nothing much. Can I come for a visit?"

Her last letter said she was planning to stay in Philadelphia. She'd found another job. A good one. "Well, sure," I said. "When?"

"I thought I'd leave tomorrow."

"Tomorrow?" I squeaked.

There was a long silence.

"Don't you want me to come?" she asked in a very small voice.

"Of course I do. You just surprised me, that's all. What happened with your job?"

I like it when she gives me catnip.

There was another long pause. "I got fired before I even started."

I looked at Marmalade, who glanced up at me and then went back to purring and licking between her toenails. "You what?"

"You heard me."

"How did that happen?"

"The boss and his wife were in the office when I walked in for my orientation about three hours ago. She took one look at me, grabbed her husband's arm and waltzed him into the conference room. The next thing I knew I was out the door."

"You're kidding, right?"

"Wrong. The guy I was supposed to share an office with said that I was the fifth or sixth in a string of women that had been canned. He couldn't understand why the boss didn't just hire a man or some ugly old grandma and forget about anybody less than fifty."

I gritted my teeth a bit at the "ugly old grandma" remark. After all, *I* was a grandmother. But I supposed my gorgeous silver-haired sister, who wore vanilla perfume and always smelled like a newly-baked cookie, didn't mean it personally.

Glaze kept going. "Then on top of that . . ."

There was more?

". . . Yuko, my roommate, told me she's getting married and needs to move out as soon as the lease is up."

"When does that happen?"

"At the end of the month. So I've been sitting here and wondering what I could possibly do, and Martinsville sounded like a wonderful solution."

With no job and no roommate, she obviously couldn't afford the townhouse. But we didn't have a guest room. I supposed I could rig something up in the sewing room–maybe get a daybed. Rats!

"Biscuit? Are you there?"

"Oh yeah, sorry. I guess I tuned out for a minute. I'm trying to figure out how I can get a daybed in the sewing room."

"Stop right there. I don't want to do that. I was hoping that you two might let me stay in Bob's old house for a while. The one on Upper Sweetgum."

"It's the only old house he had."

She ignored my snide remark. "You haven't sold it yet, have you?"

We hadn't even put it on the market, much less sold it.

"That way I can sort of take care of it for you. I'll even mow the grass . . ."

My city sister? Mow the grass?

". . . if Bob'll teach me how," she continued.

I couldn't resist it. "Tom'll probably be happy to help you there," I said.

"Well," she said, drawing the syllable out way longer than it was intended to go, "don't think I hadn't thought of that."

Hmm, maybe I'd be a matron of honor sooner than I'd figured. Tom Parkman had been head over heels ever since he met her six months ago. Any fool could see that. I just couldn't quite figure out where my sister stood. But this was looking more promising. "Sure," I said. "Come on. It'll be good having you here in town. You can join the tap dance class, too."

"Really?" She sounded considerably more interested than I'd thought she would.

"Well, we're supposed to have six in a class, and we're down to five," I said. "One of our members died."

"Don't make me feel *too* welcome," she said with a chuckle. "I just love being the fill-in person."

"That'll get you back for the ugly old grandma remark."

"I didn't say that!"

"But you agreed with him."

This conversation does not make sense.

I laughed it off. Marmalade was pawing at me. It must be time for her to eat, although, without my watch on and with no sun showing through the clouds I had no clue about the time. "Just kidding, Sis. You hurry on down here, and we'll have the house ready and warmed up for you when you get here. The place is fully furnished, so don't worry about anything."

"Give me a couple of days. I still have to pack the car, and I don't drive fast."

"Sure thing. And bring a raincoat."

As soon as we hung up, I called Bob with the good news . . .

Smellsweet is coming back. That is very good news.

. . . and Marmalade filled in the background of our conversation with her yowls for food. I flat forgot to tell him that Glaze would be staying in his old house on Upper Sweetgum, but I knew he wouldn't mind.

THE SUN, AFTER three cloudy days in a row, streamed onto the side porch, lighting the kitchen despite the wide eaves. As long as I had the phone warmed up, I called my daughter Sally and asked her to lunch while I spooned a bit of tuna into Marmalade's bowl.

Thank you, but I was not asking for food.

It was a spur-of-the-moment invitation, but she seemed happy that I'd called. "I'd love to go, Mom."

I could picture her deep brown eyes, just like her father's, raking over the contents of her closet. It was the closet that used to be mine. She lived in the house that Sol and I used to share. Last year I rented it to Sally and Jason, her football hero husband, and I moved five miles down the valley to Martinsville. "Are you in the closet?" I asked her.

"Yeah, how'd you know?"

I wanted to say *mother's intuition*, but figured that almost eight months into her pregnancy she wouldn't fall for that line. "I can hear you scooting the coat hangers back and forth," I admitted. I reached up to pat Marmalade who had finished her tuna and climbed onto my shoulders.

"Wear something nice," Sally told me. "Something that won't embarrass me."

I pulled the phone away from my ear and looked at it. "What's that supposed to mean?"

She ignored my question. "Wear your blue skirt and that blue and green blouse I gave you for your birthday." There was a pause before she added, "Be sure your sandals don't have paint on them."

I believed in cutting a bit of slack for pregnant women, but this was beginning to rasp on my good nature. I looked down at my rumpled green slacks and my tee-shirt that said *Give blood for all the little reasons.* I rather liked the bright-colored cartoon hand prints beneath the slogan. I needed to schedule my next donation, but that meant driving to Athens. Maybe Glaze would go with me. I wondered if she'd ever given blood before.

"Mother? Are you there?"

Sally brought me back to the present. I took a deep breath. "I think I'm quite capable of dressing appropriately," I told her. "I'll pick you up in an hour."

"We can go to the Braetonburg Buffet House," she said. "They have the best salad bar."

After we hung up, Marmy jumped off my shoulders and led the way to the laundry room. She must have been napping in the clean laundry again. The blue skirt, which I dearly loved because it never showed a single wrinkle, was sprinkled with a generous amount of cat hair. I brushed at it as I walked back up to the bedroom. A little cat hair never hurt anybody. The blouse was marginally better, although I did notice several pulled threads on the shoulders. I couldn't help it if Marmalade had to hang on when I turned a corner too fast.

I slipped into my off-white sandals, double-checked them, and changed to the brown ones. Nobody else would have noticed the green speckles from when a friend and I had painted the new Green Room in the library, but Sally would definitely pick up on my sartorial blunder. Nitpicky.

DESPITE ALL THAT, we had a delightful lunch, although I noticed her eyeing my shoulders more than once. I should have thrown a scarf around me so the pulled threads wouldn't show. I thought I'd bring the conversation around to something Sally would enjoy. The baby. "With this one," I told her, "I guess I'm going to have to camp out on your doorstep."

"Why?"

"Why? So I can be there with you when you deliver, that's why. I missed both of Sandra's births–both kids came so fast–so I'm not going to risk missing this one." My iced tea was sweating, and a puddle had formed around the bottom of the glass. I mopped it up with one of the extra paper napkins. Why *do* they give people so many? "Anyway," I went on, "I'm so glad they let support people be there during the birth. It wasn't like that when you were born."

Sally looked out the window and squinted. The sun was a good change from all the rain we'd been having, and it was piercingly bright. I was glad my back was to the window.

"Mom?" Sally fiddled with her fork, lining it up precisely across her plate, parallel to the table's edge. She opened her mouth and started to speak, but closed it as the waiter sidled up to refill our tea. I wondered what Sally wanted to say that the waiter couldn't witness. Surely waiters–wait persons–hear everything. It must be frustrating, though, always to hear only partial conversations. A word here, a phrase there. I picked up my fork and stabbed at some of the bow tie macaroni swimming in salad dressing.

Sally broke into my reverie. "Mom." She bit off the word. "I don't want you there."

Stopping the flow of a forkful of salad from plate to mouth can be a tricky business when the salad dressing is threatening to drip. The dressing won, leaving a trail down the front of my blue and green blouse. Thank goodness it was cotton and would wash easily.

Sally didn't see me make a mess of myself. She wasn't looking at me. I couldn't think of a thing to say. Did she mean it? Her own mother? I would have given my eyeteeth to have my mom with me when I delivered Sandra and Sally. I could feel my eyes narrowing. A blistering retort gathered speed, ready to erupt. And then I thought about my former mother-in-law. Sol's mother. The last person on earth I would have wanted with me in a delivery room. A fussy, judgmental shrew of a woman. She would have upset me so much, Sandra or Sally would have clawed back inside to keep from popping out into an atmosphere of such icy disapproval.

The volcano inside me bulged out, like Mount St. Helens about to spew lava and destruction, but it stopped short of exploding and turned itself inwards. Was I such a bad mother that my child didn't want me with her? Was I being unbearably pushy to simply *expect* to be included in this life-affirming event?

Sally still watched the people walking past the window, as if they had a particular key she needed for a subterranean vault. To lock me out. Her left hand paused a handsbreadth away from her bulging stomach. That was my third grandchild in there, and I wanted to see him come out. Was that unreasonable? A little voice told me I shouldn't take this personally, but I ignored it.

I put my fork down, pushed my plate away, and tried unsuccessfully to mop up the obvious dribble. It had insinuated itself between and under the white buttons. There weren't nearly enough napkins. I looked like a slob.

"Sally?"

She kept her eyes firmly averted. "Hmm?" she said.

"Would you please look at me?"

"Oh, Mom, you've got salad dressing on your blouse!"

"This is not about my table manners. Would you mind telling me why you don't want me at the birth?" I was proud I kept my voice even.

"We, Jason and I, . . . we talked about it. We just want the two of us there. He can support me just fine. We've taken the classes . . ."

So did I, I thought. Twenty some-odd years ago, but I still remembered the breathing.

"We don't know how this is going to work out . . ."

Nobody ever did, especially at a first birth. All the more reason for me to be there.

". . . so, we just . . . decided, that's all."

Lunch didn't look good anymore. "It's your decision, dear." I pulled three bills from my wallet and placed them in the middle of the table. "That should cover both lunches and the tip." I pushed my chair back and walked away from my daughter. I waited until I was in the car before I began to cry.

Halfway home it dawned on me that I'd left my pregnant daughter without a ride. It wasn't raining, though, and if she could have a baby without me, she could jolly well get herself the four blocks from the restaurant to her house. She could walk. Braetonburg didn't have steep hills like Martinsville. She could call that husband of hers. It was probably all his idea anyway.

I didn't exactly slam the door on my way in, but Bob came out of the office with his mouth open. "Bisque," he said, using the name he called me only when he was concerned, "are you okay?"

"Yes." I shoved my keys into the side pocket of my purse. "No." I slammed the purse onto the drop-leaf table. "Dammit!"

Bob figured out a long time ago that sometimes I need a hug before I can talk straight. He spread his arms, and I lunged into their warmth as if he could make the bears go away.

"GOOD NEWS," I told the tap dancers before class that evening, after I had resolutely decided not to mention Sally to any of them. "Glaze is moving to Martinsville, and she wants to join the class." General cheers all around. "Is that okay, Miss Mary?"

"Of course it is!" Miss Mary was unrelentingly enthusiastic. "We'll get her caught up on the steps in no time at all!"

Considering that I still was comfortable with only three of the steps we'd learned, I thought Miss Mary might be a bit too optimistic. Then again, I had no idea what sort of athletic talent Glaze had, since I'd largely ignored my five-years-younger sister for quite awhile, and then when we were both old enough to have something in common, I went off to college. Maybe she was a tap dance whiz. Of course, we weren't going that fast in class. Sadie Masters, in her yellow leotard–she always wore yellow–was eighty-one years old. And my knee still bothered me some. Miss Mary took all of that into account.

AFTER THE LESSON, we all wandered up to *Azalea House*, Melissa Tarkington's bed & breakfast place, for pumpkin pie and chitchat. We settled into our usual Tuesday night places in the white-walled kitchen, around the long table with its blue-checked tablecloth. Our Tuesday conversations were always a highlight of my week. Melissa turned on the fan that hung from the twelve-foot ceiling. Old houses were fun, but updates like ceiling fans and energy-efficient new appliances are a great improvement. I was still close enough to menopause to appreciate the cool breeze.

"How are things at the library?" Ida Peterson asked in the general direction of Sadie and me. She and her husband Ralph owned the grocery store in town. Ida was quite the business woman. "Are you busy all the time?"

I had just opened my mouth to tell her how nice it was to have so many people using the town library–it was, after all, less than two years old–when Sadie set down her fork and spoke up. "It's not too good." She must have missed seeing my mouth drop open. What did she mean, not too good? She stayed busy during the two days she volunteered each week.

"It's not?" Melissa sounded puzzled. "There are always lots of people in there whenever I go." She paused. "Well, usually," she added.

I didn't like the dubious tone in her voice. My library was doing just fine, thank you.

Sadie nodded her yellow-scarfed head. An eighty-one-year-old with a yellow bandana looked rather pert, I thought, even though I didn't agree with her. "There may be a lot of traffic," she said, "but it's always the same people, over and over again. They check out a book or two, bring them back the next week, check out two more." She reached for her fork. "We need an advertising campaign, something to get new people in there."

"I'll put up a sign in the grocery store," Ida offered. "Everybody in town ought to be using the library."

Annie McGill, with her long red braid draped over her left shoulder, waved her hand for the floor. "I'd be willing to give anybody a free cup of herbal tea if they show me their new library card." She held up her hand again, this time to stop the voices of acclamation. "The trouble is, everyone who shops at *Heal Thyself* already has a library card."

"Put a sign in the window," Ida suggested. "That might draw you in some new customers." She screwed her lips off to one side. "Potential customers, that is. But once you have them in the door and give them some tea, they're bound to look around. Maybe buy something."

Annie tossed her braid back over her shoulder, clopping Melissa's head in the process.

"Watch it, girl. You've got a dangerous weapon there."

Ida paid no attention to the ruckus. She smoothed a wrinkle in the tablecloth. "Everybody shops at the grocery store. I'll put your herb shop offer in the flyer. That way everyone in town will see it."

"We could have a Halloween party at the library," Sadie said. "And invite the whole town."

"Costumes," Ida said.

"Potluck dinner," Melissa chimed in.

Annie shook her head. "Card applications is what you really mean."

"No reason why we can't introduce people to the library in a fun way," Ida said. "Sadie and I will organize it."

"We will?"

Just like that, I had a publicity campaign.

WHEN I GOT home, I couldn't find Marmalade. Bob didn't know where she was. Said he hadn't seen her all evening. I stepped out onto the back stoop. "Marmy, bed time!"

I am quite comfortable right here.

I looked around the yard. The shed where we kept all the lawn and garden equipment was a shadowy mirage just outside the splash of light from the kitchen's bay window. I looked back at the garden and saw Marmalade peeking at me from the eggplant patch where she was nestled into the catnip that Elizabeth had planted to repel the nematodes. Otherwise they would have eaten up the eggplant.

I thought she planted it for me.

I loved this healthy garden, nourished as it was with the best fertilizer in the world–compost. I called to Marmalade one more time and watched her arch her back, stretch out her front legs, and walk her back legs up to meet the front ones. She looked like a giant furry inchworm.

Inchworms are very graceful.

My gratitude list for Tuesday, October 1st

Five things for which I'm grateful:

1. My sister
2. My husband
3. My friends in the tap class
   (I'm counting them as one item in this list)

4. My completely logical way of keeping an address book
5. My cat

I am grateful for
Widelap, my human
Softfoot, my other human
clear thinking, even though my humans do not do that sometimes
catnip
tuna

Chapter 4

Wednesday, October 2nd

"I CAN'T KEEP imposing on your hospitality," Madeleine Ames told her brother right after the nine o'clock Mass.

John looked up from the stove where he was scrambling eggs for their breakfast. "I don't see why not. It seems to be working out okay." He spooned some runny eggs out onto his plate and kept stirring the rest in the pan. His sister liked them almost crispy around the edges. He didn't even shudder anymore as he overcooked them for her. He breathed in the scrumptious coffee aroma. She made truly spectacular coffee. It was worth the trade. He'd cook her eggs the way she wanted forever if she'd just keep making that coffee every morning.

"I don't know," she said.

"Sure it is. You're not in the way of my parishioners at all." There was a long enough silence that he finally looked up at her. "What?" he asked.

"Did it ever occur to you that they're in *my* way?" she asked.

"What are you talking about? You've got half the upstairs for your very own space."

She picked up the two coffee mugs and headed for the minuscule table. He followed her with both plates. The toast, juice pitcher, butter, and other breakfast paraphernalia were already in place. "You're right," she said as she tucked one leg underneath her and settled into the chair closest to the door. "But once I'm up there, if you have someone here for a counseling session, I feel like I can't come downstairs. You never shut the door when you have a parishioner in your office." She buttered a large slab of toast. "And I don't want to intrude."

He didn't understand. Madeleine, at thirty-three, had just recently left home, and she had sought a refuge of sorts with her brother. He looked around the brown-walled kitchen. The old rectory, built adjacent to St. Theresa's Catholic Church in the mid-1800's, was a rambling building with lots of space. "What do you mean, intrude?" he asked.

"If I use the front stairs, I have to cross the hallway and go right past your office door. You're a priest. People want their privacy. I don't want them to think I'm spying on them." She pushed her hair back from her face. "And if I go down the back stairs," she added, "well, you know those back stairs."

He did. Their agonized squeaks sounded like gunshots. He always avoided the back stairs if he could.

"And if I go out the back door . . ." Madeleine shuddered.

Oh yes, indeed. The back door out of the kitchen made a grinding sound every time it was opened. Like a dog fight. Or the Alaskan ice floe breaking up. It resounded through the old rooms, bouncing off the high ceilings and echoing through the entire structure. They never used the back door if they could avoid it.

He tried to get his parishioners to make appointments for counseling sessions, but sometimes, often, they simply showed up on the doorstep and asked to speak with him. It had never before been much of a problem. But now he liked having someone to eat with. He enjoyed his conversations with Madeleine. He hadn't realized she felt imprisoned upstairs. Maybe that was too strong a word.

He didn't know quite what to say, so he settled for spooning a rather large bite of eggs into his mouth. Then he chewed in a way that he hoped looked thoughtful. Eventually, though, he had to swallow. And there sat his sister, waiting for a comment. He took the coward's way out. "What did you have in mind?" he asked.

She poured some juice and took a long swallow. It looked to him like she was buying time the same way he had.

"Dad sent me some money," she finally said, "to help tide me over. I'll need to get a day job of some sort, but I want some space to write in. I think I'd like to ask Bob Sheffield if I can rent his old house. I walked up there yesterday. It's not too big for me to take care of. There must be at least a couple of bedrooms upstairs from the number of windows I could see. I could sleep in one and write in the other one."

John nodded. She'd been writing horror novels for years. He hadn't known that until four months ago. They'd had lots of opportunity for long talks now that she was staying with him, and he'd found out quite a bit about her. She'd even let him read several of her manuscripts. They were fairly gruesome, but with a certain flair. She'd never had anything published, but her latest book–the one she thought was the most promising one so far–was being reviewed by an agent, and Madeleine had told him she was hopeful about this one.

She killed off their mother, or a character who closely resembled their mother, in every single book. He could understand the impulse. If writing about homicide kept her from actively engaging in it, he had to approve. Not that he thought Madeleine would ever truly murder their mother. Ahh, but he could see how tempting it would be to toy with the idea.

He'd been spreading butter on his toast. When he noticed Madeleine looking at him rather pointedly, he looked down at his handiwork. He had sliced the toast, mangled it, shredded it, gouged it. Madeleine burst out laughing as a distinct red tone rose up his face. “Yes,” she howled, “that’s why I write it all out!”

His mug was empty. “If you move out,” he said, “I’ll miss your coffee.”

“What? You won’t miss *me*, your little sister? You won’t miss our scintillating conversations?”

“It’s barely two blocks from here. Surely you’ll come visit once in a while,” he said. “And make me some coffee,” he added.

“I’ll call Bob as soon as we get the dishes done,” she said. “My turn to dry.”

Chapter 5

Thursday, October 3rd

ROGER WINSTON JOHNSON IV, twenty-two years old and built like a zipper if he stuck out his tongue and turned sideways, was up to his elbows in garbage. He knew his limitations. He hadn't tried to date anyone ever since his best friend Marty Owens told him that Melody Cummings, the first girl he ever loved in high school, didn't want to go out with anybody she could probably throw over her shoulder. Why did skinny guys fall for sturdy girls? For that matter, why did the tallest guy in town date the shortest girl? The world was built upside down, that was why. Or so Roger decided as an overloaded plastic bag ripped and sent a stream of plate scrapings onto the bed of his dark blue pickup truck. It gave a new, more redolent meaning to the concept of spilling the beans.

Roger adjusted his work gloves and scooped up the scattered taco remains, wedging them back into the bag so he could tie a knot to close up the torn corner. He hummed one of his melodies and sang snatches of the words here and there. . . .*call me home, two, three, lay my heart down by the river, call me home, hum, hum, always ease my aching mind, and four and hum de-dum dum, smiles and open arms to welcome me, pause, two, three, four, home.*

Miss Sadie's garbage was usually packaged better. But at eighty-something or other, she probably had an excuse, although Roger found that his older clients generally had neater garbage than the middle-aged folks. The twenties and thirties people were downright messy. After six years of taking Miss Sadie's garbage to the county dump, ever since he learned to drive, he could tell if she'd been feeling well just by whether or not each day's refuse was wrapped in a couple of sheets of newspaper. When she was feeling poorly, everything went in a plastic bag. When her garbage was a collection of news-wrapped lumps, he'd have seen her all week driving off in her yellow Chevy morning and afternoon. She didn't go many places in the evening, except to her tap dance lesson on Tuesday nights. Usually her lights, which he could see across the street from his music studio on 5th Street, went out at 8:30 or so. He knew she tucked in her husband about 7:30 and then read a good book until time for lights out. . . . *It's the people, two, three, who have known me since my childhood, it's the people, two, three, who are there to lend a hand, and they're calling me, three, four, calling me, seven eight, home.*

Miss Sadie and Mr. Wallis had been married forever or even longer. Roger didn't see much of him, except when the old man was sitting out on the rocker on their front porch. Then Roger would stop by sometimes and sit with him for awhile.

Twice a week some sort of county program sent someone to give Mr. Wallis a bath and help Miss Sadie. Naturally Roger always mowed their grass, and a couple of the town ladies came over each week to help Miss Sadie clean. This was a good town.

Wallis Masters had taught Roger how to fish when Roger was five or six. Just a simple pole with a hook and a line at first. Even back then Mr. Wallis, as Roger always called him, was already old. But Roger's legs were still pretty short, so the two of them could walk easily together down to the Metoochie

River. Mr. Wallis favored fishing near the boulders at either end of what the people of Martinsville called “the Pool.” It was easy to get a hook caught among the big rocks, but the trout favored the deep eddies formed by the water as it swirled around the boulders. Once Roger had put on some height—when he was twelve he’d sprouted up like a weed in a turnip patch—Mr. Wallis taught him to fly fish. Roger loved flipping the long line with the featherweight fly right over the dark water where the trout hid. The river had been so low in recent years because of the drought that the fishing hadn’t been worth anything. But this year all those rainstorms started in June. I’ll need to get out my fly rod and try that new fly Bob Sheffield gave me, Roger thought.

Like a current through a river, like the heartbeat in my chest, hum de-dum de-dum forever, for I know now, seven eight, one, two, three, my heart’s at rest, six, seven, eight, one, two, three. Roger liked the pauses he’d built into that song.

“Roger, what’s that you’re singing?”

“Hello, Miss Sadie. You picked a good day to go out. I see a few clouds up there, but I bet you’ll have time to run your errands before the rain starts again.”

“That’s true, Roger, but you’re not answering my question. What were you singing?”

“Just a little song I wrote. Isn’t much.”

Miss Sadie tilted her head to one side. “Do you have it written down?”

“Well, sure, but I could just sing it to you sometime, all the way through. There are a whole bunch of verses.”

“Just bring me the music, Roger. I might like to practice playing it on my harmonica. It sounds like it might have a nice melody.” She patted his arm. “Thank you for taking my garbage. I’m sorry it’s not wrapped up nicely, but I’ve been a little under the weather.”

“You’re looking mighty fine today, Miss Sadie.”

She patted her chest where a bright yellow scarf was knotted across her heart. "You make an old lady feel pretty perky, young man."

Roger watched her trundle down the walk toward her yellow Chevy. . . . *arms that welcome me and shelter me and hum, two, three, four . . .*

He drove on down Fifth Street, still singing, to Mrs. Smith's house. Judy Smith was so busy getting ready for the shows where she exhibited her quilts all over the eastern U.S. that she never could remember to take stuff to the dump until it smelled to high heaven. And her son was off at college now. Roger had figured that as long as he was taking Miss Sadie's and his own family's garbage, he might as well load up the pickup.

"Would you really?" she practically crowed when he first asked her.

"It's no big deal, Mrs. Smith. I'm headed to the dump anyway."

Then Judy mentioned it to Paul Welsh, the man she dated occasionally.

"Roger, my man," Paul had boomed out one Monday while Roger was putting up the new letters on the signboard for the Old Church. "I hear you've gone into the garbage business."

Roger rotated the M in his hands. They were short on W's, and this would do the job. "Not exactly, Mr. Welsh." He started the second word in next week's sermon title. "I've just been helping out Miss Sadie and Mrs. Smith."

"What's it worth to you to take mine as well? With all the traveling I do, I'm not home half the time. Don't know where all my garbage comes from, but there sure is a lot of it."

Roger nodded. "Sure. I'll take your garbage, too."

"What'll you charge me?"

"Oh, nothing. I'm headed that way anyhow with my own trash."

"Wait a minute. I'm offering to pay you."

"You don't have to do that." Roger felt no need to squirm under Paul Welsh's scrutiny. After all, he was just helping out neighbors. But Mr. Welsh kept staring at him until he did feel a squirm coming on. Roger turned back to the sign and snapped on the next few letters. "I really don't mind taking your garbage," he added.

"That's not the point. Here, turn around and look at me. You can take Miss Sadie's trash to the landfill for free if you want to. In fact, I think that's a downright nice thing for you to do. And when I'm a hundred years old you can stop charging me, too. But, in the meantime, this costs you time and effort. You need to look at this from a business point of view. You have to buy gas and maintain your truck. The dirt roads into the landfill are rough on cars, so you'll be saving me time and effort and wear and tear on my vehicle. That's worth something to me. Now, what are you going to charge me to pick up my trash once a week?"

Roger looked over at his sign. HOW WILL YOU KNOW, it asked. He wondered about that himself. "A couple of dollars?" he asked.

"Let's make it ten, and you've got yourself a deal."

They shook hands, and Roger was in the garbage business.

The next week Reverend Pursey called Roger and asked if he'd like a new customer. Brighton Montgomery said he wanted to be on the route, too. Then Ms. McKee heard about it and signed up because her husband didn't like trekking up to Russell Gap all that often. She asked if she could mention it to her tap dance class. By the following Wednesday Roger had three more customers, Annie McGill and Melissa Tarkington from the tap dance class, and Ms. McKee's mother-in-law. That was a full load every Thursday. Roger figured that as long as his music wasn't selling–yet–he might as well have some other way of earning a living. And it was good work. Honest work. He looked at the mushed-up beans in the bottom of his truck. It was dirty work, too. But what the heck, it was income.

ROGER HATED HAVING to say no. "I'm really sorry, Mrs. Peterson. My truck is full to the gills on Thursdays. I just don't have room for a new customer."

Ida's eyebrows moved up pretty close to her hairline, then they scrunched down really fast like a sledge hammer on a fence post. "I'm not talking about my house garbage, Roger," she said. "I want you to take the store's garbage. That's a full load all by itself."

"The grocery store?"

"That's the only store we own, last time I looked."

Roger did a quick calculation. Right now, with six paying customers, he was earning more than enough, considering all he had to do was just drive up to Russell Gap, turn west on the county road, and turn right onto the landfill road. Of course, he had to gather the trash, but everybody except Miss Sadie put it out by the curb, so that was easy. He knew the grocery store trash was out back in big trash cans. There were six or seven of them, and they had heavy lids to keep out the raccoons and possums. He could probably make it in one trip, but the loading and unloading would be hard, and he'd have to rig up some sort of ramp. He'd have to figure out a way to keep the lids from flying off, too.

Ida stood there patiently while Roger calculated. He thought it was an outrageous amount, and fully expected her to shake her head.

"Can you do two trips a week?" she asked. "Mondays and Fridays?"

Roger was really in the garbage business.

THE LIBRARY WAS closed on Thursdays, but I had to get in some work time without having to stop every few minutes to help somebody look up something. Glaze would be arriving around noon. The soup was ready for dinner. The house was clean. Relatively clean. So I had two or three hours to myself. I should have locked the front door. Sharon Armitage poked her head in. "Yoo-hoo, Biscuit. Are you there?"

"Come on in, Sharon," I said, "but lock the door behind you. How'd you know I was here?"

"I didn't, but I could see the light on while I was driving past and figured I'd give it a try." She sidled up next to the rolltop desk. I was trying without much success to bring some order to the pigeonholes. So far I'd cleaned out three. That left only a couple of thousand to go. "Would you be willing to put up a bulletin board?" she asked.

I looked around the main floor of the library. "Sure," I said. "Maybe over there near the front door. Why do you want one?"

"I've got this great idea for building business, and I need places to put my flyers."

"Try the grocery store."

"Yep. I already did. They've got one and of course I put one in my Beauty Shop window, and Frank Snelling agreed to put one up at the Frame Shop."

"What's your idea?"

"I figure if I offer a free manicure to every woman who comes in for a shampoo and set, I can build up a regular clientele that way. Yep. Sounds like a good idea, doesn't it?"

"Sharon, you already have a regular clientele. You do everybody's hair in town, and it keeps you pretty busy."

Her eyes wandered over my long ash brown, gray-sprinkled hair. I'd pulled it back into a ponytail just to get it out of my way. "Not everybody," she said. "And anyway, I've hired me a manicurist. I'll pay her a percentage of what she brings in, plus she gets to keep all her tips."

"But she won't bring in anything at first if you're giving free manicures."

"No, and she knows that, but she said she could convince any woman to get her nails done on a regular basis if she could just get her hands on their hands once. Yep. That's what she said. Her hands on their hands."

"Well, okay. I'll have to go up to Garner Creek and see if I can find one of those cork boards."

"Don't you bother a bit," she said. "I just happen to have brought one with me. Let me run out to my car and I'll help you put it up."

Her flyer was pink. Revolting pink. Eye-catching pink in an upset-stomach sort of way. She pinned it up with her own thumb tacks and said, "Pumpkin's gonna think this is wonderful."

"Pumpkin?"

"Yep. My new manicurist. That's her name." I'd never heard of anyone in town named Pumpkin, but Sharon explained before I could ask. "She came up for somebody's funeral and decided to stick around. She's renting a room from the Montgomery's."

"Brighton and Ellen? I didn't know they were renting out rooms."

"Just the one. I met Pumpkin down at the Delicious last week." The DeliSchuss, a deli owned by Hans and Margot Schuss, was something of a fixture in town. "She said she was a manicurist," Sharon went on, "and well, it all just fell into place. Yep. Just like that."

"She was renting a room without having a job?" This was nothing but gossip, but I was inordinately curious about anyone who'd call herself Pumpkin.

"Nope. I talked to her about the job and then Ariel was filling my coffee cup and overheard us and said her folks had been talking about renting out that extra room, and well, there it all was, yep, handy as you please."

"How'd she get a nickname like Pumpkin?" I asked.

"That's not a nickname. That's her real name."

"Who on earth would name a child Pumpkin?"

"Pumpkin told me her mother was eight months pregnant with her when she won a blue ribbon at the County Fair for the biggest pumpkin in the whole entire competition."

"So she named her daughter Pumpkin?" That sounded absolutely bizarre, until I remembered my own name.

Sharon looked me up and down. "You're named after a pot, and you think a vegetable is weird?"

Chapter 6

GLAZE HAD SEEN Bob's old house on Upper Sweetgum Street before, of course. When she came to town to attend our wedding last April, Bob had invited the two of us up for barbequed chicken one evening . . .

I like his chicken.

. . . but she'd never seen the upstairs. "What do you think?" I asked. She veered to the left at the top of the stairs and walked into the smaller of the two bedrooms. She went straight to the window that overlooked the hillside down to the Metoochie. Despite all the trees, we could see glints of water. Marmalade hopped onto a convenient chair and looked outside, purring contentedly.

You need a bird feeder.

"This will be my bedroom." Glaze could certainly make up her mind fast. She fingered the gray and white striped curtains. "I may need to redecorate," she added. It had been a bachelor's house for years. It was a wonder there were curtains at all. They looked like mattress ticking.

There was another window in the wall to our right, the back wall of the house. It was curtained in the same dreary fabric, and the curtains were closed, probably because that view looked out toward the side of Sadie's yellow house. Everything about Sadie was yellow, . . .

I call her Looselaces.

. . . even her tennis shoes, which were invariably untied. Not that I thought Sadie was nosy, but who wants neighbors looking into your bedroom?

"Let's go get my luggage at least, so I can feel like I'm partway moved in." Glaze scooped up Marmalade and danced around the room. "I'm going to love being here!"

We have fun when we are together.

"One suitcase," I agreed. "But then we head back down the hill for some lunch." My stomach rumbled in harmony with Marmalade's loud purr. I stayed upstairs while Glaze retrieved her dark blue suitcase. We hoisted it onto the narrow bed. "I'll help you haul in all your stuff later," I told her.

"It'll wait," she said, patting the tapestry-sided luggage. "I'm going to be here a long time, and I can live out of this one suitcase for a couple of days at least. Did you and Bob decide on the rent?"

"Oh shoot! I forgot to tell him."

"He doesn't know I'm moving to Martinsville? You forgot to mention something major like your sister's coming to town?"

"Silly." I made a face at her. "Of course he knows that. I just forgot to tell him that you'd be moving into his old house." I turned back toward the stairs. "He'll still want to be able to get into his workshop. Hope you won't mind that." Bob tied fishing flies in the little outbuilding in his back yard. "There's no place for that where we are now unless we build him another shed out back."

"An outhouse?" Glaze grinned at me. "So, he doesn't know I'm moving in. When were you planning on telling him? And when do I find out how much the rent is?"

I started moving down the stairs. "We'll tell him tonight after dinner."

THE CLOUDS WERE still heavy, although it wasn't raining.

Yet. I squeezed into the front seat of her green Civic. It was jam-packed with all her earthly goods. Glaze drove slowly down Upper Sweetgum Street to where it dead ended at the funeral home. “That’s where the barn used to be, isn’t it?” Glaze asked as we turned the corner. We’d grown up in Braetonburg, five miles up the valley, so we both were sketchy on Martinsville history. What we knew came from Bob’s lectures–he was something of a town historian–and some ancient diaries in the library that told a lot about Martinsville in the 1800’s. One of them mentioned the fire that destroyed the barn. We’d never found anything that went as far back as the founding of the town. Just the handed-down stories about building the barn and the first three babies born in the town. Hopefully somebody would discover something in an old trunk. I mentioned as much to Glaze.

“Heck, there’s probably all sorts of stuff like that in your attic.”

I sighed. Someday I was going to have to get around to cleaning out that attic. Everybody who’d ever lived in that old house had left stuff up there. I walked up the stairs every so often, took one look around at the trunks and hat boxes, the lamps and hobby horses, the doll houses and rolled-up rugs, and promptly retreated downstairs. “That can be our project,” I said.

“What project?”

“Cleaning up my attic.”

My ever-helpful sister grinned at me. “I think I’ll go back to Philadelphia tomorrow.”

> “THIS IS YOUR mid-week, early-afternoon weather report from WRRT, the voice of Keagan County, where you get all the news of the valley, all the weather that comes into the valley, and a list of all the people who

> check out of the valley. We give you the obituary listing at five p.m., just in time for you to think appropriate thoughts over your evening meal. Ha-ha! Radio Ralph Towers here, getting ready for an afternoon of good old oldies. That's why they're called oldies. Because they're old. But first, the one p.m. five-day forecast. Rain tomorrow, lots of rain. Well, it'll make the trees grow, right? And we'll have a real sunny weekend and on into Monday. Let's hear a little music now. Is early Elvis old enough for you? *Hound Dog* was always one of my favorites. Here it is, straight from the turntable of Radio Ralph Towers, the only announcer who ever had a radio station named just for him. . . ."

As soon as I could get my hands out of the dishwater I turned off the radio in disgust. We'd been having trouble getting the public radio signal. Maybe it had something to do with all the rainstorms. I'd rather listen to twenty minutes of uninterrupted static than twenty seconds of Radio Ralph. Glaze wandered into the kitchen from the little blue and white powder room.

"Who was that?" she asked a few minutes later. She looked considerably refreshed. "It sounded like a bad Walter Cronkite imitation."

"That's right. You left Braetonburg before Ralph took over the station. Believe me, you don't want to know him. And you don't want to listen to him." Not while she was in my house, that is.

"Is he that bad?"

"No. He's worse."

THE DOORBELL RANG just as we sat down to dinner. Bob started to get up, but I was closer to the front hall, so I motioned him back down.

I could see Madeleine Ames through the beveled glass panes on the substantial old front door. I loved my lace curtains, but they never kept anybody from seeing out–or in for that matter. "Come on in," I told her as I swung the door back, "and meet my sister. She just got in from Philadelphia this afternoon."

We went through all the usual hello's and how-are-you's. Of course, I asked her to stay for dinner. It was a real invitation, too, not one of those won't-you-stay-I-hope-you-won't things that seem to be a staple of Southern hospitality. She must have heard the genuine note in my voice because she accepted.

Once we had her seated, she tucked her left leg underneath her. After I gave her a big blue-ringed bowl of vegetable soup and a substantial slab of honey-oat bread, she asked Glaze about Philadelphia.

Glaze told about her various job woes, making it sound pretty funny with her imitation of the indignant wife, and she left out the ugly grandma remark. I faded out a bit, reminding myself to remember to tell Bob that Glaze would be staying at the Sweetgum house. He probably thought she'd be camping out on the couch for a while. He was such a calm man. I sure did like him.

I tuned back into the conversation when Madeleine turned to Bob and asked, "What do you want me to do with the suitcase you left in the extra bedroom?"

What was she talking about?

"I'm not sure what you mean," Bob said. "I didn't leave anything except the furniture and some kitchen stuff." He set down his spoon and slathered more butter on his bread. "And my workshop," he added.

"No," she said. "There's a big blue tapestry suitcase in the bedroom on the left. The one where I'm going to be doing my writing."

I looked at Glaze. Glaze looked at Madeleine. Madeleine kept looking at Bob. Bob ate another mouthful of bread. "Couldn't be," he said.

"That's my suitcase," Glaze said.

Bob and Madeleine did double-takes at Glaze, like a comedy team. They both talked at the same time. "Your suitcase?" "Why?" Glaze just looked baffled.

I jumped into the long silence. "I told Glaze she could move into your old house. She didn't want to stay here with us. I told her she could rent it." I tried to ignore the fact that Madeleine's mouth was hanging open. What on earth was wrong with her?

Bob didn't exactly roll his eyes, but he came close to it. "I think we have a problem here, Woman," he said. "I rented the house to Madeleine."

"You never told me that," I said.

"You never asked." He looked at me over the top of his glasses. "And you never told me you were letting your sister move in there."

"Oh. Well." I couldn't help the giggle. "You never asked," I said.

Eventually we worked it out. As Marmalade alternated laps between the two of them, Glaze and Madeleine decided they could share the house on a trial basis for a couple of months.

I can visit them there.

They laughed together over the mix-up. Glaze's gentle murmur of a chuckle blended with Madeleine's bubbly chortle and Marmalade's rumbly purr.

Smellsweet and Curlup like each other.

They were going to get along just fine.

Chapter 7

Friday, October 4

EVERYTHING ABOUT THE old Millicent Mansion was oversized. It was the town library, and we never had to worry about finding enough room for all the books. The conservatory out back, with its tromp l'oeil walls, could have been a big city library's reading room; the grand staircase where I'd found that dead body a year and a half ago . . .

I am the one who found it.

. . . had stair steps that were seven feet wide; the ceilings upstairs were all at least ten feet high, and those on the ground floor were sixteen. And then there were the windows. Tall, imposing, faintly wavy with age, and slightly blue-tinged, but beautifully shaped with arches at the top of most of them.

The fourth floor attic was originally designed to house the servants, with tiny cubbyhole rooms off a central corridor and an enormous storage room at the end where the narrow back stairs wound down to the lower floors.

It used to have many mice in it until I began my work here.

So, when I talk about the *little* room on the second floor that was tucked under the stairs, keep in mind that it was little only in comparison to the other rooms on the first three floors.

The tuckaway room was green, but I wanted it to be blue. For Astronomy and Science. We already had a Green Room that housed the gardening books. I'd had help on redoing the Green Room, but now I couldn't see how I was going to paint this one all by myself. It was too much to ask of my Three Petunias, as I called my dear but elderly library volunteers. I cocked my head to one side, visualizing blue walls fading up into a black ceiling covered with a planetarium-like display of constellations. Surely I could find someone who could paint stars on a black background. I wouldn't ask Bob. He hated painting.

"Why is my favorite librarian just standing there blocking the doorway?" Matthew Olsen, my next door neighbor, grinned at me from behind an armful of books. He must have raided the biography shelves.

"I can't wait to turn this into the science room," I told him, "but it needs to be painted black and blue first."

"Like bruises?"

"No. Like a blue sky around the sides fading into a black night above. With stars."

He peered over the top of his glasses. I could see the wheels turning. "That'll look mighty purty," he said. "I'll send Buddy over tomorrow morning."

"Matthew, you can't just volunteer Buddy's time like that. He may have other plans."

"Mm-hmm. He did. He was planning on helping me clean out my attic. I rooked him into it. I figure he gets room and board from his ol' dad, so he can help me when I need it." He glanced up at the ten-foot ceiling where the underside of the staircase ended its upside down stair steps. "Believe me, he'd rather be painting, even *this* place."

"But, how will you take care of your attic?"

"It's like every other attic in this town." I nodded, thinking of my own mess. "It'll get cleaned when it's good and ready, and not before." He gave a wicked grin. "I was hoping something more promising would turn up. I'll come along and keep him company."

Matthew had more energy and a great deal more artistic talent than I'd thought. Between the two of them, he and Buddy cleaned out the room, painted it, and created the prettiest set of stars, complete with a sprinkle of the Milky Way. They put up the shelves late Sunday night so Rebecca Jo and Esther and I could arrange the books on Monday.

A LAZY CURL of steam from Sam's soup-sized mug of coffee wafted its earthy good-morning smell through the compact beige-walled kitchen. Coffee? It could just as well have been chili or vegetable soup or spiced apple cider for all the notice Sam took of it. A plain white envelope. Sam Hastings paused only long enough to set down the rest of the mail beside the coffee, then ripped open the letter. A real letter this time. Not a postcard.

9/23/96

Dear Sam,

I finally figured out the only way I'm ever going to make as much money as I want is to marry it. Or steal it. But neither one of those is very appealing. I hate where I work, but it pays the rent. With my luck, if I married anybody, he'd end up being like Daddy. And if I stole anything, I'd get caught. So I just keep on having fun (not counting my job).

"What job? What job?" Sam practically shouted at the two sheets of paper that lay crumpled on the kitchen table, took a long sip of coffee, and looked again at the equally crumpled envelope. No return address and a smudged postmark. The letter had probably been in a pocket for several days before it was mailed.

> *I'm gonna quit smoking. Costs too much and the prices keep going up. You never smoked, so you don't know how hard it is to quit. Isn't it funny the way we keep in touch even though we never see each other? . . .*

"In touch? You call this keeping in touch? I don't know where you are. I can't write you letters. This isn't a conversation; it's a frigging monologue."

> *. . . Once Daddy dies, do you want to go back to Martinsville? . . .*

"Why are you asking me questions when I have no way of answering them?"

> *. . . I bet it hasn't changed a bit. Except I'm pretty sure the boogeyman doesn't live there anymore. Ha-ha. Oh! Forgot to tell you–I got a phone finally. Call me.*

"Finally? After two years?"

> *You keep on keeping on. Me, too.*
>
> *Your little sister,*
>
> *Easton*

Sam Hastings let out a long breath. More than two years had passed since Easton had run off with somebody's husband. Sam hadn't liked the sleazeball, but Easton wouldn't listen.

She'd stormed out the door into the warm July evening, and that was it. When Sam got back home from work the next day, all her clothes had been cleared out. Her bottles and jars, soaps and lotions, toothpaste and makeup were gone from the bathroom. She'd left the fry pan and the popcorn popper. She'd taken the pizza cutter and the CD player and her pillow. The note said, "Don't forget to feed the birds."

Two weeks later, just before Sam considered filing a missing persons report, Easton sent a postcard from Macon. "Having a great time," it said. The next card, as uninformative as the first, came from southwest Georgia, from Columbus. The husband came back to town after the first few months and his wife took him back. Easton stayed on the road, though, despite Sam's entreaties the few times she called–collect.

There were a series of cards from Alabama and Mississippi. Lately she'd been back in Macon. The postmarks (when they were legible) told Sam her location. Nothing more.

The late afternoon sun spilled onto the table, bathing Easton's letter in red-gold light. Sam missed that massive head of fiery hair and her wonderful singing. The house was so quiet now. Had been for two years.

Why would Easton want to go back to Martinsville, Sam wondered. They hadn't had an idyllic childhood. Sam was sure that some kids did have perfect families. Take Bobby and Tommy, for instance. Sam smiled. Three childhood friends. The thought started a movie in Sam's head–one that didn't run often, but once it began, Sam couldn't stop it. It had all started with Pepper. Bobby and Tommy came later, but Sam never would have gone way back in the caves if it hadn't been for Pepper. And then Sam wouldn't have shown Bobby and Tommy the caves. And Bobby never would have asked that question of his. The first time Sam ran away from home might have been the last time, except for Pepper.

SAM HEARD THE narrator of that internal movie.

"I'm talking to you, Sam. I'm talking to you. When you're five and you're scared of your father and you run up the street and across the footbridge, you don't want to stay very long. But you're afraid to go back and then it starts getting dark and by then you've wandered down to where the cave opens into the hillside, and you can see the town across the river and you can see your father out there shouting and looking for you, and he has his belt in his hand. You peek between the trees and see the other people turning away, not looking at your father because he's shouting and stumbling again and then you hear a sound behind you and you're scared to turn around, but you have to because it's close. And it's a dog a little ways inside the cave, whining and licking her bottom. That looks funny, and you laugh some until you see something coming out of the bottom, and it's a baby dog. And you watch it and watch, and it gets dark and starts to rain, and you don't care because you're inside the cave now and it's dry and the dog lets you pat her head. And you watch the baby dog eating and you get hungry, but it's too soon to go home. You know that. And anyway it's real dark now, so you curl up beside the dog and she lets you. And she even licks your face and that feels good. The next morning you tell the dog you're going to find her some food, and you creep home.

"The house is quiet. You can hear your father snoring. And you go to the kitchen and climb up on the counter and find some food. And you open the icebox and get out whatever you can find and you take it all across the footbridge again and you eat some and you give some to the mama dog and she's feeding her baby again and it feels good to be there. So then, every day you bring her food and you get to where she trusts you to hold the puppy and you name him Pepper because he's sprinkly black and white.

"And after a lot of time one day the mother dog isn't there any more but Pepper's waiting for you and you go in the cave just a little bit farther than you've gone before, down one of the tunnels that lead off to the side, and Pepper pushes you away from one of the deep holes on the tunnel floor."

GOOD OLD PEPPER was long gone. Sam glanced at the phone number Easton had scrawled under her signature and reached for the phone just as it started ringing. Half expecting it to be Easton, Sam was shocked to hear Aunt Myrtle's voice. "Sam? Can you and Easton come home? Your dad died last night. They found him out behind the house this morning. Looks like a heart attack or something."

Advanced cirrhosis, Sam thought, then glanced over at Easton's letter. Was she psychic?

"You need to come back," Aunt Myrtle was saying. "You kids are the closest relatives since that wife of his went and died two years ago."

"Can we stay with you for awhile, until we can throw out everything in the house?"

"Sure you can, dear."

Sam glanced at the letter one more time. "Is Bobby still around? And Tommy?"

"Of course they are," Myrtle said. "Bobby—well, we call him Bob now—is the town cop."

"Just like his dad?"

"Yes. And Tom runs the best restaurant you've ever seen."

Sam could almost taste avocado slices on rich wheat bread. "Figures."

"You'll see them at the funeral, I'm sure."

"No," Sam said. "No, we won't be there that soon. You'll have to do the funeral without us."Myrtle argued, but Sam wouldn't budge.

When they hung up, Sam saw Pepper dancing through a shaft of light in the cave. Then Bobby stepped into the light and asked, "Sam? You think you're ever gonna . . ."

Am I? Sam wondered and reached for the phone. Am I? Easton picked up on the third ring.

"This is Sam. . . . Yeah, Sam. . . . We're going home."

Saturday, October 5th

MELISSA LEANED AGAINST my kitchen counter. "I can't remember Sadie's number. Do you know it right offhand?"

I was busy piling some cheese and crackers on one of my blue-ringed plates. The library closed at 2:00 each Saturday, and she and I had formed a habit of having a mid-afternoon snack together if she didn't have bed & breakfast chores. Bob was up at his workshop doing fish things, the way he usually spent Saturday afternoons. "It's in my address book. In the desk–the top drawer," I said and pointed with my nose toward the office. "Feel free to rummage."

She walked past the laundry room door. I could hear Marmalade in there scratching around in her litter box. This rain was getting to be inconvenient, since Marmy almost never went outside when the weather was drippy.

It is too wet out there. I prefer dry paws.

I was tired of cleaning out the box every day.

I appreciate a clean box. I cannot flush the way you can.

Marmalade meowed quietly, and Melissa hummed a catchy tune as she bent over the desk. It sounded familiar, but I couldn't place it.

"Are you sure you've got her number?" she called around the corner. "I can't find it."

"I don't list people under–"

"I know that. You use the first names, but she's not under S for Sadie."

"The S section was getting full, so I put her under Y. It's snack time; come on," I reminded her.

"Y? Why?"

"You sound like an echo."

"I know. Why Y?"

"For yellow," I said. It made perfect sense to me.

She brought the book with her and settled into her usual seat.

I tooth-picked some cheese cubes onto my plate. "What's that you were humming?" I asked.

"Something I heard Ariel singing in the deli the other day while she was cleaning the counter. The tune just sort of stuck."

"She has a good voice," I said. "I wonder if she'll go into music after she graduates."

"Who can tell with kids."

"Any words to that tune?"

"Not that I'd know. She was just lah-lah-lah-ing it."

What does that mean?

"Catchy lyrics," I said. Marmalade hopped onto my lap and stuck her nose in the cheese on my plate. I intercepted her before she could complete her raid . . .

You gave some to Goodcook. Why not to me?

. . . and dropped her unceremoniously onto the floor.

Humph.

The sound she made was surprisingly like Grandma Martelson's favorite snort.

Chapter 8

Monday, October 7th

"YOU WOULDN'T HAPPEN to want to invite me for dinner, would you, Mom?"

My son, standing there munching on a brownie, was definitely shifting to a new phase. He used to show up in the early evening, admiring the smells coming from the kitchen, hinting without asking. Now he was being more direct. Twenty-two and still changing.

The dinners he liked so much were almost always soup. That was one of the few things I knew how to cook well. It's amazing how many types of soup there are–and all of them yummy. Particularly with all the goodies coming from Elizabeth's garden. The zucchini was still growing prolifically. All that rain hadn't slowed it down a bit. Each day I could step out the back door and pick something, cut something, or dig something up. Beans, leeks, squash, potatoes. I was going to have to ask Elizabeth what her secret was. Compost always worked wonders, but hers must have been super-charged. My three-bin system had been producing finished compost only for a few weeks. It takes a while to get a compost pile up and running. Elizabeth got simply spectacular results from her veggie patch in the back yard and I had inherited it (or bought it, rather).

My good luck. I hoped her garden would keep producing as well next year. Maybe it was the way she interplanted different varieties.

Scott watched me with his eyebrows raised in hope. "Sure," I told him. "We won't eat for another half hour or so, but you can go ahead and set the table." Bob wasn't home from Rupert's funeral yet, but I expected him momentarily.

Scott had been here often enough over the last six months to know where everything was. I watched him open the correct door and lift three small plates and three big bowls out of the cabinet. I pulled out the silverware drawer and handed him the knives and spoons as he turned to amble past me.

"Mom?"

His voice was half an octave higher than I expected it to be, a sure sign of stress. I looked at him, trying to gauge what was going on.

"Mom?" He paused.

"Yes?" I prompted.

"Mom?" Maybe he'd get past the first word before we sat down to eat. "You wouldn't happen to have a phone book around, would you?"

Phone book? Why did it take him so long to ask about a phone book? "Sure," I said, "it's on my desk."

"Oh good." He loped past me toward the office. "I thought I'd ask Mr. Montgomery about renter's insurance for my new apartment." His voice sounded a little too bright, a little too high. A little too fake.

"Renter's insurance?"

"Yeah. Because I have a new apartment."

"Yes. You said that."

"And you're supposed to have insurance on the contents, just in case something happens."

"Good thinking." Whatever was he getting at? A moment later I heard a stifled groan.

"What happened to the M pages? They're all stuck together."

Oh drat, I'd forgotten about Verity Marie and the glue. I was a soft touch when it came to my grandkids and what Verity called their "experibents." Scott was a good uncle, but he didn't have children. He wasn't at all forgiving until I told him I had Brighton's phone number in my address book. "Pull open the top drawer. It's in there."

Pause. Rustle. Rustle. Groan. "No, it's not. I looked under B for Brighton. And E for Ellen."

At least he remembered my filing system. "Look under I."

"I?"

"For insurance." It made perfect sense to me. What didn't make sense was why my son was acting so funny about a simple phone number. I looked at him. What, after all, did I know about the inner workings of my son's mind? I was fairly sure his nervousness had nothing to do with getting insurance. Hmm . . . Ariel! That had to be it. At sixteen–or was she seventeen now?– she was bright, and so drop-dead gorgeous that she stood out like a lighthouse lamp in the fog. Of course, she was a little young for him. She looked a lot older, but she was still only a junior.

Why didn't he just call her at the deli? Or drop in and ask for her phone number directly? Maybe he believed a circuitous approach would be better. Not scare her off.

"Scott?"

"Yeah?"

"You can call from here."

"That's okay, Mom. I'll do it later this evening."

He was sounding suspiciously bright. "Mr. Montgomery won't be home this evening," I told him. "He's on the Town Council and they meet on Monday nights."

"Oh?" He didn't sound surprised. He sounded devious. He probably planned it this way so he would have a better chance of talking with Ariel if her dad was out. "Guess I'll have to call him tomorrow on my lunch break."

I eyed my son's casual stance and decided not to press the issue. I'd find out soon enough if he started dating Ariel Montgomery. It was hard to have a secret in a small town.

"Are we still planning on having that family picnic next week? The one at Bluebottle Falls?"

"Yes," I said. "As long as the weather cooperates."

"Think I could bring a guest?"

Hmm. Did I want to encourage him to date Ariel? I doubted Ellen would want her daughter going out with a twenty-two-year-old. But that way I could keep an eye on them. "Fine with me, son," I said.

Chapter 9

Tuesday, October 8th

MARMALADE PRANCED AROUND the front door and meowed, so I let her out and watched her cut across the yard, skirting the flower beds that surrounded the dogwood tree. She headed up the hill like a power walker wearing little white socks. She was on a mission of sorts. Guess I'd never know where she was headed.

GLAZE OPENED THE front door, intending to wipe the streaks off the window pane that let the wan light of a cloudy afternoon into her new house. Well, old house, but new to her. She had to catch herself so she wouldn't step on Marmalade. "What, little one? Are you here again?" She called back over her shoulder, "We have a visitor."

Hello, Smellsweet.

Glaze watched her roommate back out of the closet where she was rearranging the cleaning supplies. Madeleine looked around the kitchen. "Who?" she asked.

Hello, Curlup.

Marmalade meowed from behind the butcher-block island.

"Oh. You mean the cat?" Both women smiled as Marmalade strolled to the far end of the long galley-type kitchen and headed for the cabinet just to the right of the sink. "This is what we get for showing her where we keep that jar of catnip," Madeleine said.

You do not have to show me. I can tell it is there.

"We're both suckers, I guess." Glaze pulled out the jar and extracted a fuzzy cat-toy that nested in the aromatic leaves. She tossed it high over her shoulder and watched Marmalade catch it in mid-air. "Wonder if she'd consider trying out for the Dawgs? . . ."

Dogs?

". . . She wouldn't even need a catcher's mitt."

Madeleine shook her head. "Wouldn't work. A baseball's a far cry from a catnip toy."

Baseball?

"Too bad. Biscuit and Bob could have retired on Marmy's salary."

Celery? Humans are hard to understand.

Glaze went back to cleaning the window while Marmalade played quietly and expertly with the ball of fake fur. Eventually she meowed to be let out, and a rather bemused Glaze opened the door for her.

THAT EVENING, BOB offered to walk with me to tap dance class. He was headed that direction anyway. He strode out the front door ahead of me. My knee was in pretty good shape, but I didn't want to jinx it by hurrying on the steps. Halfway down, I paused to look out across the front yard. Just enough trees to make it interesting, just enough flower beds to make it beautiful. Well, the trees made it beautiful, too. And I still wanted another flower bed out there, where the afternoon sun encouraged the grass to grow deep and thick. I hated mowing. Maybe more zinnias and some dwarf sunflowers, coneflowers and scarlet Crocosmia–all the bright colors.

Bob waved to the Snellings who were out for their evening constitutional, as they called it. Must have been a good idea because they were both in their seventies and still active as could be. Neither one of them wanted to retire. Frank had slowed down a bit in his frame shop, but Myrtle was still writing for the *Keagan County Record* and apparently still enjoyed gadding about the town for juicy bits of news for her weekly “Musings from Martinsville” column.

They paused as they reached our front walk. Myrtle waved at me as Frank said, in his usual stentorian tones, “Hey Bob, did you hear Sam’s coming back to town after all these years?”

Sam? The only Sam I knew was Sam Casperson, but he hadn’t left. I wondered who they were talking about. I didn’t hear Bob’s words, just the neutral tone of his answer. By the time I reached them, they were discussing the weather report. Always the weather. Didn’t anyone ever get tired of talking about the weather?

As soon as they were out of earshot down the hill, I turned to Bob. “Who’s Sam?”

“Just . . .” he cocked his head to one side, “just somebody Tom and I used to hang out with a long time ago.” He kept walking, but slowed down his usual long stride to match my steps.

WHEN WE PILED out of the dance studio en masse after the tap class, Marmalade was sitting on the sidewalk with her orange tail curled around her white toes.

I like to be tidy.

“Would you look at that, girls?” Sadie bent slightly and reached out her hand. Marmalade stood up on her hind legs and rested her front legs against Sadie’s thigh, then arched her neck into what looked like a thoroughly satisfying scratch session.

"She always does this, whenever I pat her," Sadie explained. "I think she knows I can't bend over as far as I used to."

"Nonsense," Ida snorted. "You're a lot more limber than you let on. Look at the way you do that essence thing." The *essence* was a particularly frustrating step that the rest of us struggled with. Sadie danced circles around us, with her arms out to the sides and her rather substantial hips twitching. Maybe Ida was just jealous.

Sadie drew herself up to her full five-foot one. "I don't have to bend over in that one," she said.

Ida humphed again, and we started up the street while Sadie got into her car. She drove everywhere. The rest of us walked everywhere. How could she be in such good shape?

Marmalade followed us up the hill and right into Melissa's kitchen.

I would like some chicken.

She meowed quietly, and Melissa lifted a little gray saucer from the cabinet and opened the fridge. "Would you like some chicken, sweetie-pie?" she asked.

Yes. I just said that.

". . . I just cooked some up for a pot pie."

Annie the vegetarian laughed. "When she visits me I feed her organic tomatoes."

"Tomatoes?" Ida interrupted. "Cats don't like tomatoes."

Yes I do.

"I usually give her meat scraps in a green dish," she continued.

They are good, too.

". . . and then she goes in and sits with Ralph while he watches his White Sox game. I've heard him explaining baseball to her."

He likes white socks. I have white socks.

Glaze laughed. "She's been up to see Madeleine and me a couple of times, when it wasn't raining. We bought some catnip toys for her."

Sadie walked in a few moments later, and we asked her if Marmalade ever visited her and begged for food.

Excuse me? I do not beg.

"Cream," Sadie said. "In a yellow bowl."

Why did my cat ever come home for cat food when she had such a progressive feast around town? I knew she visited Tom at the restaurant, too.

He gives me fish.

Where else? I wondered as I watched Marmalade licking her paw and swiping it over her face and whiskers.

If you would listen to me I would tell you my schedule.

Chapter 10

Thursday, October 10th

THE EARLY MORNING sun streamed in through the kitchen window over the sink and puddled on the linoleum. I'd been folding towels and sheets in the laundry room for longer than I cared to think about. Why did I always leave the laundry until there was such a pile it became a chore? I wanted to get it finished, though, before Glaze and I left for our shopping trip to Athens. When I came out into the kitchen, Marmalade was stretched full length on the floor, luxuriating in the pool of warmth.

It is not particularly warm. It is simply beautiful.

What a gift after so many days of drizzle. There was a glow around her head, almost like a halo, where the rays illuminated the fringe of soft hair on her ears and the whiskers that stood out from the side of her face. As I stepped closer to soak up a bit of the sun myself, a stray glint bounced off my watch and sent a flicker of light across Marmy's paws. She slapped at it before it skittered across the room. I could almost see her thought process.

Do I want to leave the sun to chase that little critter?

She was obviously wondering if she was fast enough to catch it.

Mouse droppings! You do not understand the way I think.

I brought my arm back into the stream of sunshine, and Marmalade pounced on the reflection, only to miss it as it disappeared in the fur of her back. She whirled and I eased my watch over my wrist so I could maneuver it better. I sent the little splotch of light bouncing up the side of the counter, and Marmy leapt after it, paddling her paws as she tried to scoop it into the air. This was much more fun than folding laundry.

> "THIS IS YOUR mid-week, mid-morning weather report from WRRT, the voice of Keagan County, right in the middle of your AM dial, where you get all the valley news and all the valley weather. Your reporter today, and every day, is Ralph Towers, better known in the valley as Radio Ralph. Heck, folks, WRRT is this valley's only station, and I'm the only reporter, so what you hear is what you get. And you get the best there is. It may have started out sunny this morning–that's Thursday in case you haven't looked at your calendar yet—and we're going to have lovely weather all the rest of today. But it looks like it's going to rain all day tomorrow. And Saturday, too, clearing on Sunday. What do these clouds think we are? Ducks? Don't think it's time to start building an ark yet. If it gets to that point, you'll hear about it first on WRRT, here in Garner Creek and all up and down the Metoochie River Valley."

"Isn't somebody going to strangle him someday?" Glaze asked as she looked for other stations on the car radio.

"Save your energy," I told her. "People like him."

"This people doesn't."

"Uh-huh."

Glaze poked the *Off* button with great relish. "Have you ever met him?"

I'd met Ralph–hadn't everyone?–and he did have some endearing traits, but his radio chatter was not one of them. "It wasn't my favorite event," I told her. Neither were his forecasts, which were invariably wrong.

Glaze had agreed to go with me to Athens for my Red Cross appointment, as long as we spent some time looking for a leotard and tap shoes for her. We filled in the drive time with general conversation. It felt good to have such a connection with my sister. Too bad we lost all those years when she was growing up under the storm clouds of manic depression. I wondered how many other people needed help and weren't getting it simply because nobody around them recognized bipolar disorder.

Finding the tap outfit for Glaze turned out to be a breeze. She opted for white shoes and an icy blue leotard–a great color for her with her silver hair. We ate lunch in Athens before we went to the Red Cross Center where we each donated a pint. I was on my ninth or tenth gallon–I'd lost track. This was Glaze's first time, and she did just fine. We drove home through the rain at a leisurely pace, glad to know that the next two days would be sunny. Ralph, after all, had predicted nothing but rain.

Chapter 11

Friday, October 11th

SAM WAS DRIVING. Easton hummed and fiddled with her fingernails. "Did you ever wonder about the caves?" Sam asked her.

"What do you mean?"

"You know, the caves."

"I *know* the caves," Easton drawled. "I just don't know what you're asking."

"Did I ever tell you how I started going there?"

Easton looked out the window at the pine trees that lined the road. Sam could almost see what she was thinking. *It's going to be a long trip. I might as well listen.* "No," Easton said, "I don't think you did."

Sam didn't care if she was an unwilling audience. There was this need to talk it all out. To rewind that movie and play it again. "Bobby and Tommy were always scared of the caves," Sam said by way of introduction. "They didn't exactly creep along behind me, but they didn't walk completely upright, either. You know those caves. Those treacherous spiked ceilings." Sam looked over at Easton. She seemed to be listening. Good. "Those gray tunnels were *my* territory. I think I knew every twist in every passage."

Sam laughed. "Bobby Sheffield. Bobby swore I had a built-in compass. I never got lost. Never. It didn't matter how dark it was, I never needed a flashlight. Bobby and Tommy always had those things. You'd think the flashlights grew out of the ends of their arms. But the dark never slowed me down."

Easton stirred in her seat. "The bats always scared me," she said.

"They eat lots of bugs."

"I know, but they scared me. They'd go flying in and out of those vents and I'd hug your legs and cry." She looked over at Sam. "They didn't slow you down at all. But I did. You must not have liked having me tag along."

"You were okay," Sam said. "And anyway, I had to get you away from Rupert."

Easton turned her head away. "He loved me," she whispered.

"He was mean," Sam said. "He was a drunk. He hit both of us. He . . ." Sam's voice faded off and the noise of the engine took over for a moment and kept the silence from engulfing both of them. "He was a mean man, and a poor excuse for a father."

"He loved me, he did. I know he did." She swallowed and Sam saw her clench her fists on her lap. "He did. He loved me."

Sam could never figure out how to get past this insane side of Easton. How could she equate *that* with love? Sam tried to neutralize the moment. "Those caves, though; they were really something. Pepper and I had a great time there."

"Tell me more about Pepper," Easton said.

Sam knew she'd heard this part of the story, but it was obvious that Easton wanted to change the subject away from Rupert. "He could walk on his hind legs," Sam said, "sort of hopping along. He did that from the time he was just a little tyke. He had this short silky hair that was mostly white, mostly black."

"Which?"

"Which what?

"Which was it, mostly black or mostly white?"

"Kind of both," Sam said. "Maybe half and half by the time he grew up, but when he was a puppy, he was mostly white with this big sprinkle of little black spots all down his back. Like a pepper shaker exploded over him." Sam took a deep breath, remembering that first night alone in the cave except for mama dog and the one brand new puppy. "So, I named him Pepper."

Easton didn't say anything. Sam wondered if she'd tuned out. "When did Bobby and Tommy find the caves?" she asked after a few minutes.

"I doubt they ever would have been brave enough to go in there if I hadn't led them in." Sam wasn't bragging. That's just the way it was. "We were all about six years old. We'd made friends before that, and they used to let me follow them up into the woods. That was their territory. The caves were mine. Bobby tried branching off on his own once, when he was eight or nine, but I had to follow the sound of his hollering and lead him back to the main room. He never tried that again."

"I need to pee," Easton said.

"Yeah. We need some gas. I'll stop at the next station."

"Remember where you peed in the cave?" Easton asked.

Sam felt a bit sheepish. "Uh-huh. Those deep holes."

Easton shuddered. "Once Tommy and Bobby pushed a couple of stones over the edge of one of those holes and it took a long time for it to hit the bottom. I know we just imagined it, but it sounded like it went all the way to China."

China. The word hung between them. Sam could practically see it there above the stick shift.

Easton shook her head and turned back to her window.

Sam tried for a light tone. "I feel bad about the peeing now, and we shouldn't have tossed our garbage in there either, but we just didn't think about it."

"The holes scared me," Easton repeated. "I don't think I ever went to the bathroom in the cave. I think I always just held it." She pointed up ahead. "There's a gas station. My bladder's gotten smaller as I've gotten older. Do you think that's possible?"

Sam saw the shaft of light one more time and smiled. "I suppose most anything's possible."

EASTON CLIMBED BACK in the car. "What are you chuckling about?" she asked.

"Oh, just remembering things."

"Like what?"

Sam put the car in gear and pulled out into the light stream of traffic headed north. "I was remembering how you used to gurgle when I fed you at night. You were a funny baby."

"What do you mean you fed me at night?" Easton said. "Mama fed me."

"That mama of yours was usually falling down drunk every night, right along with Rupert. Your screams used to wake me up at night. I started feeding you in the middle of the night when you weren't more than a month or so old."

"You couldn't have. You were just a little kid."

"I never had a chance to be a little kid," Sam said. "I was six when you were born, in case you've forgotten. And your hunger cries were loud enough to wake me up, but not loud enough to stir that mother of yours."

"She fed me. She used to hold me in the middle of the night and rock me. She loved me."

"Easton, that's a fairy tale you made up. Would you please wake up to the facts? I'm the one who held you at night. I fed you a cold bottle because I didn't know you were supposed to warm up the milk. I changed your diapers and dressed you and later on when Rupert started . . ." Sam gulped and plunged ahead.

". . . started acting up with you too, I hid both of us in the caves until he was too drunk to notice."

Easton picked at the side of her finger. "You know what? You're crazy. It wasn't like that at all."

Sam shrugged.

"I've got a hangnail," Easton said. "Wonder if I can get a manicure in Martinsville."

IT WAS A long trip. Every time Sam tried to talk about the way things really had been growing up, Easton would fly off into denial with a discussion of hair or nails or movie stars. Finally Sam gave up and just enjoyed remembering alone. Easton started singing in her low, rich molasses voice, something slow and soft. It was a good background for Sam's memory.

> SAM WOKE BOBBY most Saturday mornings by calling to him from outside Bobby's bedroom window. "Grab some food and let's go!" Bobby would come barreling out of his kitchen, slamming the screen door in the process. He'd have a paper bag full of bread and peanut butter and maybe an apple or two and a banana and some cookies. He'd holler to his mom, "See you for supper, Ma!" and off they'd scoot out to Tommy's house and issue the same invitation. They'd always have to wait while Tommy chose what to bring. Sandwiches, usually, with mayonnaise and things like avocado and thin-sliced meats that Bobby and Sam couldn't always identify, but always ate, since they shared all their meals when they were adventuring. Bobby and Tommy always brought the food. Sam brought the built-in compass.

The Big Room, as they called the cavernous grotto deep inside the hill, had pillars formed by eons of stalactites dripping down from the high ceilings, joining with the calcified stalagmites that had built up over the centuries from the ground floor of the cave. There was a shelf-like formation on the far side of the room that the three friends had commandeered as their club house. They gradually stockpiled old blankets and playing cards and a battered Monopoly game. The bats stayed in the side caves, mostly, so there wasn't that thick layer of guano in this room. That made the clubhouse shelf much more attractive, particularly when they ate their meals there. Once–only once–Bobby said, "Let's paint a white stripe from the entrance to the clubhouse." Young Sam imagined Rupert following the stripe and threw such a fit, Bobby never mentioned it again.

Bobby and Tommy and Sam. What a trio. They had hills and forests and caves to play in. They could roam on those lazy summer days and never be called home until it was getting almost too dark to see. Sam had a built-in timer as well. "Time to go, guys." And they'd all scramble down out of the trees or come dripping out of the river, or load up anything the cave mice might eat, throw their garbage down one of the deepest holes, and head home.

Sam clutched the steering wheel hard, fingers white against the dark leather. Bobby and Tommy would head home to meat loaf and fresh corn and new-hulled peas and baked potatoes oozing with fresh butter. The kind of meals Sam longed for but didn't get. Rupert never cooked, barely showed up sober enough to eat. The only things Sam learned how to make were tuna fish sandwiches and spaghetti with store-bought sauce on it. Back when Sam was five, Sam's mom left, or died (Sam never knew which since Rupert said one thing one day and something else another day, and nobody in the town ever talked about it). She left Sam with a burden too heavy for any child.

Sam looked up at the face looking back from the rear-view mirror. No wonder these eyebrows branch straight out from two deep worry lines, Sam thought. They seem to be cemented there. They'd been there a long time.

> Of course, Sam couldn't keep Rupert's secrets forever. Bobby and Tommy eventually noticed what passed for groceries in Sam's kitchen cupboard. And they started working on their moms. Sam could almost hear them wheedling. "Can we invite Sam to dinner, Ma?" "This is a lot of food you're cooking, Mom. What about if I run over and get Sam to come help us eat it?"

Sam downshifted on a steep hill and remembered with deep gratitude the mothers of Martinsville who sent clothing and food and books, and all those other necessities for any child, to Rupert Hastings' small house near the bottom end of Willow Street where it nested against the overhanging cliff.

> They couldn't keep Sam from running away, though. When Rupert was rip-roaring drunk and his howling anguish reverberated through the sturdy walls of the little cottage and out onto

Willow Street where all the neighbors could hear, or when Rupert was sober and visited Sam's bedroom in the middle of the night, young Sam would get away as soon as possible, slip out the front door, and scurry to the corner. But it was never soon enough. Little feet pounding the sidewalks, Sam would run all the way up First Street to the footbridge, eluding anyone who tried to stand in the way. Of course, once across the Metoochie, there was no way anyone could follow. Sometimes Sam would be gone for a day, walking the hills and exploring the caves with Pepper.

Sam remembered the sounds of the people calling *Sam! Sam! Where are you?* that first night, the night Sam found Pepper. Sam always stayed hidden until Rupert was civil again. And eventually the search parties stopped. Sam was grateful on the one hand. And incredibly lonely on the other.

SAM LOOKED OVER at Easton. She'd finished her songs and fallen asleep, curled up against the car window. She looked so vulnerable. Not a quality she liked to show.

Sam hadn't liked it very much when Rupert brought home a new wife, and then when a baby showed up less than a year later, when Sam was six, almost seven, it had been awful. But the baby's screams were pathetic, and maybe Sam needed somebody to take care of. Somebody more than Pepper, who got by on his own pretty well by then. Pepper hung around the yard, out of hitting range of Rupert, and was always ready to go off on an adventure with Sam. Poor Pepper didn't understand when Sam had to start school, but he was always waiting when Sam came home.

Easton was usually there, too, when Sam came home. Usually.

Sam glanced at her, still sleeping against the window. That kid sure could hide.

The caves scared her, so she never went there by herself. That much Sam could count on. But there were so many other places. One night, when Sam came home from playing at Tommy's house, Rupert sat at the kitchen table holding his bloodied head. That woman, his wife, was hollering at him about what he'd been doing to Easton. Sam didn't want to hear that part. Sam spent homework hours searching the town. She could have hidden anywhere. All her favorite places were empty, though. The cemetery, the woods behind the Millicent mansion, their secret path up through the cliff. How could such a tiny town be so immense? Sam finally gave up and headed back toward home. Not a block from the house, Easton burst out from behind the big tree at the corner and grabbed Sam around the waist. "I saw the boogeyman," she wailed. "The boogeyman! He was digging a hole to China!"

China, Sam thought. *China*. That had been a dirty word between the two of them ever since.

> It took a long time to settle her down. After that, she didn't run off too much at night unless they went to the caves together. Instead, when the brawling downstairs woke them, Easton would cling to Sam and cry. By the time Easton was twelve, Sam couldn't stand it any more. The day after high school graduation, Sam loaded up the '57 Chevy, convinced Easton to climb into the front seat, helped old Pepper into the back and drove north out of Martinsville, found a job, put Easton in school that fall, and made it work for both of them.

Thank goodness for Aunt Myrtle, Sam thought, and cringed, remembering how much money she'd sent them those first few years to help them along. *I paid her back, though. A little bit each month.* Sam stretched, as much as one can stretch behind the wheel of a Mazda. It would be good to be home again and see Aunt Myrtle. Home. Sam hadn't thought of Martinsville as home in years. Funny how things could change. All it took was somebody dying.

Chapter 12

MY KNEES WERE not up to kneeling in the children's section for fifteen minutes. It always took me awhile to shelve the little books scattered around on the low colorful tables. At least the children were reading. I supposed I should have tidied up before I left on Wednesday, but I'd just wanted to get home before the drizzle turned to a downpour. Today it was finally clear again, and I was stuck inside shelving books. Rebecca Jo and Sadie were still trying to catalog the boxes of donated books. Every so often I heard a burst of laughter drift down from the third floor.

When a square-faced young man walked in the front door, I used it as an excuse to stand up and stretch my legs out. "I didn't mean to bother you, Ma'am," he said. "But I wanted to get a library card if that's okay with you."

"Of course it's okay with me." I looked him over briefly. "I don't think we've met. Do you live here in town?"

"Yes Ma'am, I do, and I heard I could get a free box of blueberry muffin mix at the grocery store if I brought in a new library card." Ida was taking this publicity campaign seriously. And probably getting rid of some nearly outdated merchandise. He ducked his head and shuffled his feet. "I'm not much at cooking," he said. I could identify with that. "So I thought some blueberry muffins would be a good thing to try."

"It'll be tasty, I'm sure." I handed him an application and waited while he filled it out. It didn't take him long. His handwriting was legible, so I ignored the fact that he hadn't printed anything. His name, though. It looked like Reebok Garner. "I'm not sure of this spelling," I said.

He laughed and the lines around his eyes crinkled. "Nobody ever is. I was named for the antelope. My dad thought that was a fine-sounding name. But then somebody borrowed it for shoes."

"You must have gotten teased a lot." It was hard to feel sorry for him, though. He sounded so jolly.

"Not after they found out I could make more jokes about my name than they could."

"Good strategy."

He leaned against the counter. "My dad taught me that. He said he'd given me a name with a lot of character, and I had to decide if I could live up to it."

"Well, Reebok, you sound like an inspiration."

"No. My dad was the inspiration. I'm just following in his *shoes*." He had a merry twinkle to his eyes. I was pretty sure I was going to like Reebok. And our publicity campaign was off to a rousing good start.

RIGHT AFTER I got home, Glaze waltzed in and plunked down two metal coat hangers on my kitchen table. "You have to see this," she said. "Do you have a pair of pliers I can use?"

"Sure." I rummaged through the junk drawer until I spotted the red handles.

"You'll never believe what Sadie taught me." She twisted around the hook until it detached itself from the other end of the wire. Then she used the pliers to straighten the hook. Next she tackled the "body" of the coat hanger, straightening that whole piece until she ended up with an elongated L. When she held the straightened hook part in her hand, the rest of it stuck out in front of her parallel to the floor.

"What on earth are you doing?" I asked as she started in on the second coat hanger.

"Getting ready to dowse," she said.

"Dowse? I thought you needed a forked willow wand or some such thing."

"That's one way to do it." She stuck out the tip of her tongue between her teeth while she unwound the top of the hanger. "This is another."

"What are you dowsing for?"

"Well, Sadie told me that she knew how to dowse for bodies in old graveyards . . ."

"Bodies?"

"Uh-huh. And I asked her to teach me. It's really simple." She kept working as she talked. "We went over to the cemetery by the Old Church. Radio Ralph is a farce," she said. "The weather was beautiful for dowsing. Anyway, I held the short part of the hangers loosely in my hands so they could wiggle easily. Every time I got to a grave, as soon as the wires were over where the corpse was, the tips would rotate in and click together."

"You were probably doing it unconsciously," I said, "making the ends hit each other. After all, you could see where the bodies were just because of the headstones."

Glaze nodded. "I told Sadie the same thing. She had me close my eyes and walk across a long row of graves. She kept talking so I could follow her voice, and she warned me if I was getting ready to run into a headstone or anything." She paused and took a big breath. "It worked! Every time the tips got over a body, they swung in toward each other. I could feel them move and hear them click together. Sadie thinks I'm a natural."

"Glaze, this is bizarre."

"Yeah, but it's also lots of fun. It's supposed to work for water, too. Let's do your yard and see if you have any hidden springs."

"If I do, maybe that will account for the success of Elizabeth's flower beds."

THAT EVENING I couldn't help laughing as I recounted the ridiculous experiment to Bob. "We ended up deciding that Glaze was very good at dowsing for flowers. Daisies, dahlias, daffodil bulbs. Every time she got over one of the flower beds, her little dowsing rods clicked together. And they clicked beside the front dogwood, too."

"Water, maybe?" Bob offered.

"Silly! We can't have that many springs in the yard. Poor Glaze was thoroughly disappointed. She thought she was going to have a new hobby, I guess. She left the rods here. Maybe I'll have a go at them in the back yard."

Bob didn't exactly roll his eyes, but he came really close.

"Oh, don't be an old poop. Come on outside. Let's try this. It's a good excuse to enjoy the evening."

Grumbling under his breath, Bob picked up his coffee mug. "Let's go, then."

I started off from the back steps and headed in the general direction of Elizabeth's vegetable garden. Someday I would probably think of it as mine, but it truly was her work of art, and I was just reaping all the benefit from it. Always buy a house from a gardener.

As I approached the edge where the marigolds were planted to help repel bugs, the coat hanger rods stayed fairly steady in my hands.

"Go on down one of the rows," Bob offered from the porch where he perched on the top step, in his orange shirt, like an orangutan on a tree stump. An orangutan with a coffee mug.

Two feet, nothing. Three feet, nothing. Four feet into the garden, the tips clicked together. I backed up and tried it again. Same result.

"Keep going," he said. "We might have a dozen springs in there. We have to find them all before we leave for CT's."

"Quit laughing at me." I tossed the words over my shoulder and moved a little faster. I'd almost forgotten we had a dinner date and I needed to change first. Chef Tom's wasn't too fancy, but my faded old blue jeans weren't appropriate. Bob was going to have to change that orange shirt he had on, too. Orange is not his best color. By the time I criss-crossed the garden several times, we'd located four places where the rods always came together. Over the zucchini patch, beside the thornless blackberries, right in the middle of the leeks and onions, and where the string beans climbed their poles.

Bob was thoroughly amused. "Far be it from me, Woman," he said, "to denigrate this folklore system . . ."

I loved this man I married. He used the word *denigrate* in regular conversation.

". . . but don't you think your subconscious mind is making those things click? You want to find underground springs, so you're making yourself find springs."

"I am not! These things really are clicking on their own. And quit raising your eyebrow at me."

"We're downhill from a pond," he said at a measured pace. "There's probably a high water table under this whole block."

"Then why do the rods keep clicking in only a few places?"

"Because that's where they clicked the first time and now you have a predilection to having them repeat their performance."

Why on earth did I marry such an insufferable skeptic who used ostentatious words in ordinary conversation?

LATER, THOUGH, I decided to forgive him his skepticism. And his vocabulary. Dinner at CT's on a Friday night wasn't a hard and fast rule, but we liked to eat there. It was the sort of place where people took their time over their food. We'd driven instead of taking our usual stroll. The parking lot was full–everybody must have heard the weather report. Radio Ralph had said it would be clear all evening, so we all brought umbrellas or drove.

The rambly old house that Tom Parkman had turned into the Chef Tom's restaurant could accommodate loads of people, but each little room held only a few tables, so no one felt cramped or hurried. The old parlor was a lounge of sorts, with a bar down one side and comfortable chairs ranged around low coffee tables. We never minded waiting to be seated because we usually ran into friends, and the conversation was good. Except when all anyone could talk about was the weather. This summer had been bad for hurricanes. Of course, we never got the full force of the winds this far inland, but the rains were another matter. The funny thing was that the last of the hurricanes had ended a month ago, and we were still getting rain.

Bob dropped me off at the front door and went to park the car. By the time he joined me I was ensconced in one of the well-padded wing chairs across from Monica and George Ingalls, who had invited Melissa to join them for dinner. "No guests this weekend?" Bob asked as he slid into the chair between Melissa and me.

"Nope. I'm free," she said. "The Pontiacs will be here Sunday, so I'm living it up in the meantime."

George leaned forward to pick up his wine glass. He laughed as he looked at Bob from the gap between his bushy eyebrows and the tops of his heavy glasses. "Did you hear the good news? Sam's moving back to town. Any plans?"

What was so funny?

"Nothing to speak of," Bob said. Turning to me he asked, "What can I get for you to drink? The usual?"

"Yes. Thank you."

He scooted back his chair. "Be right back."

I didn't want to sound totally ignorant, so I didn't ask about Sam. Everybody in town seemed to know something about this guy, and I didn't have a clue. By the time Bob brought back my mineral water with no ice, the conversation had moved on.

After we ordered, I waited for our server to leave. "Who's Sam?"

"Sam? I already told you. Just somebody Tom and I used to pal around with. It was lots of years ago."

"Well, everyone seems to think it's funny that Sam is coming back to town. What am I missing?"

"Missing?"

"Yeah. What's the joke?"

"Oh, that." Bob shook his head. He was not being helpful at all. "We used to get into a lot of scrapes, that's all. All three of us. Remember I told you how Tom and I got lost in the caves that summer when we were twelve?"

"Yeah."

"Well, we got lost because Sam was the only one who knew the way around the caves really well. They may be just across the river from here, but believe me, they're like a foreign country. That day, Sam got mad at us because of some jokes we made, and left us there. Just ran off."

"What a terrible thing to do! You could have starved."

Bob pushed his glasses more firmly up onto the bridge of his nose. "Naw," he said. "Sam wouldn't have left us there more than a day or two." He chuckled. "Served us right. We'd said some awful things. We were bragging about how we could spit so much farther than Sam could. I guess we laid it on a little heavy. Poor Sam. Never did learn to spit worth anything. We were pretty hungry the next day, but we finally got out when Sam had second thoughts and came back to get us."

"Were you really that lost?"

"Not lost exactly. But we knew if we wandered around we would be, so we pretty much stayed put. We got kind of chilly those two nights, but we'd brought in enough food for all three of us, so Tom and I ate it and played card games."

"In a cave? How'd you see to play cards?"

"There are these . . ." Bob's hands sketched a vague shape in the air, "vents. Narrow openings here and there that let in plenty of fresh air. There was enough light that we could sort of see each other. But the vents were way overhead and looked too small for even a kid to get through. The bats could fly in and out through them, but the big central room where Sam left us had smooth walls and a really high ceiling, so we couldn't climb up and follow the bats out at sunset."

The bats of the Metoochie River Valley were a miracle. They were one reason our summers were so pleasant. Between the bats from across the river and the purple martins that lived in the bird houses all over town, the mosquitoes didn't stand a chance. I hadn't realized the hillside was riddled with those vents–sounded downright dangerous to me. I'd have to be sure I never took Verity Marie over there.

"Weren't you scared?"

Bob drew himself a little straighter in his chair, as if he were planning on denying it. But then his basic honesty won out. Or maybe he saw my eyebrow inching upwards. "We tried to pretend like we weren't, but halfway through that first night Tommy asked me what would happen if Sam had fallen in a hole and gotten killed on the way out. Nobody would know where we were."

"Your parents must have been frantic when you didn't come home."

Bob thought a moment. "Don't think so. Tom and Sam and I were always taking off into the hills for a day or two at a time. We'd raided the kitchen that morning, so Mom knew we were off on an adventure. Doubt she worried."

I decided I'd have to ask Rebecca Jo about *her* side of the story sometime. He must have run his mother ragged. The funny thing was that it never occurred to him that she might have lost sleep over his shenanigans. Of course, he'd never had children to raise. That was the difference.

Sol, my first husband, and I had let our son Scott go cliff climbing, of course, but he had safety gear for that. And there *was* that time he'd burned down the backyard workshop trying to make fireworks, but at least I usually had known where he was.

"What are you thinking about so hard?" Bob took a crispy cracker, spooned some spinach dip on it, and handed it to me.

"I was just thinking that I'm very glad I wasn't your mother."

Bob's eyes crinkle up at the side when he's amused. He reached across the table and touched the inside of my wrist. "I can agree with that, Woman. I'm *very* glad you're not my mother."

We finished most of the spinach dip, but then we had the waiter put our entrees in doggie bags and we went straight home.

Chapter 13

Saturday, October 12th

MYRTLE SAT BESIDE the substantial maple coffee table that she'd inherited fifty years before from her grandmother and stared at the two offspring of her second cousin Rupert. Two different mothers. She could see it in their eyes, their foreheads, their noses. Maybe the chins were from the Hastings side. Rupert had been square-jawed from day one. Sam's cheekbones were definitely from the first wife. Easton's hair was from wife number two. Of course Myrtle hadn't seen the kids in years. Kids. Ha! They were all grown up, practically middle-aged. Almost.

Myrtle sighed. She sincerely hoped Easton hadn't inherited her mother's temperament. Far be it from her to speak ill of the dead, but that woman sure took liberties. Land sakes, she could stir up a room just by walking into it. Had enough chips on her shoulder to start a bonfire with. Myrtle hated to admit it, but she'd admired that woman's pizzazz. Until she started drinking so heavily. Of course, married to Rupert, who wouldn't?

EASTON LOOKED ACROSS the dreary old coffee table at her cousin Myrtle. Why hadn't they bought some pretty furniture instead of this heavy old stuff? Something white would brighten up the whole room. Easton went back to picking at a snagged cuticle on her right index finger. Every time she ran her hands through her hair, the little piece of skin caught and pulled. It wasn't comfortable, and she didn't like it. She hummed a jazzy tune. Where, she wondered, would she find a manicure in this hick town? She wished she'd thought about that before she agreed to come back here.

SAM LOOKED ACROSS the shiny polish of the obviously well-loved coffee-table from Aunt Myrtle to Easton and back again. One had spunk and the other had attitude. One was all mousy gray coals and the other was live fire. One was full of anecdotes and old stories, while the other knew all the soap operas. Sam hadn't really noticed before. All Easton had was her hair. And her nerve. And her gorgeous singing voice.

How will I ever get her to face reality, Sam wondered.

Sam offered to help Myrtle refill their tea glasses. Easton just sat there fiddling with her fingernails and humming.

Once they were in the kitchen, Myrtle looked up at Sam. "I'm sorry you missed the funeral."

"Don't think I missed much."

"He changed a lot these last few years. Once that wife of his died he sobered up. Went to AA meetings. Even started trying to fix up the house."

Sam raised an eyebrow. "Humph."

"Believe me, it used to look a lot worse than it does now."

"I grew up there, remember?"

"Yes, dear. I do. I know you had a hard time, you and your sister both." Sam had to admit, Myrtle tried to be fair. "But Rupert did the best he knew how," Myrtle added.

Sam looked at her. "His best wasn't good enough. Not for either one of us. He was a mean man."

Myrtle took a deep breath and reached into the pocket of her gray cardigan. "When they found him, he had this in his hand." She pulled out two crumpled sheets of paper, folded as if to go in an envelope. "They said I should give it to you if I ever saw you again."

Sam eyed the letter. Curiosity overcame caution, a second or two before Easton rounded the corner into the kitchen. "What's the holdup on the tea?"

Myrtle slid the letter into Sam's outstretched hand, picked up two glasses and handed one to Easton. Sam said, "Thank you." Easton didn't say anything.

THE ENVELOPE WAS impressive. Montreal Literary Agency, it said. Madeleine ripped it open and pulled out a single sheet of heavy ivory paper. "I can't stand it." She held it out at arm's length. "Read it and tell me if it's any good. If it's another rejection, I'll go slit my wrists."

Glaze frowned as she put down her coffee cup and reached for the letter. "That's not funny."

"I'm serious. I don't think I can bear one more turndown."

"Of course you can. That's what happens to writers." She looked over the letter. "It's not exactly a rejection, but I don't think you're going to like this."

"You might as well give it to me." Madeleine took the letter, turned her face up toward the ceiling. "Please, please, please, please . . . On second thought, I don't want to see it." She rearranged her legs, tucking the left one underneath her and lifting her right foot onto the left side of the chair seat. She handed the letter back to Glaze and wrapped her arms around her right leg, resting her chin on her knee. "Read it to me," she said.

Glaze peered at her for a moment, wondering how anyone could manage such contortion comfortably, and then read,

> Dear Ms. Ames:
>
> Your manuscript *A Slaying Song Tonight* has distinct potential. Your writing shows a defi-

nite flair for both story line and dialogue. I would be open to discussing the possibility of representing you.

There is one condition, however. If you want me to sell your book, you will have to do some extensive rewriting. I have built a strong reputation in my field, and I know what sells and what doesn't. I suggest you either completely rewrite or else eliminate "Elyzabeth." The death scene at the end is unacceptable. I realize she is a major character in your book, but she does not ring true. The ring of truth is something that I require of all books I represent. It makes them so much easier to place with a major house.

Once you have completed this rewrite, please resubmit your manuscript. After reviewing it, I feel confident that we will be able to reach a mutually satisfactory arrangement.

Cordially,
Agatha Montreal

Glaze dropped the letter on the table and looked up with only a little hesitation.

"Where's my razor?" Madeleine asked.

"Oh for crying out loud, stop the melodrama," Glaze grumped.

"I was just trying to be funny."

"It's not ever funny to talk about killing yourself. I know. So quit it."

Madeleine unwrapped her arms and leaned back in her chair. "Whoops!" she said. "I must have pushed the wrong button. I'm sorry."

"Apology accepted," Glaze said with only a modicum of good grace. "Don't ever do it again."

The two women looked at each other, measuring the strength of the tentative truce. Then Glaze smiled. "You *did* push a button. I'll tell you about it some day. But not now." She stood up to get the coffee pot for refills. "So, what are you going to do about that rewrite?"

"I can't delete Elyzabeth," Madeleine wailed. "She's my murderer who gets mutilated at the end."

"Sounds like you're going to have to delete her if you want this Agatha Montreal to be your agent. Didn't you say she's really good at what she does?"

"Yeah. She's supposedly one of the best in the industry. The agent I signed with last year quit her job. I had to start over again. This is my first halfway decent letter."

"Then couldn't you give it a try?"

"I think I need to go cry about it for awhile." Madeleine tucked the letter back into the envelope. "Then maybe I'll *think* about considering it." She unwound herself, stood up, and drained her coffee cup. "It's a completely stupid idea. I don't think I like this Agatha Montreal very much at all."

"You don't even know her."

"What's that got to do with anything?"

"Sorry. I thought logic might be a possibility here."

"Not when I'm pissed off, it isn't." Madeleine turned and stalked up the stairs, pausing first to drape herself dramatically across the newel post. "I will retire to my desk and slash my murderer to bits. Then I will completely rewrite the entire book, inventing new characters right and left. And I will be back within an hour. Or two." She flipped her hair back away from her eyes. "Or make that a year."

Glaze laughed and rolled her eyes. "Writers!" she said as Madeleine disappeared up the staircase.

Dear Sam and Easton,

Myrtle tells me you two stay in touch, so I'm going to write one letter for both of you. I've been going to AA meetings for almost two years now. It's taken me all this while to get up to the ninth step, the one where we're supposed to make amends. I guess that's what this letter is supposed to do. These meetings don't let me make any excuses for myself. I hurt both of you. I guess I hurt you bad. And they tell me I can't blame it on the drinking. What I did was wrong. That must be why you left and why you've never come home.

I'm taking responsibility for my life now, and that includes the drinking and everything I did to the two of you. I know the beatings were a horrible thing. I know the fighting that went on between your mom (step-mom) and me must have scared you. I know that other stuff–well, it was bad, and I don't expect you to forgive me. I just hope there's some way you can understand that I was a weak man. And I took all of that out on you two kids because you couldn't defend yourselves.

Myrtle says she hears from you once in a while. She says you're doing okay. I'm glad. I know it's not because of your old man. You didn't inherit anything good from me, because I didn't have anything good to give you. So what you've done, you be proud of it because you got there on your own steam.

There aren't any debts for you to pay off after I'm gone. The house is yours Sam, and I hope some day you'll consider living here after I'm gone and making it a good home for both of you. I've cleaned it up. It's been handed down in the family from father to son right back from the beginning of this town. I don't know if I ever told you this. Four generations back we came from a second son, so we didn't get the main property, but what we got was good enough. Now I guess it's up to you, Sam, to keep it going.

My heart isn't doing very well. All those years of living wrong put a lot of strain on the old ticker, I guess. I'm glad I wrote this. I hope it can undo some of the damage I caused. I'm going to give this to Myrtle to send to you. She won't give me your address. I don't blame her. I wouldn't trust me either.

Your old man

Sam blinked hard a couple of times and handed the letter to Easton. It didn't change a thing. Rupert thought he could make it all okay somehow by apologizing? Well, he was wrong about that. Sam felt icy cold and too warm at the same time. How could you spend your whole life hating someone, fearing him, and then just say, "It's over. Move on." Rupert wasn't just dead. He was dead wrong. What he was right about was that they'd made it without his help. And now he was dead and buried. No. It didn't change a thing, but somehow Sam was glad to have the letter.

Easton read the letter, threw it at Sam, and slammed Myrtle's front door on her way out. She hadn't said a word.

Two hours later Sam went looking for her and finally found her in the back yard of the old house on Willow Street, huddled on a dilapidated lawn chair. "He must have died right about here," she said as Sam walked up beside her. "Myrtle said it was in the middle of the back yard."

Sam couldn't see that it mattered much.

"I don't know if I can live here," Easton said. "I've been trying to imagine going through a day in this house without thinking about everything that went on. I've tried so hard to believe that he loved me. And that she loved me, too. But sitting here, it's hard to hold onto that dream."

"You're in your own private fairy tale when you think that way," Sam said.

Easton nodded once, twice. "Yeah," she said. "Remember the blood when Mama brained him with the liquor bottle that night? I think if I walked into the kitchen now, that's all I'd see. The blood. And remember the times he chased us up the stairs . . ." Easton's voice wound down. She twisted to her right and wrapped her arms around Sam's waist. "I can't face it, Sam. I want to stay here in Martinsville. I want to feel like I have a home town. It's safe here now. But I can't live in this house. Can we find another place?"

Sam hugged her back. "We'll clear out the house. Maybe if we paint all the rooms it'll feel different."

Easton pulled away and looked back toward the house.

Sam took a deep breath. "We don't have to decide right now. Let's hold off for awhile." Sam saw Bobby stepping into that shaft of light and heard his question echoing through the cave. "I'm glad we came home. It feels good just to be back here. I want to hook up with some of my old friends. I want to see the caves again. I want to see if there's anything left for me here."

Easton didn't have anything else to say. They walked in silence back to Myrtle's house.

Chapter 14

Sunday, October 13th

FATHER AMES PROPPED his sister's umbrella so it could drip onto the mat beside the door. He held out a dry hand towel. She looked like a bedraggled puppy. "I'm glad you're here," he said. "But why did you come out in all this rain?" Thunder punctuated his question.

She curled herself onto the couch. "What do you really think of my books?"

Gory. Ghoulish. Ghastly. "I like them," he said. Even to him, that sounded inadequate.

She raised an eyebrow at him.

"I just don't understand why you torture people in so many devious ways," he said.

Madeleine shifted from having her left leg curled underneath her to having her right leg curled underneath. She plumped up the extra couch pillow and leaned against it. "Why do you say that?"

"Come on, Squidling." He reverted to the pet name he'd tagged her with so many years ago. "Don't you ever wonder what people will think of you with all this killing you do on paper? How can you sit there at your computer hour after hour and think . . . mayhem? Especially when you always do it to Mother."

"First of all, it's not Mother, . . ."

He mirrored her earlier expression as he raised one eyebrow.

". . . regardless of what you think. And secondly, that's what I do. I kill people in horrible ways. On paper. I've been doing it for years. And I intend to keep doing it until I get a book published." She shifted back onto her left leg. Father Ames couldn't figure out how or why she always seemed to curl herself into a pretzel. He wondered about it as she kept talking. "And I plan to have a lot of books published." She leaned forward to rummage through her purse and extracted an ivory envelope. "They love it," she said. "They want to be my agent," she added. She opened the letter and looked it over, almost as if she hadn't read it lately. "All they want me to do is a tiny rewrite."

He waited for her to go on, but she just punched the cushion again. "What does that mean?" he asked.

"I have to get rid of Elyzabeth," she wailed. "Write her out and invent somebody else."

He'd read the book. "But she's Mother."

"She's *not* Mother. She's my psychotic maniac murderer, and she gets thrown into that wood chipper at the end, and she deserves it, and it's such a deliciously ghastly way for her to die, and I want to leave it in, and I don't know what to do now, because I don't think I'll ever be able to do this." She balled up the letter and tossed it at him.

She should have gone into baseball, he thought. Father John the priest warred for several seconds with Johnny the brother. Father John the priest didn't know what to say. Seminary hadn't prepared him for his sister in tears. "You'll figure it out, Sis," Johnny said. "I believe in you."

The pretzel stayed curled up without saying anything else while thunder reverberated through the old rectory. John grabbed the box of tissues and plopped it on her lap as he went to pour them some coffee. It was all he could think to do. Anyway, he needed some caffeine.

"Thanks," he heard her mumble as he rounded the corner into the kitchen.

MAYBE IT WAS the rain that put me in such a lousy mood. I felt caged. Martinsville is such a small town. In the relentless downpour, though, I'd stopped walking and started driving to and from work and on every errand I had to run. I couldn't garden. I couldn't walk. I was ready to climb the walls. But thinking of climbing was a mistake because it reminded me of my attempt at rock-climbing four months ago. That had ended when a woman plunged to her death. Ghastly thought. And that reminded me of poor Harlan, the young man who'd been stabbed in the library a year and a half ago.

I shoved the little booties I was making into my knitting bag and interrupted my husband's reading. "Bob, I can't believe there have been two murders in this town in the last couple of years." I was in a sour mood, thinking about deaths. Violent deaths. "First Harlan. Then Diane Marie last June. How can that happen in Martinsville?"

He looked at me over the top of his glasses and folded his paper shut. "Beats me. It's almost as much a mystery as what happened forty-odd years ago. Remember?"

"Remember what?" I could see the wheels grinding as he processed my question.

"That's right," he said, "I keep forgetting you're just a youngster."

I stuck out my tongue at him. "At least I'm not an old codger like you." Still, forty years ago, when I was nine, Bob would have been in his early teens, old enough to recall something dramatic. "So, what happened?" I asked.

He shook his head. "At the time I thought it was pretty exciting. My parents were freaked out about it, especially my dad.

He probably felt like he had to solve it since he was the town cop. He never could figure out what was going on, though. About all he could do was ask everybody to keep their doors locked. That even worked for a while, but after it all settled down, nobody did anymore." He paused and drummed his fingers against the folded paper. "I wish I knew . . ."

Since he obviously wasn't going to finish his sentence, I tried jump-starting him. "You wish you knew what?"

"What happened to those seven traveling salesmen."

What is a salesmen?

Marmalade sat up in my lap, almost as if she were listening. "Salesmen? What are you talking about?"

"There were so many traveling salesmen in those days. Somebody was always knocking on doors, selling brushes or cleaning products or encyclopedias. Of course, most of the women were home during the day, and most of the men were gone, but nobody thought much about any risk. And most of those guys were just hard workers trying to earn a living. Oh, there were occasional shysters, but they usually gave themselves away with shoddy samples or poorly printed pamphlets."

Get to the point, I thought. "Were they harming the women, is that what happened?" I asked.

It is not nice to hurt women. I will protect you, Widelap.

"No, quite the opposite. They'd make their rounds through most of the town, and then they'd just disappear."

"Well, naturally. If they were travelers, they'd leave town. Of course they'd disappear."

"No. They'd never make it to the next town on their route. Usually salesmen would start here in Martinsville because it was at the bottom of the valley, and work their way north toward Russell Gap. But one day a detective hired by one of the companies came to town and talked to my dad. Told him that one of the men hadn't shown up in Braetonburg. Dad and the detective checked around and found that the orders women here in town had placed were never turned in. Then they called some of the other companies that employed travelers and found out they'd 'lost' salesmen, too. Dad even called in the state to help, but no trace of those men was ever found. They'd hit every house in town, and then they'd be gone, almost like they'd been abducted by a UFO."

What is a yuefoh?

I patted Marmy, who was meowing almost louder than Bob was talking.

"What do you think happened?"

"Wish I knew." Bob set the paper on the coffee table and scratched his head. He needed a haircut. "I'd love to find the answer someday," he said.

I thought about it as I scratched Marmalade. "Seven murders. That's a lot."

I can count to eighteen.

"Technically, it's not a murder if you don't have a body," Bob reminded me.

"Okay. So, seven not-murders."

"Seven disappearances."

"Bob?"

"Yeah?"

"How would locking your doors help if the *salesmen* were disappearing?"

He cocked his head to one side. "Guess you're right. But Dad always was a cautious soul. Didn't want anyone to get hurt on his beat. And, of course, that all happened right after Augustus Welsh vanished."

"Augustus Welsh?" I asked. "Any relation to Paul?" Paul Welsh was our neighbor across the street. He lived in a house tucked behind a huge hedge of *Ligustrum lucidum.* Glossy Privet to those who didn't use botanical names. Which meant most of the USA, I supposed.

"Yeah. His grandfather. They all lived together after his wife died. He walked out of the house one day when Paul was just a kid. Told his son, Paul's father," Bob added for my benefit, which was just as well, since I was getting lost in all the pronouns, "told him that he was going visiting. And he never came back."

"Who was he visiting?"

"Nobody knew."

"Let me get this straight. Mr. Welsh lived with his son and grandson?"

"They lived with him. After old Mrs. Welsh died, Paul's parents moved in to take care of the granddad. Paul was just a baby at the time. Once the old man vanished, my dad had to investigate it. It was one of his first cases. Couldn't find any trace. They figured he must have walked down to the river and been swept down the Gorge. Heavy rains that year."

"And the body never showed up downstream?"

"Nope. They did find a dead body, but it wasn't Augustus. He had a distinctive bent leg from some sort of accident. Walked with a horrible limp ever since he was a kid. The body they found had two perfect legs, and it finally turned out to be somebody from up in Russell Gap who'd gotten drunk and fell in the river."

"But he said he was going visiting, didn't he? Augustus, I mean."

"They didn't pay too much attention to that. The old man hadn't been right in his head since his wife died. About tore him up with grief, or so my dad always said."

I had a brief thought about the old man bumping off his wife and then drowning himself from remorse, but I always did have too active an imagination. "What does all this have to do with the dead salesmen?"

"*Missing* salesmen."

"Okay. How does it connect?"

"It doesn't." Bob scratched his chin. "Just the timing, that's all. Old Mr. Welsh one month, and the salesmen starting the next month. It doesn't make any sense."

I yawned and stretched. "What does make sense is bedtime."

"Good idea," Bob said. Then he caught the look in my eyes and stood up rather quickly, dumping Marmalade on the floor in the process. "Good idea, indeed."

Chapter 15

Monday, October 14th

"GOT ANY TIME for an old friend?"

Bob looked up from the application on his desk. "Sam!" He jumped to his feet. "Sam! I heard you were back in town."

"Couldn't wait any longer to look you up. You haven't changed a bit."

Bob ran his right hand through his hair. His left hand still held the application form. "Are you blind?" he said. "Look at all this gray."

Sam studied him for a moment. "Naw. You still look like my Bobby."

"Have you seen Tom yet?" Bob clasped Sam's hand across the desk and held it for several seconds. "Gosh, it's good to see you." He nodded at one of the paper-filled chairs. "Just dump that stack of papers on the floor."

Sam did as directed and sat. "No, I haven't seen him. Heard he's a chef."

"Naturally. Did quite well in New York. Finally sold out there and came back here to start a great restaurant. Up on Third Street."

Sam drummed three fingers on the chair arm. "What about you? Did you ever marry Sheila?"

Bob shrugged. "It only lasted a few years. She divorced me, but I . . ."

Melody Cummings stuck her head around the open door. "Bob, the guy's here for his job interview." She looked at Sam's big smile and back at Bob. "Reebok Garner, remember?"

"Melody's our general do-everything town clerk," Bob told Sam. "Couldn't get along without her. She keeps all our appointments straight, handles all the disgruntled taxpayers before they get to the assessor's office, answers the phone, types up letters." He glanced back at the application he held. "Drats! I haven't finished looking this over. Town thinks I need a deputy." He shook his head. "Sam, I'd love to talk some more, but this isn't the time for it. Are you in town to stay?"

"At least for a month. We have to get Rupert's things cleared out and do something about the house. After that, I don't know. Find a place. Get a job. See what happens."

"Well, let's get together for dinner or something. Maybe we can all go up to Tom's some evening. Real soon. It'll be good to talk over old times."

Sam nodded. "Great idea. I'll call you tomorrow."

"I'D LIKE TO get a library card."

I looked up from the ancient rolltop desk. I was still trying to put some semblance of order into the pigeonholes that were stuffed with old receipts and grocery lists and letters. Part of me wanted to throw out everything, but the librarian side of me felt like I was holding history in my hands. I shoved the small pile of receipts back into the fourth hole from the left on the top row. This job could wait till later. Till tomorrow. Till next year.

The woman who had requested my attention stood there, quietly looking me over. Her gaze seemed particularly intent, but not hostile, so I decided not to worry about my faded blue jeans. I normally wore a skirt, blouse, and sandals to work, but hadn't wanted to deal with trying to keep my feet warm in this cold rain, so I'd opted for my roomy old jeans, a sweater, and warm socks with my tennies. Marmalade had elected to stay home. She was probably going to snuggle up on my pillow all day.

"Do you live here in the Upper Valley?" I asked. "Anyone can use the library facilities, but you have to be a Keagan County resident to check out books." Why was I sounding so insufferably stuffy? We were trying to increase the number of library patrons, weren't we?

Her long chestnut hair slipped from behind her ears and swung forward as she nodded. "I'm moving back to town. I grew up around here." She stuck out her hand. "My name's Louise Cronin. But I was born a Hastings. I'm going back to that name officially as soon as I can get to the lawyers."

"Bisque McKee," I said. Her handshake was firm. "People call me Biscuit."

"McKee?" She cocked her head to one side. "I don't remember any McKees from when I lived here before."

"I'm fairly new here." I stood up and motioned her over to the check-out desk that held the application forms. "I moved here from Braetonburg. Ended up marrying a Sheffield, but I kept my maiden name. Didn't want to be saddled with such unfortunate initials."

As generally happened when I made that statement, it took her a moment to figure it out. Her laugh, when it bubbled out, was what I can only describe as throaty. It reminded me of the smell of coffee. Rich and dark and flavorful. Luckily most people never thought about my current monogram–just as unfortunate.

"There's a good law firm in Garner Creek," I told her, "if you want to change your name legally. They've been in business quite a while, and I've never heard any complaints."

"Are they still around?" She smiled. Her teeth were exceptionally white. "Bushy, Bagot, and Green? I knew them a long time ago. When I was a kid." She took the form I handed her and wrote in her name. Strong handwriting. Well-formed letters. I could read them easily, even upside down from my side of the counter.

"Louise is my middle name, but I hate my first name. I'm not going to put it on here."

"That's okay," I assured her. "We're not real formal around here. I think we'll need to use your last name as it is now, though. We can always change the card later."

"My husband was a louse, but he was hard to hate." She filled in an address up on Third Street. "One of those charmers that make you feel like heaven until you find out he's been running around on you with everything in a skirt. It was a mistake right from the start. My little sister used to live with me, but she wasn't much help where the rent was concerned. I think she's pathologically unable to hold onto money." She sighed, and pointed to her application. "Cronin," she said. "I was only married for a couple of years. Right after the divorce I stopped using his name. It had too many bad memories associated with it. It's about time I reclaimed my birth name, even though it never did me much good."

It's amazing, I thought, what women who've just met will tell each other. I supposed that was all part of the networking we do so well. The connecting. The inter-connecting, rather like spider webs, with the strands stretching between us, thrown out on the waves of conversation. I was getting entirely too lyrical.

"So you married Barkley," she said.

"No. I married his brother."

"You married Bobby?" Something that looked surprisingly like pain flicked across her face.

Bobby? She was calling him Bobby? Of course she was. She would have known him way back when. I pointed to the address she'd given. "Isn't that Myrtle Snelling's house?"

"Um-hmm," she said. She shook her shoulders. They must have felt tight. "She's a great-aunt of some sort, or maybe a cousin. I never paid much attention to all that stuff." She wrote in a phone number. "We just got into town Saturday night. We're staying with Aunt Myrtle until we get our father's place cleaned out."

"We?" I asked. I knew I was being nosy, but it felt like she expected me to know what she was talking about.

"My sister and I." She paused. "We kids always stuck together. And now that Rupert is dead . . ."

She let the sentence dangle there, like an unbaited fishhook. I had the distinct impression I shouldn't ask any more questions. I'd read about Rupert Hastings' funeral in Myrtle's column. There hadn't been any of those flowery death notices that tend to blossom in small-town newspapers. I'd wondered about it at the time. Bob said he had to be at the funeral, but it was a library day, so I went on to work and let the Petunias attend the service. I hadn't known the family after all, except for Myrtle, and she was only Rupert's second cousin. It wasn't like losing a brother.

Louise straightened up, stretched, then leaned against the counter. "If I stay in town . . ."

If? She'd just gotten a library card. Why do that if she didn't know whether or not she was staying for good?

". . . I'll probably be working at that catalog company up in Russell Gap. A cousin of mine owns it. I called him from Atlanta last week, and he told me he might have something available. It won't pay much, but I'll have the house. And I need a simpler job for a while, I guess. I have a lot to think about."

I wondered what she did that she needed to get away from her old work. "Small world," I told her. "My son works there, at the catalog company."

"You and Bobby have a son?"

"From my first marriage. I was widowed six years ago. Bob and I married last April," I explained. "I also have two daughters and two granddaughters. And one on the way," I added, for good measure.

"Last April?" she said. "That's all?" She handed me the form. "I never had kids. Maybe that was just as well."

The phone number wasn't Myrtle's. It wasn't even our area code. "We need a local number," I said.

"That's my cell phone. It's the best way to reach me."

"Louise, I hate to be the one to tell you, but cell phones don't work in this valley."

"Crud-buckets," she spluttered. She pulled a slender, shiny blue lump from her purse, flipped it open, and pushed a button. "I paid a minor fortune for this baby, and you're telling me it won't work?" Before I could answer, she read from the tiny screen. "Roaming . . . roaming . . ." Her hair swung forward again.

Bob and I had had several discussions about cell phones. The geographics of this narrow, cliff-enclosed valley made cell phone transmission almost impossible. Bob and all the other police officers and volunteer firefighters up and down the valley had pagers that were somehow or other serviced by the local independent phone company, but cell phones were way beyond their capacity. We'd had private phone lines for only the last two dozen years. Before that, everyone was on a party line. Hopelessly out-of-date, I supposed, but then again, we didn't have to put up with rush-hour traffic or high crime rates or high school dropouts. I could live without cell phones.

"I can't live without my cell phone," Louise grumbled. She turned the little blue implement toward me.

No signal I read in minuscule letters. I guess you'll have to, I thought. But I didn't say it out loud.

She stuffed the useless blue box back in her purse. "I guess I'll have to," she grumped.

NOT FIVE MINUTES after Louise left, another new patron came in asking for a library card. She'd seen a sign in the grocery store. "They'll give me a free bunch of bananas if I have a new library card. I need to do more reading anyway," she said. "I'm on my lunch break. Will this take long?"

Ida must have run out of muffin-mix and started on her overstocked bananas. I'd have to thank her the next time I saw her. I turned my attention back to Melody. She was the indispensable clerk at the town hall. I'd met her there and seen her around town. I wondered if Louise had seen the flyer, too. I should have mentioned it to her. I'd hate for her to miss out on her free bananas. That afternoon I gave out three more library cards. I hoped Sharon's ploy to get new customers for her manicurist at the Beauty Shop was working just as well as our library card campaign.

Chapter 16

I SAT, AGAIN, at the ancient rolltop desk, wondering just how old it was, trying to put off the chore of sorting all the odd bits of paper, mostly receipts so far, that crammed into the pigeonholes—five rows of them—under the rolled back lid.

I can help you.

Marmalade swatted at some papers that hung out of one of the middle cubbyholes toward the right hand end of the fourth row. A minor cloud of dust rose around both of us. Marmalade sneezed and I went for my bottle of water.

"Bless you." Sadie pushed the reshelving cart toward the children's section. She didn't usually work on Mondays, but we were trying to catch up with a lot of picky little chores.

I took a satisfying slug of water and pulled out a wad of papers that, if the dust spoke the truth, had not been dislodged for years. Change that to decades.

I unrolled and unfolded for a moment or two and ended up with a pile of curling papers, many of them yellowed a bit along the edge that had stuck out from the wooden confines of the pigeonhole. These looked like they might be more interesting than the receipts I'd found in the top row.

Marmalade stuck her paw far back into the now-empty pigeonhole. "What's in there, Marmy?" I asked her, . . .

More paper.

. . . almost as if I expected her to answer me.

Mouse droppings! You do not listen to me.

She interrupted her purr with another sneeze. More dust, I supposed. But there did seem to be something else in there. I took scissors from the wide drawer and used them to dig into the narrow space. I pulled out a crumpled piece of paper that had been folded and refolded. It was a bill for $6.83, addressed to Benjamin Millicent, handwritten in an old copperplate script. Beneath the amount, there was a note that stated *Remaining Balance for One Rolltop Desk of Fine Maple, with Secret Drawer, bought on Account.* The date was August 12, 1834. The letterhead, printed at the top, said

Moon's Fine Furniture
E Moon, Prop.
Established 1803

A secret drawer? Hmm. I wondered if we were talking about the desk I was sitting at. Maple. Rolltop. Millicent. Probably. I wondered what the E stood for. Edward? Eugene? Elijah? "Sadie," I said, "come look at this."

She set down the stack of Learn to Read books and trundled over to the desk.

"I think our desk has a secret drawer." I poked around a bit. I'd have to get Bob to help me find it. "Do you know anything about an E Moon Furniture Store? I've never heard of a Moon family in Martinsville." I handed her the bill and rummaged through the pile. Another bill from E Moon—Ernest? Erskine? Estus? Lots of old-fashioned names started with E—specified a bedstead. And a third listed various tables and chairs. "Mr. Millicent must have been a loyal customer of Mr. Moon," I said.

"Mrs. Moon."

"What?"

"*E Moon* was Eliza," Sadie said.

"E for Eliza? Not for Edward?" Or Elias or Elkin or Elijah, I added to myself.

"Yes. You see, she'd been the local . . ." Sadie paused and looked around the empty library, then lowered her voice to a conspiratorial level anyway. "The local madame. Or she was up until the flood of 1802 washed away the house she maintained down on First Street right across from where Ida's grocery store is now. The flood swept it away with hardly a trace left of the foundation." Sadie shook her head and chuckled. "I can just see all those prim, proper ladies in the town deciding that Mrs. Moon had been judged and come up lacking."

"What happened? Was she killed in the flood?"

"Oh, mercy me, no. She lived another 60 years almost. Died close to ninety years old."

"That doesn't sound like much of a judgment to me."

Sadie laughed and handed back the bill. "I have to get to Sharon's for my perm. If you find anything else interesting, let me know. And if you find that hidden drawer, don't open it until I get back."

"I wouldn't dream of it," I said. Luckily, I didn't have to test my integrity, because I didn't find it, even though I looked for a long time.

"GIRLS, YOU WON'T believe what Biscuit and I found out this morning at the library." Sadie poked at the towel that wrapped her wet hair and shifted her ample bottom in the chair next to Ida.

Sharon clipped another snip from Ida's hair. "Something good?" she said.

Sadie spread her fingers wide. "This is the prettiest manicure I ever had, Pumpkin. Thank you so much."

"Are you going to tell us what went on at the library?" Sadie knew Ida had no patience with suspense. "And, by the way, that's the only manicure you've ever had."

Sadie chose to ignore Ida. "There's a secret drawer in the rolltop desk."

"What's in it?" Ida asked.

"Ooh, I love secrets," Sharon said.

"How do you get into it?" Melissa demanded.

"Well, we haven't exactly found it yet," Sadie admitted, "but we're sure it's there."

Ida snorted. "Right."

"We are! We found a receipt that listed the *rolltop desk with a secret drawer*. It was from Eliza Moon."

"Is she from around here?" Sharon asked.

"Eliza Moon," Ida said. "Wasn't she the town hussy?"

"No, dear," Sadie said. "She was the town *madame*, until she started her furniture store, that is."

"This sounds good," Sharon said. "Tell me more."

"She used to live here in the 1800s," Sadie said. "She was the local lady of the night, had a house right here on First Street. But then she turned respectable."

"Respectable?" Ida snorted. "Ha! Bet nobody let her forget what she'd been."

Sadie glared at her friend. "Hush your mouth Ida, and listen. Eliza Moon turned out to be the prettiest corpse anyone had ever seen."

"You ought to know," Ida said. 'You know more about cemeteries and obituaries than any woman I've ever known."

Sadie took a deep breath. "I heard from my great-grandmother, who lived to be almost a hundred years old, that every woman in town got mad at Eliza Moon's funeral."

"Why was that?" Sharon wasn't even pretending to work on Ida's hair any more.

"Because she was the most graceful dead body anyone had ever seen. Her hair was the color of those Irish Setters up on Pine Street. And even with a lot of gray in it, it was still full and long and absolutely gorgeous. And she had a face like an angel."

"Ha!" Ida wasn't impressed. "I don't believe that. The woman was ninety when she died."

"She was still beautiful," Sadie said. "And all the women went home from the funeral and took it out on their husbands. At least that's what I heard." From where Sadie sat she could look right out on Main Street. She halted her narration to watch a young woman get out of a dark blue sedan. "I swear I'm looking at a ghost, girls," Sadie said.

Everyone turned and watched the red head cross the street. Her hair melted down her back. Its fire raised such heat that the rain turned to mist, to steam, before it even made contact. Or maybe that was just Sadie's imagination. "It's Eliza's ghost," she said.

The bell over the door jingled as the woman walked in.

"Welcome to the Beauty Shop." Sharon's voice quavered a bit.

"My name's Easton Hastings," the new woman barked in a voice that threatened to drown out the whine of Melissa's hairdryer. "I need me that free manicure. And I need it fast," she added, plunking herself down on the worn pink seat at the shampoo station. A room full of pink, orange, and red-fingered women stared at her. "I'll take that shampoo, too," she growled.

All the women looked at Sharon. "We'll be with you in a minute, honey," Sharon cooed. "I just have to finish a couple of these other ladies first." Pumpkin started to stand, but Sharon shook her head. "Pumpkin, honey," she said, "you need to put that second coat on Miss Sadie's nails."

Sadie looked down at her Petal Pink nails that Pumpkin had finished ten minutes ago. Sharon didn't like being pushed around, that was for sure. "I don't think it's a ghost, after all," Sadie muttered.

Easton fidgeted while Sharon spent more time than necessary checking Ida's brown hair and Sadie's gray hair, fussing with a comb-out and fiddling with Melissa's dryer. Pumpkin applied two more coats of clear polish over Sadie's Petal Pink and took an unconscionably long time doing it.

Easton tapped her toe, looked at her watch, shifted in her seat, and shook her head. It was obvious that she was in a hurry, but Sharon wouldn't budge.

Sadie peered from under the rim of the dryer as Sharon lowered it over her curlers and saw Easton laid out in a coffin, with her luminous hair spread around her narrow face. Easton shifted sideways in the shampoo chair and Sadie added a dramatic streak of white to the ninety-year-old head in her vision. Yes. Easton would look as pretty when she died as Eliza Moon had done. Too bad her manners didn't suit her looks.

"There must be *something* nice about her," Sadie mumbled, but nobody seemed to hear her.

MADELEINE SET THE manuscript exactly in the middle of the kitchen table and tapped her index finger on it twice before she started crying. "It's awful," she said to the sink. "I don't know why I ever thought I could write," she told the refrigerator. Turning all the way around on her heel, she addressed the stove. "Maybe I should eat roast book for dinner and never have to look at this mess again."

"Who are you talking to?" Glaze stood in the doorway with her hands full of dripping wet grocery bags.

"With all that thunder, I didn't hear you come in." Madeleine gave a loud sniff. "Here," she said, swiping at her eyes. "Let me take a couple of those."

Glaze handed over two bags. "These are all the upstairs things–toilet paper and such." She set the rest on the counter beside the sink and started unpacking bell peppers, leeks, leaf lettuce, garlic, lemons. "I left the cans and boxes in the car," she said over her shoulder. "We can bring those in later, if the rain ever slows down." Her voice dropped to an obviously nonchalant pitch, as she put two dark red potatoes off to one side. "So, who *were* you talking to?"

Madeleine shrugged, even though Glaze wasn't facing her. "I read my whole book again. I decided it's fairly awful. How could I ever write such drivel?"

Glaze turned around. "It's . . . it's not *that* bad."

Madeleine's eyes narrowed. "That's not much of a recommendation."

"Well. . . um . . ." Glaze stuttered a bit. "Maybe it's just that I don't read a lot of blood and gore sorts of books."

Madeleine set her two grocery bags on the nearest chair and leaned against the back of it. "No. You're right. It's not that bad. But it's not that good, either." She pulled her hair back from her face as if she were making a ponytail. "Maybe Ms. Montreal is right. I need to start over."

"She didn't say that."

"No," Madeleine said again, giving one last tug at her hair. She shook her head and sank onto the other chair. "She didn't. *I* said it. I just can't get excited about killing off Mother now that I don't live with her anymore."

"But I like the way you have that chase scene through the cemetery in the ice storm."

Madeleine raised one eyebrow. "So, keep that scene and ditch the rest of the book?"

"I didn't say that!"

Madeleine placed both hands flat on the table. "You didn't have to." She picked up the grocery bags in one hand and her manuscript in the other. "I'll put the toilet paper away, and then I'll flush *this*."

"How about a nice cup of coffee?"

Madeleine winced. "I don't know how to write and you don't know how to make coffee. We make quite a pair. Here." She held out the toilet paper. "You take this up, and I'll make us some *good* coffee."

Glaze grinned and flounced out of the kitchen.

Madeleine pulled the coffee maker closer to the edge of the counter. "Maybe I could *start* with the cemetery scene and do some flashbacks," she said as she poured in the water.

By the time Glaze got back, clad in a comfortable set of blue jeans and an icy blue sweatshirt, Madeleine was crossing out entire paragraphs, entire pages.

"I don't have to kill her off and chop her up in the wood shredder," she muttered. "I could have her go quietly insane and fall into that ditch by the cemetery at the end."

"Be sure she's drooling and gnashing her teeth," Glaze suggested. She poured herself a cup of coffee and took a sip. "This coffee is divine." She looked out at the swirling rain clouds. "You could have her sinking into the ditch at the end, unable to hold herself up. The water could be rising . . ." Glaze took another sip. "Horrible death," she added.

"Good touch. Now all I have to do is write the entire book over again. Piece of cake."

Chapter 17

Tuesday, October 15th

IT WAS ALL anyone could do to get through class. Everybody wanted to talk about Easton Hastings and the furor she'd caused at Sharon's Beauty Shop. Miss Mary kept us quiet enough during class, but afterwards we descended on *Azalea House.*

Ida was in full gossip mode. "And Sharon just left her sitting there for a good five minutes. Easton kept shifting around and tapping her foot and doing everything she could to hurry Sharon up."

Sadie broke into Ida's commentary. "It was more like ten minutes," she said. "And the more Easton fiddled with her watch, the slower Sharon worked. So did Pumpkin." She held out her pink-tipped fingers. "She gave me two extra coats of polish I didn't even need. Some people just don't know how to behave."

"Are you talking about Easton or Sharon or Pumpkin?" I asked.

Sadie took a moment to answer. "Well, none of them would have won a prize."

"That's right," Ida said. "Pumpkin was just following orders, but Easton was rude and Sharon was vindictive."

And we were gossipy. Before any further snipping at Easton could surface, I changed the subject. "Glaze," I said, "what did you think of the tap class?"

Glaze shook her head. "I know I'm not the most coordinated person in the world, but how could I have sprouted two left feet in the past week?"

We all nodded. We knew just how she felt.

"WHO ON EARTH is this Easton Hastings?" I asked Bob after I got home from class. "How does she fit into the family?"

Bob looked up from his *Keagan County Record.* "The Hastings family? She's Sam's little sister." He went back to reading.

"When am I going to meet Sam?"

He looked back up at me over the top of the paper. "I'm surprised you haven't already. Sam always did love books. Probably in the library . . ."

His mind was obviously on his paper, so I let it rest. Everybody else in the world was taking out library cards, thanks to my publicity campaign. Well, Ida and Sadie's publicity campaign. So why not Sam? I'd meet him eventually, I supposed. Especially with Ida and Sadie planning to hold a Halloween potluck party for the whole town at the library.

I turned back to my knitting. Bob rustled the paper. "Sam didn't call me today. Wonder why not?" And went back to his reading.

My gratitude list for Tuesday the 15th

1. Glaze
2. Sadie and all the other tappers
3. Bob - naturally!
4. The acorn squash that is ripening despite all this rain
5. My glorious healthy garden, even if it is soggy.

I am grateful for
the birds who chirp and awaken me before dawn
catnip from Smellsweet and Curlup
Widelap who lets me outside when I want to go out
water in a bowl
tuna

Chapter 18

Wednesday, October 16th

IT WAS STILL raining that first day she walked into the library just before closing time, but the rain had turned cold. I watched her pause just inside the heavy mahogany door and shake herself, dog-like, sending a spray of droplets from her massive halo of red hair. The wide hardwood floorboards glistened from the excess moisture as she floated across that oaken expanse. This must have been the sort of moment that Haggard wrote about when he first saw the ethereal *She* of his 19th century novel. That was perhaps why when Easton's voice came, gravelly and hoarse, it shocked the heck out of me. I had expected dulcet vibrations instead of a construction site rat-a-tat-tat.

"I'm Easton Hastings," she croaked. "I need me a library card and I need it fast."

Hello.

"Does that cat bite?"

I retract my greeting.

"Of course not. She's a library cat."

I am more than that.

"I don't like cats very much. They eat birds."

I do not. I do not like feathers stuck in my mouth.

I'd never seen Marmy chase a bird, but I didn't say anything. It's hard to talk people out of unreasonable prejudice. Oh well, I didn't have to like her in order to give her a library card.

This was quite the week for issuing new library cards. Maybe it wasn't just the publicity and the free food. Maybe it was all the rain, too. People appreciated reading so much more when they weren't lured by lovely autumn weather. And the periodic power outages that had left so much of Martinsville without television had helped, too. Of course, Bob and I didn't have a TV set, so it didn't matter much to us. And we had a hand-crank emergency radio, so we could always get the news (gloomy) and the weather report (rain, rain, rain). Radio Ralph kept saying clear, clear, clear, but we all knew what that meant.

I called my wandering mind back to my job and handed the woman an application form as Marmalade stopped meowing and jumped off the counter onto the seat of the chair I'd just vacated. "As long as you live here in the Upper Valley, all you need to do is fill this in." I knew who she was, of course, after the discussion on Tuesday night in Melissa's kitchen. There couldn't be two heads of hair that color in this small town.

There are three. Do you remember the Irish Setters?

"Yeah, I live here now. We're staying up on Third Street for a while, but we'll be getting our own place soon."

I watched as she wrote her name in crooked block letters. Childish handwriting. The house number she wrote down was Myrtle's. "Are you Louise's sister?" I asked.

"Louise?" Her look could only be described as quizzical. She must have been surprised I knew her sister. "Yeah," she said. "Louise." Surely it wasn't so astonishing that people in a small town would know what was going on.

"Your aunt must be delighted to have you staying with her."

"My aunt?" She sounded distinctly like an echo.

"Louise told me that Myrtle was her aunt."

"Not a chance. She's a cousin of some sort, two or three times removed." She crossed out the phone number and rewrote it. I could see that she still had Myrtle's number wrong. I could always correct it later. "My sister calls her Aunt," Easton added, "but she's wrong about that."

I wondered what Easton called her seventy-two-year-old cousin.

"I just call her Myrtle," she added, as if she read my mind.

She cannot do that. She is thinking too much about herself.

Easton frowned at Marmalade, who had let out the cutest little yarp. I swallowed the snide comment that came to mind and handed her the small map of the library that we keep on hand. "I'll have your card ready by the time you find your books." As she walked–glided–up the staircase, I glanced at her birth date. Easton was Sam's sister, too. I wondered if Sam was older than Louise. Or was he the middle one? I always wanted a brother. Would Sam have red hair like Easton or brown hair like Louise?

Those are too many questions.

Marmalade pushed her head under my hand for a scratch. Her ears were twitching. It was time to lock up the library and head for home as soon as I could get Easton to leave.

WHY ON EARTH couldn't I remember Melissa's phone number? I'd lived there for a whole year when I first moved to Martinsville. But the number was gone, lost in the dead air space between my ears.

I picked up my little address book and turned to the B's for bed & breakfast. She picked up on the fourth ring. "Melissa Tarkington. *Azalea House.*" She sounded out of breath.

"Were you outside? What took you so long?"

"No, I was up to my elbows in flour. I've got a family coming in this afternoon. They're vacationing here for a week.

It always surprised me when people came to Martinsville for a vacation. First of all, how did they ever find us in our narrow, dead-end valley? We weren't exactly a tourist destination. And Melissa never advertised, as far as I knew.

She answered my question before I asked it. "They're here to meet up with the Pontiacs."

Maggie's in-laws. They visited occasionally from out west somewhere and always roomed at Melissa's so they wouldn't have to impose on Maggie, or so they said. But we all privately believed they did it because Melissa was a much better cook than Maggie. And because Doodle-Do, Maggie's rooster, tended to be over enthusiastic too early in the morning.

"Why did you call?" Melissa asked.

The clank of her spoon against her metal mixing bowl was unmistakable. "If you cook while you're holding the phone like that, you'll get a crick in your neck."

"Thank you, Dr. Biscuit. Now, why did you call? Besides wanting to run my life, that is."

Phooey! "Never mind. You have guests coming, so it won't work. I wanted to see if you'd go up to Garner Creek with me and help me pick out some clothes that won't embarrass my daughter."

"You are entirely too intimidated by that child," she pontificated.

"Now who's trying to run whose life?"

She laughed. "Truce! We both do it."

She tapped the spoon against the rim of the bowl and plopped something–probably the spoon–in the sink. I heard the distinctive whoosh, whoosh, whoosh as she washed her hands. "Why do you need new clothes anyway?" she asked me. "Something big coming up?"

"Just a family picnic at Bluebottle Falls this Saturday if it doesn't rain. With Auntie Blue and Uncle Mark settled in, we decided to celebrate." We loved Bluebottle Falls, just up the valley a few miles, between Braetonburg and Hastings. It was probably the smallest state park in Georgia. There were hiking trails through the ferns beside the twisting stream that wound its way into the Metoochie. At one point, the stream cut between two huge outcroppings of moss-covered rock and plunged a good thirty feet into a deep pool. In the summer the swimming was perfect. Of course, in October the water would be too cold for swimming, but the flat-topped boulders surrounding the pool held the sun's warmth deliciously.

"Just wear blue jeans and a tee-shirt," she said. "And take a sweatshirt. Bluebottle's liable to be chilly this time of year."

"Sally doesn't like blue jeans."

"So what?"

"What about my dark blue skirt? It's denim."

"Sure. Put it with that red and white striped top you have, and you'll be just fine. And take your white sweatshirt."

"What about shoes?"

"Your white sandals. But take tennies along in case you want to hike."

"I can't wear white sandals. It's after Labor Day."

"Oh pooh! Nobody pays attention to that silly old rule anymore."

Sally probably would. "And besides, they have some green paint spots on them."

"They'll be fine," she assured me.

Not if Sally's going to be there, I thought. Of course, Sally might not be there. Eight and a half months pregnant. She wouldn't risk the steep path down to the picnic spot.

Chapter 19

Thursday, October 17th

> "THIS IS YOUR mid-week, early-afternoon weather report from . . ."

Radio Ralph sounded particularly chipper. I wondered how he maintained his upbeat tone in the face of so much public derision. People were beginning to grump about him, as if he *caused* the weather, and didn't simply report it.

> "You've been hoping the weather would be clear for the weekend. Well folks, I hate to be the one to tell you, but you weren't praying hard enough. We are going to have storms all weekend. Translated, that means wet, wet, wet. Too bad we'll all get soaked. But let's have a fun weekend anyway. So more lousy weather Friday through Monday. You heard it here on WR . . ."

I sincerely hoped that Ralph was wrong as usual. We were so used to his backward forecasts. Everybody would be wearing shorts and tee-shirts. If he was somehow right this time around, he was going to be the most unpopular man in the valley.

SADIE SET THE small stepladder under one of her many

birdfeeders. "I hope you don't sink halfway into the ground when I step on you," she muttered. The ground was so wet. But several of her birdfeeders had run out of sunflower seeds, and her little friends depended on her. Maybe she could get just one of them filled. In all this rain, she'd have to take it inside, dry it off and refill it there so the seed wouldn't get soaked. She balanced on the second step and lifted the feeder from its hook.

"Can I help you with that?"

Sadie dropped the feeder. "Oh! Where did you come from?"

Easton Hastings stood there with her red hair tucked up into a floppy blue rain hat. The wide brim dripped all the way around the edges. "I'm sorry, I didn't mean to scare you."

"You look like a waterfall," Sadie said.

"Feel like one, too." Easton bent to retrieve the bird feeder. "I was passing by and it looked like you might need some help. I like birds, and I'd be happy to fill your feeders for you."

The sweet words, so at odds with Easton's previous behavior at the Beauty Shop, startled Sadie. She glanced around at the dangling suet feeder, the tube-like thistle feeder for the finches, the four-pronged twirling corn cob holder she'd installed to lure the squirrels away from her sunflower seeds. They still raided the feeders, but she enjoyed their antics as they tried to nibble off the corn kernels. It was so much effort these days to keep all the feeders cleaned and filled. "I'd appreciate that," she said. "Thank you for offering."

Easton lifted down two more of the feeders. "We might as well fill them all while I'm here."

"Well, look at you! You're tall enough not to need the stepladder."

Easton glanced at the ladder, sunk into the lawn a good three inches. "Guess all this rain has left you with a swamp, huh? Good thing I have my boots on."

"Yes," Sadie said. "But next year we'll probably have another dry spell, so I don't worry too much. Why don't you come inside for some cookies while we fill up the feeders? Leave the ladder. I can bring it in later." She reached for the thistle feeder. "Let me take this one. Your hands are full."

Easton didn't say thank you.

Sadie pushed her front door open and led the way into a narrow entrance hall. She paused by the coat rack and started unbuttoning her raincoat. Her hands felt stiff. Must be all the humidity, she thought. "Set those feeders on the floor and hang your raincoat here."

Easton plunked the feeders down on the pale yellow linoleum. "These feeders are big. Do you have enough seed?" She took off her hat, stuck it on the top of the rack, and shook out her hair.

That hair, Sadie sighed. Just like Eliza Moon. "Don't worry about that. I have plenty of seed. One of the sweet men in town buys it for me. He says that he likes to help the birds but he doesn't want to bother with feeders." Sadie was pretty sure that Paul Welsh didn't care one way or the other about birds. But he, like so many of the younger folk in town—forty seemed pretty young to her—was like a son to her. It felt good to be old and appreciated.

Easton shrugged out of her raincoat and shifted from one leg to the other. "Who is it?"

"Who is who, dear?"

"The man who buys you the seed."

"Paul Welsh."

"I haven't met him. Yet." She looked at her own reflection in the wavy old mirror behind the coat rack. "Is he cute?"

Sadie went on working at her buttons. She didn't appreciate the question, or Easton's tone. But the child *was* helping her with the birdfeeders. She ignored the query. "He sells farm equipment, so he might get some sort of a discount at the feed store."

Easton rotated her head. "I've got a crick in my neck." Before Sadie could express her concern, Easton added, "Is he married?"

"Goodness gracious, you're full of questions, aren't you? Let's go fill the feeders and get those cookies."

SADIE WATCHED EASTON survey the bright yellow living room. She'd lived with this color for so many years, sometimes she forgot that newcomers to her house could be startled by it. She patted the sunflower-gold afghan draped across the daffodil-yellow couch. The end table was the color of legal pads, and the lamps had butterfly-yellow shades. There was a rocking chair, painted a soft lemon shade, with a needlepoint cushion the color of the stripes on a honeybee.

Sadie watched her look up and down the pine knickknack shelves. Wallis had wanted to buy maple ones, but Sadie hated to paint good maple.

"You collect salt and pepper shakers?" Easton asked.

"Yes. I've never traveled much, but friends bring me back little souvenirs from their vacations." She picked up an Eiffel Tower, dusted its dust-free surface, and set it back next to its twin. "I almost feel like I've been there."

"You must like yellow," Easton said. "It's awfully bright in here, even on a rainy day."

Sadie wasn't sure whether that was a compliment. She looked back down at the Eiffel Towers and moved them ever so slightly closer to a pair of cows that said *Ben & Jerry's* on their black and white rumps. "Yes," she said. "Yes. Yellow is . . . special. The kitchen is through here." She led the way across the living room, but Easton stopped beside the piano.

"Do you play?"

Sadie turned back. "Not much. The piano was always my husband's joy. He can't manage anymore. Oh, he picks out a tune or two, now, but that's about it." Sadie brushed her hand along the keys. "He never learned how to read music, but he could hear a tune once and play it just like that."

Easton peered at the sheet music propped above the keys. Her voice dropped to a whisper. "I love music."

"Well sit down and play me something," Sadie said. "But put the soft pedal on. We have to be quiet because Wallis is taking his morning nap."

"No, I can't play. I always wanted piano lessons, but that . . . that just never happened."

"But you like music," Sadie prompted.

"Oh, I sing. That's about it." She looked back at the handwritten sheet music. "I had a wonderful music teacher in school. She taught us to read music. It was the only thing that let me escape from . . ." Her voice dwindled to silence.

Sadie nodded. Rupert's children had a hard time of it. But now Rupert was dead. He'd looked peaceful in his coffin, so maybe he'd managed to put the past behind him. She hoped so.

Easton raised an eyebrow. "This looks interesting. Did you write it?"

"Goodness gracious, no. Roger Johnson wrote it. The dear boy must be tone-deaf. He can't sing worth diddly-squat, but he writes a good tune. I've been practicing it on my harmonica."

"Harmonica?"

"Don't sound so surprised, dear. Old ladies can do some amazing things."

Easton cleared her throat and hummed a little. "Is this in a minor key or am I reading it wrong?"

"Let's fill the birdfeeders and get them back outside. Then I'll play the melody for you and you can sing along."

"You're supposed to dry out the feeders before you fill them."

Sadie wondered sometimes why she didn't speak up for herself when young people acted so superior. She might be eighty-one, but she certainly wasn't stupid. She *was* well-mannered, however. "Yes, dear. I know that."

"That's so the seed won't rot."

Sadie thought of several blistering things to say, counted to three, and settled for, "Well, then, I'll just let *you* do all the drying."

Sadie led the way into her yellow kitchen. The color of summer squash.

Friday, October 18th

WHEN IDA STORMED into the library, I braced myself. She was usually a placid person. Something awful must have happened. "That Easton Hastings is going to be sorry." She drummed her fingers on the check-out desk's white laminate surface. Some day I'd love to have the top replaced with a mellow, deep-grained oak or maple. It would probably take a while, considering the teensy budget the town allotted me.

"Take a breath, Ida. What's wrong with Easton?"

"That vixen? What do you mean what's wrong with her? Just because she hasn't set her sights on Bob," she paused before she spit out the word "yet," then left her sentence hanging in the still morning air of the old Millicent mansion's high-ceilinged main room. The building was obviously built for grand receptions and parties, and this room, with its elegant staircase and tall arched windows, had to have been used as a ballroom. I could see women in hoop skirts twirling on the arms of their escorts. Waltzes are so lovely.

Ida's spluttering pulled me back into the conversation. ". . . to put it bluntly."

What had I missed? "Bluntly?" I hoped that sounded neutral enough. Ida didn't like it when I tuned out.

"You don't think calling her a slut is blunt enough?"

"Well, I guess I see what you mean." That sounded awfully limp to me, but Ida let it pass.

"Bless his heart," Ida said, using the Southern euphemism, "I love Ralph, but he just stood there with his tongue hanging out and let her fiddle with his top button and then unbutton it."

That was too many buttons in one sentence, and I was afraid to ask what article of clothing Ida was talking about.

"She rumbled at him in that gravelly voice of hers. He obviously thinks it's sexy as all get-out, but I think it sounds like a cement mixer. She told him she knew a secret about him."

"A secret?"

"Yeah," Ida snorted. "She said she knew his chest hair was so manly he ought to let it show more. And now Ralph's mad at me."

"What did you do?"

"I did what any self-respecting wife would do. I grabbed Ralph's arm and told him he didn't have enough hair left to make an eyebrow brush with." She dabbed at her eyes, blew her nose, and tossed the tissue toward the wastebasket behind the desk. She missed.

"He looked so miserable, Biscuit. How could I have said such a hateful thing to him? We've always been fair to each other. Even when we argue, we've never said anything to undercut each other's . . . dignity. And here I went and ripped his ego to shreds in front of that red-headed . . . Why? Why did I do it?"

I shoved the tissue box closer to her, then waited for the tears to slow down a bit. Three more soggy tissues joined their compatriot on the floor. "You were never very good at basketball, were you, Ida?"

When laughing combines with crying, the result can be pretty loud. The front door opened and Louise walked in, pausing a moment to assess the situation. "Hey there, Biscuit," she said. "Am I interrupting anything?"

"No. Come on in. It's just . . ." This was, after all, Easton's sister. "Just an inside joke." I glanced over at Ida, who nodded and took one more tissue.

"I didn't know you two knew each other," Ida muttered.

"Sure, Ida," I said. "We're old friends. Ever since she took out a library card four days ago. This is the second time I've seen her."

Louise stepped closer. "You're Ida? Of course you are. I don't remember your last name, but I'd recognize those pretty blue eyes of yours anywhere. They haven't changed a bit since you were a little kid."

What a kind thing to say. Ida's eyes were as faded as an old pair of blue jeans, and they never did shine much, although when she laughed they twinkled. Right now they were bleary-looking from all the tears. I admired Louise's tact. She turned to me. "I haven't seen Ida since the year I graduated."

"Yeah," Ida said. "And you didn't say goodbye to anybody. What did you mean just up and leaving like that?"

A shadow crossed Louise's face, or so I thought. "You know how impulsive kids can be," she said. "I didn't grow up until I was thirty."

"You were grown up when you were eleven," Ida said. But she said it kindly. I probably only imagined the pain that dimmed Louise's eyes for a moment.

"MA'AM, DO YOU think I could get a library card?" I had to stop myself from gasping when I looked up. The man standing across the desk from me had the biggest ears I'd ever seen. They stuck out at an outrageous angle. The poor man. I bet his life was miserable in grade school. He looked around the empty library. "I want some books about mental illness," he added in an undertone.

"Do you live here in the valley?" I asked.

"Well, I'm moving back here. Been gone a long time. My mom lives in the retirement center up the way. I've been too far away to visit much. She's going downhill fast."

"I'm sorry to hear that. Illness in our parents can be hard to deal with."

His mouth twitched to one side and mumbled, "You don't know the half of it." He shook his head. It reminded me of an old mule my grandfather used to have. I took a better look at him. If it hadn't been for his ears, he would have looked almost invisible. He was wearing brown pants and a light brown shirt. His thin hair matched his outfit. His eyes were brown, his eyebrows as sparse as his hair. He must have been in his sixties. So his mother would have been in her eighties.

"How about that library card?" he asked again.

"As long as you have a local address," I said.

"I'm renting up on Pine Street. And the sign in the grocery store said I could get a free bunch of bananas if I had a new library card."

Ida was really taking this publicity campaign seriously. When she wasn't planning on killing Easton Hastings. I picked up an application form. "Just fill this in." I'd have to print off some more before we ran out.

I was getting very good at reading upside down. Lyle Hoskins, he wrote. "Are you Elizabeth's son?"

He smiled, and I could see a resemblance to Elizabeth. His eyes. They were the same oval shape as hers. And his smile was a little lopsided. "Yes," he said. "She's my mom."

"My husband and I bought her house."

Some sort of shadow crossed his face. It looked like he didn't have happy memories of the place. "That old barn?" he said. "Too bad. You're going to get socked with the heating bills this winter."

I didn't like the sound of that. We'd moved in last April, so I had no clue what the house was like in the cold. The ceilings were fairly high, and there were a lot of windows. Maybe I could get Glaze to help me make some heavier curtains. And we'd have to get some ceiling fans to circulate warm air downward. Too bad fireplaces don't heat efficiently. Maybe we should look into a wood stove.

He handed me the application. Horrible handwriting. I asked for an explanation of a couple of the numbers. I couldn't tell his ones from his sevens or his threes from his fives. "This address is Sadie Masters' house," I said.

"Yes it is. I used to know them real well. Miss Sadie said I could stay with them until I find another place. Of course, I'm paying them rent. And I can help out with some of the chores," he added.

"I'm sure you'll be a big help."

I handed him the next to the last library map and pointed the way upstairs to the psychology section. By the time he came back with three books in hand, I had his card finished. "Enjoy your bananas," I told him as he left.

Chapter 20

Saturday, October 19th

THE DAYS WERE shorter and the dawns came later this time of year, and I wanted to stay in bed. But Doodle-Do had been crowing his fool head off for the last thirty minutes, and Marmalade was kneading my tummy.

I am ready for food.

I padded over to the window to admire the clear sky above the trees in the backyard. The weather was cooperating. Of course, Ralph had said rain. My denim skirt and striped tee-shirt would be perfect, and who cared what Sally thought. But at eight months pregnant, I wouldn't bet on her holding her tongue. If she even showed up.

SHE SHOWED UP. All the men went to help her down the steep path. She headed straight for me.

"Mother!"

Oh no. She caught me. I leaned forward, hoping my skirt would cover my feet. "Hello Sally," I said. "You made it down the path. Where's Jason?" Not that I cared, but it might divert her attention from my sandals.

"I'm going to kill that Easton Hastings," she said.

My feet were safe. "Why? What's she done this time?"

"We stopped by the church social on the way here. She stood right behind Jason's chair while he was competing in the pie-eating contest. When he won, I thought she was going to kiss his blueberry-covered face. Would have served her right to get all stained. But he . . . he . . . he . . ." I wondered whether or not I was ever going to hear what he'd done. "He pushed her away and said . . ." Her voice took on Jason's improbable tenor. ". . . 'now sweetie, you don't want to get all messy.' He actually called her sweetie! That's what he calls *me*!"

I saw Jason talking with Bob and Uncle Mark at the bottom of the path. At six foot two, with his football player build, Jason towered over the other two men. They all seemed to be watching Scott and his date who had turned out to be Pumpkin, not Ariel. Now all the fiasco about Brighton's phone number made sense. He could hardly have walked into Sharon's Beauty Shop and asked for Pumpkin's phone number. They were skipping stones across the pool, not very successfully because the currents set up by the water plunging over the falls made skipping almost impossible. I had relaxed considerably when the two of them came laughing down the path. At least he was dating someone more age-appropriate.

Sally seemed to expect me to say something. "Why weren't *you* standing behind his chair?" I asked. Wrong thing to say.

"Mother! I'm eight and a half months pregnant! I was sitting down at the end of the table resting my feet." She brushed ineffectively at her voluminous maternity top. It had several small blue splotches on it–nothing that wouldn't wash out. "And I'm the one who got splashed with blueberries!" she wailed.

It didn't seem fair, but it was hardly the end of the world.

"At least he didn't kiss her," I said. Wrong thing to say.

She stepped back and looked me up and down, as if I had just crawled out of the woodwork. "Mother! What are you doing wearing those sandals?"

I guessed her humiliation and her pregnancy and her anger at her husband made her mother as good a target as any. Whatever happened, though, to the good manners I insisted on when she was a child? I should have stayed home. "I like my sandals," I said, and put them to good use by walking away from Sally, toward the picnic table.

Glaze wandered my way, waving a hot dog in a bun. "Want one? They're yummy."

"I'll pass for now," I said. "Why did you get two? You don't usually eat that much."

"Thought you'd want one." She licked some mustard off her upper lip. "What was Sally in a snit about this time? Didn't like your tee-shirt?"

"Hubby problems," I said. "Easton and hubby specifically."

"Poor thing," she said in a voice that contradicted her words.

"Who? Sally?"

"No. I meant Jason. With Sally mad at him, he doesn't stand a chance. Hope she makes his life miserable."

"Sally's not that bad." One minute I was furious with my daughter. The next minute I was defending her. The mama bear syndrome, I supposed.

"You're right," Glaze admitted, and started on the second hot dog. "It's really Jason that's the problem."

"Could be. But Ida said Easton was after Ralph. Sounds like it's Easton that's truly the problem."

Glaze took one more bite of the hot dog. My hot dog. "Jason tried to hit on me last week," she said.

"Jason? On you? But you're . . ."

"I know," she said. "Almost old enough to be his mother."

"What did he do?"

"It was all just a bunch of suggestive language, but it made me uncomfortable."

"Did you tell him to back off or you'd clobber him?"

Glaze set her plate on the picnic table. "No," she said. "I felt like . . . like a deer in the headlights. I think I was so shocked by what he'd said, it just immobilized me."

"So, what did you do?"

"I just stood there and looked at him. He finally must have realized how shocked I was, because he sort of laughed about it and tried to pretend it had only been a joke. Only it wasn't. He frightened me. He was so tall. Just like . . . Grandpa."

What was she talking about? "Grandpa's not nearly that tall," I said. I wasn't worried about my shoes anymore. Poor Sally. I was worried about my daughter. "Grandma always said we needed to be tough. But somehow I don't think she ever had to deal with anything like this."

Glaze looked at me for a long time.

"What?" I asked. "What are you looking at?"

"Don't you know?"

"Know what?"

Glaze shook her head. "Are you going to be home this evening?"

"Sure," I said. "But what does that have to do with anything?"

"There's something I need to tell you." She turned, tossed her napkin in the trash bin, and walked up the path toward the parking area. She didn't say goodbye to anyone. Glaze always was hard to understand. Even as a little kid, she'd clam up over the stupidest things. There was that one time I remembered when she didn't say a word and she still got me in a lot of trouble. I was ten. She was five.

"BISQUE MCKEE! YOU get back in here and finish your lunch before you go up to your Grandma's house."

I didn't like cauliflower, but I knew she wouldn't stop hollering unless I went back inside. I could have gotten away with it if I'd already jumped off the back porch, but she could see me out the kitchen window. Just my luck.

"And take your sister with you when you go."

"Ma! I don't wanna. She just gets in the way." I was whining. I knew I was whining. I didn't like it when Glaze whined, but there I was doing it. Of course, I had a good reason to whine. Not that it did much good. I was gonna get stuck with her anyway. Baby-sitting. I walked as slowly as I could back into the kitchen. I hated baby-sitting. Anyway, she wasn't a baby anymore. She was five. And she could take care of herself. Ma might as well have tied her to me. Sewed her to me. She was a bother, a bother, a bother.

I wasn't really all that mad, but I wasn't going to admit it. Glaze was a pain, but I could almost remember what it was like being five when my big cousins wouldn't play with me. Almost. But this was different. We were just walking up the road to Grandma's house. Why did she need a baby-sitter for that?

I took a big forkful of cauliflower and shoved it in my mouth.

"Take smaller bites, Biscuit. You look rude with your cheeks puffed out like that. And eat with your mouth closed."

What was this? Dump on Biscuit Day? I kept chewing. When Ma turned back to the sink, I spit the cauliflower into my napkin and shoved it in the pocket of my old pants. They were all stained 'cause I wore them whenever I helped Grandma plant. She was going to divide her irises today and make a bigger flower patch to wind around the side of the house. She said I was always a big help. I knew how to put the plants in the ground just right. Glaze always stepped in all the wrong places. She really was a pain in the butt. I wasn't supposed to say that, but I wasn't talking. I must have been thinking pretty loud, though, 'cause Ma heard my brain.

"Now you remember what I've told you. You keep Glaze right with you all the time. I want her to be safe."

What could happen to a little kid walking three blocks? I thought. But I said, "Okay Ma. I'll keep her with me." Before Ma could tell me to hold her hand as we crossed the lazy old streets, I added, "I'll hold onto her at the crossings, too."

Ma actually smiled at me. Made me feel guilty, since I knew I was planning to dump Glaze as soon as I got to Grandma's. Glaze didn't like gardening. She didn't understand it. She was in the way. I'd drop her off at the tool shed, like I did the last time. I knew she wasn't supposed to touch anything there. And I think I sort of knew that if something fell on her, it could hurt her bad. But she'd be safe. Grandpa would keep her from getting hurt. I'd make sure he was there before I let go of her.

I used to ask Ma to let me go look at the tools in the shed when I was little, and she took me there a couple of times, but she kept hold of me, and it wasn't that much fun. She wouldn't let me go there by myself. And she wouldn't let me touch anything. The shed was really big and kind of dark and stuffed with lots of work tables and racks of screwdrivers and rakes and hoes and wrenches and these great big iron hole-diggers. And there were some machines I wanted to know about, but Ma always dragged me away from there before I got to learn anything at all. There was an open space at the back of the shed. Grandpa called it his workshop. He got a lot of work done there. That's what he told me once. Anyway, I think I always liked Grandma's garden a lot better than Grandpa's shed.

"Glaze! Come on honey," Ma called out. "You and your sister are going to Grandma's house."

"Don't wanna." That was my dumb sister mumbling as she sat on the top stair. I could see her feet from where I sat at the kitchen table. She'd finished all her cauliflower. Yuch! So *she* got to leave the table early. Goody-goody. That's what she was. And why did I have to watch her all the time? I was only a kid.

"Glaze, sweetie, you have to go. Mommy's going to be gone for a while this afternoon, and you need to stay with Grandma." Ma finished cleaning off the table with a couple of swipes of one of the blue-striped towels she always used. She didn't notice the napkin bulge in my pocket. "Come on. I don't want to have to tell you again."

Glaze's eyebrows were squished together as she walked into the kitchen. "I wanna go with you, Mommy," she said and held out her arms to be picked up. She was too big for that. She was pouting. She was a brat.

Ma shook her head and bent over to kiss Glaze on her forehead. "Run along, sweetie. Stay with your sister. She'll take good care of you."

"No she won't," Glaze piped up. "She's only a kid."

"I am not! I'm ten!" I stuck out my tongue at her. "And you're only five, so there!"

Ma swatted both of us on our fannies. Not hard, but it sent us scooting over toward the door. I took Glaze's hand. "Come on, brat," I said under my breath.

Grandma was already on her hands and knees in the iris patch. Her back was all bent over. She hadn't seen us. I made a quick left turn and hauled Glaze with me down toward the shed. I could see somebody moving around in the shadows. "You go on, Glaze," I told her. "Stay with Grandpa. He'll play a fun game with you." Glaze pulled back against my arm and tried to turn around. Brat. "Go on. Remember you said last time he played a game."

"I didn't like that game." She was mumbling again.

"Maybe he'll think of a new one," I grumped. He never played games with me. He probably liked her better. Anyway, Ma never gave me a chance to play in the shed. She was always saying he was too busy. Well, he couldn't be too busy to watch a little kid.

I turned on my best big-sister authority voice. Daddy called it that once when I was bossing Glaze around during a Monopoly game. She never knew what to do with the houses. "Go on in the shed. And you sit really, really still and do everything Grandpa tells you to do." She looked like she was going to cry, so I shook my finger at her. "If you complain about this, you'll get us both in trouble." That didn't sound right. She might be willing to get me in trouble if she was mad at me. "But you'll get in the biggest trouble," I added and nodded my head just like I knew something she didn't. Ma would whale the day-lights out of me if she thought I'd left my sister alone like that. But I wasn't leaving her alone. I was leaving her with Grandpa.

I watched as she disappeared into the shed. I saw Grandpa's arm come out of the shadow and take her hand. And then I ran back up to the front. I took just a few seconds to dump the cauliflower out of my napkin. "Hey Grandma! Here I am!" I hollered as I rounded the corner.

We divided irises for a while. I was very good at it. And then Grandma asked what I'd been hoping she wouldn't ask. "Where's Glaze? I thought she was coming with you."

"Oh, she went with Ma. She didn't want to come. Can I run in the house and get a cookie?"

"I was pretty sure your mother said she needed me to watch both of you." That wasn't fair. It wasn't Grandma watching Glaze. It was me. She was ignoring my cookie request, too.

"May I get a cookie, please ma'am?" It worked. She forgot about Glaze.

"Of course dear. And pour yourself a glass of milk." She wiped the back of her hand across her forehead. It left a streak of dirt. "We'll sit on the porch for a short while."

By the time we went back into the garden, I was full of cookies. I'd eaten three or four in the kitchen before I brought a little plate of them out onto the porch for the two of us. Grandma liked her cookies almost as much as I did.

A long time later we heard the phone ringing. "Run inside and grab the phone, dear," she told me.

It was Ma. "Biscuit, I'm home now. You and Glaze finish whatever you're doing with Grandma and come on home." Boy, was I lucky that Grandma hadn't answered the phone.

"I'll be right there," I told her. I skipped out to the garden, told Grandma that it was time for me to go home. "I'm going to cut across the back way," I told her. That would give me an excuse to go by the shed.

Glaze was sitting on an old straight-backed chair just inside the door of the shed. I could tell she'd been crying. "What kind of trouble did you get into?"

Grandpa walked around from the back of his workbench. "Glaze fell down," he said, but he wasn't looking at me when he said it. He was looking at Glaze. "Isn't that right?" he asked her.

My bratty sister didn't even answer. She just slipped off the bench, grabbed my hand, and headed out the door.

"Thanks for watching her, Grandpa," I said over my shoulder as I trailed behind my little sister.

Once we were across the street, I pulled back on her hand. I didn't want to get a spanking just because of my prissy little sister. I stood up as tall as I could and glared at her. "If you tell Ma you got hurt in the shed, I'll put a spider in your bed," I told her. "And it'll kill you," I added for good measure. I knew that would work. She was afraid of spiders.

When we got home, Ma could tell Glaze had been crying, and she got mad at me anyway, just because Glaze hurt herself. And I couldn't even tell her it wasn't my fault. And later on, after Ma talked to Grandma, she gave me the biggest spanking I ever got, all because I'd let Grandpa do the baby-sitting. It didn't make a bit of sense to me.

Chapter 21

I RINSED THE soap suds off the last plastic plate from the picnic, and set it in the drainboard to dry. At our family picnics I always provided all the plates, cups, and utensils, and cleaned them up afterwards—I refused to use paper plates and those dinky plastic spoons—and everyone else brought the food. Soup doesn't work at picnics.

"I found this poem," Glaze said without preamble as she walked into my kitchen. I heard Bob head back into the living room. We have that one board that squeaks anytime anyone steps on it.

It does not squeak when I walk on it.

"I want to read it to you," she said. "You might want to sit down first." Her mouth, usually so ready to laugh, was pinched in at the sides. Her nose, pert and narrow from birth, flared out as she took two or three easily audible breaths. She didn't look like the sister I knew. Or thought I knew.

I sat and put my arms around Marmalade. She had a quiet way of showing up in my lap.

Glaze waved the small book of poems in my general direction. I didn't want to point out that it was a volume I'd given her for her 43rd birthday last year. An anthology of southern poets. I'd read the first few poems and liked them.

"*The Inheritance*," she read. I didn't recall that name, but noticed that it seemed to be toward the end of the book. "See if this sounds familiar," she added.

From the look she gave me, pointed in a way I'd never seen from her, I was fairly sure I wasn't going to like this one.

Inheritance

Rocking, beneath Grandma's pecan trees,
I sat with him discussing wisdom of the ages.
He held a black book,
its leaves as frail and dry as hands.
Almost every word was underlined in red.
We spoke a while that day.
The other times, we didn't talk.
He was seventy,
with a neck like the chicken my grandmother
hacked off for Sunday dinner.
Mother hinted that Grandma had her own story to tell,
but didn't tell it except to the womenfolk,
and I wasn't a womanfolk yet.

He held his arms close to his side,
protecting his godliness
with elbows I never saw
because of long-sleeved blue shirts
(except on Sunday of course,
when shirts and reputations were white).

He never smoked.
It was ungodly, he said. Un-god-ly.
That black book he held
held his lists of what was godly and what was un.
It held lists of children born.
I was in it though I never saw my name,
not wanting to know which column he put me in.
It was all my fault, he had told me each time.

In his seventy years he tallied more
of the ungodly than the opposite.
Uncle Daniel bears scars of his righteous retribution.
I look at my grandfather's rocking chair,
the one I inherited.
The left armrest has *J. Dani* crudely carved in it.
That was when Grandpa caught him.
My father's eyes gleamed
when he told of John Daniel being dragged
out behind the tool shed -
where I had to put
the flea powder on the barn cats each summer.

They squirmed and yowled as I sprinkled
the white, white powder in childish abandon.
It sifted through their eyes and nostrils.
In just such a way, John Daniel must have hated
the white hot godliness raining down on his bare back.

Grandma's pecan trees offered no conclusion.
They shaded, instead, an old man,
and a little girl, there at his behest,
hugging her own questions,
bent over her own knees.

She handed me the book. "Now," she said, "will you quit asking me about Grandpa?"

It didn't make a bit of sense to me. "What," I asked her, "do pecan trees have to do with Grandpa?"

She spent another few moments looking at me, shrugged, and sighed. "Never mind," she said. "Maybe it's just as well."

Chapter 22

Sunday, October 20th

AUNTIE BLUE AND Uncle Mark had bought one of the few houses in the Upper Valley with an in-ground heated swimming pool. It was a bunch of bother if you asked me, all that cleaning and filtering and adding chemicals. From what I'd heard, it detracted from the resale value of the house, too. But Auntie Blue loved her pool. "I've been out swimming every single morning," she told me a week or so before. "I get in about twenty laps, and then I'm ready for breakfast."

If I did twenty laps in the morning, I'd be ready for a nap, but I didn't mention that to my seventy-six-year-old aunt.

On Sunday, though, after church, she drove down the valley to Martinsville, plopped herself down at my kitchen table, placed both her hands over her face, and shook her head. "You're never going to believe this," she said. Her shoulders were vibrating. I hate watching someone cry, especially when I don't know what the problem is.

I raised my eyebrows at my sister. I'd invited Glaze for lunch, to make up for whatever I'd done yesterday to upset her, although I still didn't understand just what that was. She hadn't been too communicative. But she must have forgiven me, because she'd shown up for the meal. She shrugged. "Don't ask me," she mouthed.

I turned back to Auntie Blue. “Okay, what’s wrong? Can you tell us?” Her whole body was shaking by that time. The news must be horrible, I thought. “Are you sick?” I asked her, all the while dreading the answer. “Is something wrong with Uncle Mark?”

“He . . . he . . .” Her voice quivered. “He bought a boat motor,” she said.

“What on earth are you talking about?” I looked up at Glaze who seemed as puzzled as I was.

Auntie Blue wiped at her eyes. It took me a few seconds to register that she wasn’t crying. She was laughing. “Oh lordy, girls, he’s gone and done it this time. He’s lost his mind.”

“Not another of his inventions.” Glaze pulled out a chair and eased into it. “What’s he come up with this time?”

“He wanted a hot tub,” Auntie Blue explained. “One of those things you can relax in.”

“We know what a hot tub is,” I told her.

“Well, we already had a perfectly good heated swimming pool. He figured all he needed was something to stir up the water.”

Glaze was already rolling her eyes. “A boat motor?”

Auntie Blue nodded. “Only trouble is the dang thing’s so loud there’s nothing relaxing about it.”

“To say nothing of the danger,” I said, picturing Verity Marie and her sister being sucked up into the propeller.

“No, no. He worked that out. He put the motor in the deep end and built a cage around it, so nobody can get close to it.”

“So, other than the noise, what’s the problem?”

“He . . . he . . .” Here we go again, I thought. “. . . he wanted to clean the pool, so first thing this morning he dumped in a box of soap flakes and started the motor.”

“Good grief, that’ll take forever for the filter to clean it out.”

Auntie Blue looked over at Glaze and back at me. “It’s worse than that. When we got home from church, we couldn’t even see the pool. When I left, there were suds about four feet deep covering the pool and the patio and the outdoor furniture, too. All I could see was the top half of the umbrella. I told your uncle that I’d be back next week sometime, and I’d better be able to swim my laps when I got there, or else.”

“Or else what?” we both asked at the same time.

“Lordy, girls, I don’t know. It just sounded like such a good exit line, like Clark Gable walking out on Scarlett.”

Chapter 23

Monday, October 21st

"THAT EASTON HASTINGS is going to be sorry."

Wait a minute, I thought. Hadn't I heard those same words from Ida? "What's wrong, Sharon? You sound really upset." Positively homicidal was more like it.

"I took a long lunch today and walked up to the kenaf field to take Carl a sandwich. He's been trying to get the field harvested for weeks, but there's been so much rain. With four clear days, though, the field dried out enough for him to start the combine. But he forgot to take his lunch box this morning, so I decided to walk up there." She looked around the empty library, then lowered her voice anyway. "You know I've been trying to lose some weight, and Doc Nathan told me walking more would be good for me."

I nodded. Everybody in town knew about Sharon's various weght-loss regimens.

"Well, I got to the top of the path and there was Carl's combine, idling off to the side. I figured he'd stopped to pee or stretch his legs or something, so I tiptoed around the combine and there they were."

"Who?" I asked, even though I knew what the answer was going to be.

"Him! And her!"

He and she I thought. But my inner editor had no place here with a friend's anguish. Did I want to ask this? I was getting way more information about Easton Hastings than I needed. "What were they doing?"

"She had her hands up on his shoulders. Both of them. And she had her head kinda tilted up in that invitation way. You know what it looks like."

Yes, I knew. I'd done the same thing right after breakfast. Except I was doing it with my *own* husband, not somebody else's.

You like Softfoot a lot.

Sharon sniffed. I reached for the tissue box under the counter. Marmalade was just depositing a dead mouse next to the waste basket. Well, it was her job, after all. I was glad she took it seriously.

You are welcome. There are not many of them left.

I nudged the mouse body closer to the counter, hoping that Sharon wouldn't notice it.

"What did you do?" I asked her.

I trapped him as he was coming out of a hole under the stairs.

"Do? What do you think I did? I barreled around the edge of that combine so fast you'd have thought I was a jet plane. 'Just what do you think you're doing here, missy?' I asked her. And then I glared at Carl, and he stuttered something about her needing some help with a sticky door lock on her car. Humph! Some poor excuse for her to get her sticky hands on my husband."

Marmy hopped up and pushed her face close to Sharon's. I hoped she didn't have mouse breath.

I did not eat it.

"What did Easton do when you caught them?" That woman had an amazing amount of gall.

"She laughed, and said *thank you very much* to Carl, and then she just turned around and walked away, twitching those hips of hers. At the corner of the combine, she looked back over her shoulder at Carl and said, 'I still know a secret about you.'" Sharon's voice came close to duplicating Easton's low vibrato, but then her voice shifted up an octave. "She even batted her eyelashes at him!"

Batting? Does she play baseball?

What was I supposed to say–so, did you haul off and clop Carl upside the head? I elected to remain silent, and simply pulled Marmalade away from Sharon.

"I . . . I . . . I could kill her!"

Easton is really in trouble, I thought.

My gratitude list for Monday the 21st

1. Waking up next to Bob
2. Going to sleep next to Bob
3. Waking to a rooster instead of an alarm clock (I'm glad he's a block away from here, though)
4. Marmalade
5. This wonderful old house

My gratitude list for today

waking up next to Widelap
taking naps all by myself
being the caretaker here and at the library
killing the intruders
Softfoot

Chapter 24

Tuesday, October 22nd

ARIEL DEPRESSED THE lever on the ancient coffee maker for what felt like the billionth time. She did enjoy her work at the Delicious, afternoons after school and four hours on Saturdays, but there were days like this when she wondered what it was all about. How many pots of coffee did she have to brew, how many cups did she have to fill before her own cup would runneth over like the sign said? To hear Reverend P talk, you'd think the cups were already full to the top and more. But as old as he was, what did he know about life the way it really was? Her remaining time in high school loomed ahead of her like that wall of the Red Sea that he'd talked about last Sunday. Well, she hoped it wouldn't come crashing down on her.

She hummed a few bars of her favorite tune, the one Roger wrote, and took her time wiping down the counter while the pot filled. The song always managed to lift her spirits, even though it was written in a minor key. She loved Roger's music. Oh, she knew he couldn't sing worth a darn, but his music. His melodies. She paused in the middle of a swipe. She could see herself standing with Roger on a stage. He'd be playing his 12-string guitar; none of that loud electric stuff he was always trying out. She'd be singing his songs.

The bell over the door jangled, and she looked up with a smile. Her smile was usually automatic but she always tried to make it genuine. This time it was fueled by her dream, and Reverend Pursey, in for his afternoon coffee, grinned back at her. She watched him thread his way between the tables to his regular booth at the back, where Father Ames already sat with the steam from his own coffee rising in front of him. Ariel lifted a white saucer from the top of the stack, filled it with the small white creamers, picked up the now-full pot, hummed a few more bars, and went to do her job.

"AFTERNOON, JOHN," HENRY said. "How's it going?"

"Fine. You?"

"Fine." He eased out of his raincoat, hung it on the hook next to the booth, and sagged into his usual spot across from his friend. He wasn't fine, but it wouldn't do to say that with so many of his parishioners sitting within earshot.

Instead, he turned the white mug upright, watched Ariel fill it to an imaginary two-thirds mark, and started dribbling the first of five creamers into the steaming cup.

He did take a moment to appreciate that Ariel always remembered to leave room in his cup for all the cream he liked to add. That was good, the mark of a conscientious worker. But it also seemed like a metaphor for his life right now. His cup certainly wasn't running over. Why he'd picked that as a sermon topic for next week, he'd never figure out. He'd even had Roger post it on the church signboard. That signboard, he thought, was one of my least inspired ideas. Nobody ever paid any attention to it. Nobody except Roger, who was paid a measly amount to change it each week.

Maybe it was all this rain, too, he thought as he poured in the fourth creamer. Maybe it was the river, washing right up over the sandy park and over the dock, and even over the boulders. Cups running over were supposed to be a good thing. But he doubted anything good would come from this unceasing rain. Or from his signboard. Or his sermons. Good grief!

FATHER JOHN AMES looked across the table at his friend diligently lacing his perfectly good coffee with all that cream. Why even bother with coffee if you had to cover up the taste? And now it wasn't hot and steaming. It sat there in the cup looking anemic and flat and probably cold. At least Ariel left enough room in the cup when she poured it for Henry. He glanced down at his own fresh mug, filled right to the brim and practically running over. All my thoughts this morning are about liquids, he thought. The rain. It must be all this rain. The river had already washed halfway up the town beach and looked to be rising more. Everything, including his spirits, felt damp. He didn't think this was what the psalmist had in mind with that line about *my cup runneth over*.

He watched Henry pour in the last white carton, lift the mug, and slosh some on the table. "Your cup running over, Henry?"

Henry grabbed a paper napkin and managed to contain the puddle. "You must have read my mind."

"No. I read your signboard."

THANK GOODNESS FOR my sturdy old house. Funny, I never thought much about my house in Braetonburg. It stood there and kept the rain off me and my family and my things, but I'd always just accepted that without noticing it. Maybe the difference was those gratitude lists I wrote every night.

I have a gratitude list, too.

Marmalade lifted her chin off my knee and looked at me with her clear green eyes. "I'm grateful for you," I told her . . .

Thank you. You are special.

. . . and felt as much as heard her rumbly purr. As I sat on my bed stroking her, I thought about my kids, my grandkids, my loving husband. "My cup runneth over," I murmured, . . .

I do not see a cup. Where is it?

. . . and Marmalade added a quiet meow. "I'm putting you and this house on my list tonight," I said.

That is a good idea.

I looked out the bedroom window at the trees in the back yard. There was no wind to speak of, just a steady downpour. All of a sudden, I wanted to be out walking in it, splashing in puddles the way my sweet granddaughter had re-taught me to do. I'm sure I used to have fun in the rain when I was a child, but at forty-nine I'd forgotten how until Verity Marie took my hand one day and said, "Grannie! Let's make splashes and watch the water dance!" Rain changed for me that day and never went back to feeling drab. I loved rain. Any kind of rain.

I hopped up from the edge of the bed where I'd been folding laundry. Again. "Want to go for a walk with me, Marmalade?"

She sat up, looked out the window almost as if she were considering my question, . . .

No, thank you. The rain is wet and this bed is soft.

. . . then turned around, meowed once more, and settled back down between the piles of clean laundry, resting her chin on her back legs and curling her tail around her nose. I ran my hand along her supple spine and went downstairs. Going out in the rain was probably a mistake, but there wasn't any lightning, and I was drip-dry. Wasn't it Helen Keller who said, *Life is either a daring adventure or nothing at all*?

I paused on the wide front porch, donning my bright pink raincoat. I debated putting on my boots, decided on my plastic gardening clogs instead. The rain was fairly warm, after all. I left my shoes by the front door, slipped into the clogs, and headed down the steps into the rain. The hood, fortunately, was big enough that when I pulled it forward, it shielded my eyes from the deluge.

For once I ignored the sidewalk, stepped off the curb into the gutter, and waded downhill through the ankle-deep water. My clogs filled up on the first step, of course. So what? They were meant for mud and water, and my socks and pant legs would dry out eventually. The sound of the rain was comforting. I was bound and determined to make it all the way to the Delicious for a cup of tea or, better yet, their luscious hot chocolate. I should have called Melissa, I thought, to see if she could join me. Halfway down to Second Street, though, I stepped in a hole hidden by the rushing water. My bum knee gave out, and I fell, hard. I don't deserve this, was my first thought. No, that was my second thought. The first one was unrepeatable in polite company.

My pants legs filled with water up to and above my knees as I knelt in the gutter, stolidly trying to ignore the pain and watching the water course past me–around me–through me. This was no fun at all. My cup was supposed to be running over, not flooding. Despite Verity Marie and her four-year-old enthusiasms I was fairly sure that I really didn't like rain at all.

BECAUSE OF MY bruises, I took it easy at tap dance class that evening. Afterwards, all anyone could talk about was how every woman in town wanted to rip Easton Hastings to pieces. "Claw her eyes out," was the way Ida put it. "Shave off that mop of hair," was Annie's suggestion. She went on to tell us that she'd talked to three women in the herb shop, any one of which would gleefully have run that Easton right out of town.

"She can't be that bad," I tried to say, even though I'd heard Sharon's story, too.

Ida had no patience with my attempt at pacification. "Just you wait." Her voice, normally a light soprano, sounded like one of those bells you hear in scary movies. Although I didn't say it out loud, I was positive I'd never have trouble with her. Bob just wasn't that kind of guy. Of course, neither was Ralph

Peterson. I wasn't sure about Sharon's husband Carl, though. Maybe he'd invited Easton up to the kenaf field.

Sadie sat there and listened to all the complaining. When she raised her hand, there was something almost regal about her. "You're not being fair," she said. "I've known Easton since she was born. She had a hard time as a kid."

"That's no excuse," Ida said. "Lots of people have hard childhoods. That doesn't give her the right to prey on my husband."

Sadie shook her head. "This afternoon," she said, "Easton came by and filled all my birdfeeders for me. She loves birds more than anybody I ever knew." Sadie looked around at us. "I think it's because they can fly."

Ida grunted and stood up. "Wish she'd fly away from here," she said.

"Before you leave," Sadie said, "I probably should warn you. Easton and I are planning a surprise for the Halloween party."

No matter how much we asked, she wouldn't say another word about it.

Chapter 25

Wednesday, October 23rd

SADIE WAS FULL of herself at the library that morning, talking about her new tenant. “He’s renting the spare bedroom,” she said. “I told him he could just stay with us. He didn’t have to rent the room. I’ve known him since he was knee-high to a grasshopper.” She shook her head. “He insisted on paying us, though. He’s such a sweet young man.”

Young man? I’d met him the previous Friday when he came for a library card. “Sadie,” I said, “Lyle’s not young.”

She set down the date stamp she was adjusting. “At my age, dearie, everybody I know looks young. And he’s certainly been a help around the house. He nailed that loose upright on the porch railing back into place. It’s been crooked for the past year, ever since Wallis fell against it.” Her eyes clouded over for a moment. “It never seemed worth it to ask anyone to do it for me. He just did it without being asked.”

“I’m glad he’s helping you,” I said. I wondered what else she needed that nobody had thought to ask her about. “Is there anything Bob and I can help you with, Sadie?”

She gave a trial stamp on a scrap of paper, to be sure she had the date right. “Not a thing,” she said. “That sweet Easton has been cleaning out my bird feeders and filling them up. Last week she told me the big one in the front yard needed to be propped up better. The post was rotting or something. I told Lyle, and he took care of it right away. Put up a brand new post and hung that feeder just like he was a professional. He's really handy. I don't imagine there's anything he couldn't do if he put his mind to it. Easton was right pleased with the new feeder post."

Maybe I'd been unfair to judge Easton, I thought. Then I remembered what Ida and Sharon had said about her. Even a bad penny could be shiny on one side, I thought.

"THAT EASTON HASTINGS is going to be sorry."

Hello, Smellsweet.

Marmalade and I had been retrieving an armful of returned books from the bin under the checkout desk and hadn't heard Glaze come in. Marmalade was in charge of sniffing each book thoroughly.

I can tell where they have been. There are many dogs in town. And many people eat while they read.

When I looked up, bumping my head in the process, Glaze was leaning across the desk. Making sure she was talking to me and not to one of my Petunias, I supposed. She rubbed my head before I could set the books down and rub it myself. "That looked like it hurt."

"Not too bad," I told her. "I'll probably have only a minor goose egg . . ."

Egg? Where?

"It'll match my bruised knees."

"Good." She obviously wasn't listening to me. She patted Marmalade. "So what am I going to do about Easton?"

I looked around the main room. It was early afternoon and there was nobody else in the library, other than Sadie and Esther, who were upstairs cataloging more of the donated books.

"You're the third or maybe fourth woman I've talked to who's upset with Easton."

"Three? Four? Is that all?" My normally urbane, gorgeous sister narrowed her eyes at me. "She's going to end up a corpse, and I can guarantee the murderer will be one of the wives she's ticked off."

"So . . ." I debated whether or not to finish my sentence. What the heck. "So, you're not a wife." *Yet*, I thought. I wished she'd hurry up. I wanted to buy that perfect matron of honor dress I'd seen at Mabel's.

I had never before understood the saying about the cat that ate the canary, . . .

A canary? Where?

. . . but Glaze definitely looked, for just a moment, like that self-satisfied cat. Then she turned to a silver-haired panther. "She's treading on thin ground," she said.

Thin ice, I thought.

Canaries do not like ice.

Before either of us could say anything else, Bob's sister-in-law, soon to be his ex-sister-in-law, came in. Just last week she had told me to change her library card. She didn't want to be called Diane Marie anymore, probably because that was also the name of the woman who was murdered a few months ago. Call me Dee, she had said. Today she didn't say anything, just waved at us and walked upstairs, pausing for a moment on the double-branched landing. I wondered if she knew she was standing right where I'd found the body . . .

I am the one who found it. You came in later and I led you to the body.

. . . of that poor young man who was murdered last year. I was thinking too much about murder recently. Yuch. After a few seconds, she turned to the right and continued upstairs toward the history section. I always wondered what books people were going to check out. I pushed Marmalade away from my face.

"What's Marmy upset about?" Glaze asked.

You do not listen to me.

She quieted down and sat with her tail curled around her toes, looking like a bookend.

Glaze lowered her voice to an intense whisper. "As I was saying, she's going to get what's coming to her if she's not careful."

"Why are you so upset?" I whispered back at her.

"I looked out my window this morning and saw Tom headed up the street. He was coming by for . . . for a chat . . ."

A chat? Right.

". . . and that Easton woman stopped him right outside my walkway. She walked up close to him and put her hand on his arm. I couldn't hear what she was saying, but Tom was nodding like one of those bobble-headed toys."

"What did you do?" I asked for the third time in less than a week.

She raised one eyebrow and did a good imitation of Queen Elizabeth. The *first* Queen Elizabeth, getting ready to behead Mary Queen of Scots. "I picked up a letter I needed to mail, walked elegantly, if I do say so myself, out my front door and down the path. Tom looked downright guilty, and Easton just stared at me like I was a bug or something. I smiled at her, put the letter in the box, took Tom by the arm, and headed back up my path."

"Sounds like a good way of handling it," I said.

The tears started up. I was going to have to buy a new box of tissues. "Right then Celia came by in her little white mail van. She took the letter out of my box, and hollered loud enough for the whole street to hear her, 'Were you plannin' on puttin' a stamp on this letter anytime soon?'" I was impressed. Glaze did a great Celia imitation. But then she dropped back into her own voice and said, "I was completely mortified. And Easton just stood there laughing at me." Glaze gulped back a sob of sheer frustration. "I . . . I . . . I could kill her!"

"What did Tom do?"

My dear sister looked positively murderous, even more so than she had a few seconds before. "He laughed, too."

Oh dear. Maybe I should cancel my matron of honor dress.

I WAS BEGINNING to think that the library had an echo of some sort. After Glaze left, Dee came downstairs carrying *The Blade and the Chalice* by Riane Eisler. She plunked the book down on the white counter and waited while I stamped the envelope pasted inside the front cover. "Do you enjoy reading anthropology, Dee?"

I might have been speaking to one of the stone lions outside the main door. "That Easton Hastings is going to be sorry," she said.

Not much of a reply to my question, I thought.

"I . . . I . . . I could kill her!"

This was ridiculous. She sounded like a recording of every woman in town, threatening the same thing as all the others, and showing the same sort of despair. Poor Easton was going to melt from all the acid poured her way. I listened to yet another story of Easton's infringement–had the woman no boundaries?–and wondered if I should have become a counselor.

"But, Dee, you're divorcing Barkley," I argued.

"What in the world does that have to do with anything?"

I'd make a lousy counselor.

FROM WHERE I stood in the middle of Children's Books, I could see the heavy front door swing open on its custom-made hinges. I loved this library. I sincerely hoped the door-opener wasn't another wife coming in to complain about Easton. I was lucky. It was Nathan, our wonderful town doctor. He stamped his feet on the heavy-duty mat we'd installed to soak up some of the rain. "Whew!" he said, "this is duck weather for sure."

"I've heard it's supposed to get a lot worse before it gets better."

"Well, that just means healing is on its way." The good doctor smiled. "And we won't shrink," he added.

"How's your new staff addition working out?" I asked. Even though I'd been surprised when Marmalade got rid of Tank, the kitten I'd picked up on my way out of Savannah several months ago, it seemed to have been for the best. Nathan was genuinely fond of his office cat.

"The patients love him," Nathan said. "And so do I. My cup runneth over," he quoted. He dumped four or five books in the return slot and walked over to join me. "Did I tell you I've changed his name?"

"Why? I thought Tank was a great name." Right from the start he'd been such a sturdy little guy.

"It just didn't fit him any more. He's still as big as ever, in fact, more so, since he's grown so tall," Nathan said. "But did you know he likes classical music better than anything? Sometimes I find him with his head snugged up right against the speaker listening to Tchaikovsky or Rimsky-Korsakov or Rachmaninoff. If I put on jazz or something else, he moves away, but those symphonies get to him every time."

"So, what did you decide to call him?"

"Well, I thought about Tchai, for Tchaikovsky, but he doesn't look like a Tchai. And I couldn't make a sensible name out of Rachmaninoff. So I settled for . . ."

I could almost hear the drumrolls in Nathan's voice.

". . . Nicholai Rimsky-KorsaCat!"

"It'll never fit on a name tag." As we chuckled, the door swung open again, and Easton walked in.

"Oh, Doctor," she gushed. She ignored me. "Can somebody be allergic to rain?"

"Rain is good for the earth, Ms. Hastings," he said.

"Call me Easton."

"And I've never known anyone to be allergic to it," he added.

"It's just getting me down," she complained, a little too sweetly for my taste. "I've been feeling restless. You wouldn't happen to make house calls, would you?"

Something was wrong with her antenna. Nathan must have had the same thought because he looked at me and grinned wickedly.

This unending round of complaints from her bright red lips was enough to turn any self-respecting, normally supportive female's stomach. We were *all* tired of the rain.

"Maybe Dr. KorsaCat, my new assistant, could help you out," Nathan said.

I laid a hand on his arm. "He can't, Nathan," I said. "He doesn't make house calls, either." We both burst out laughing. Easton didn't have a clue.

Chapter 26

Thursday October 24th

> "THIS IS RADIO Ralph Towers, broadcasting from Garner Creek, Georgia, bringing you the WRRT mid-afternoon, mid-week weather report. You don't need me to know that it's raining outside. We haven't seen rain like this in years, folks. In fact, the Metoochie River is so swollen, two towns have lost their docks. The Hastings Town Dock broke to pieces early this morning and swept away down the rapids. Martinsville must have built their dock better. It's still pretty much intact, or so we hear, but it's flopped on its side, jammed up against the cliff by the opening to the Gorge. It'll be awhile before they can repair it. Rain's due to keep pouring on us for the next five days."

Good. I turned the radio back to NPR. We'd have a sunny weekend.

Friday, October 25th

"THAT EASTON HASTINGS is going to be sorry."

I'd never seen Melissa this distraught. Well, I had seen her even more distraught than this when her favorite nephew was killed by a drunken driver. What could Easton have done that came anywhere near such a tragedy? "Why," I asked her, "would you be upset with Easton? You don't have a husband for her to steal." It sounded like a reasonable question to me, so I wasn't prepared for Melissa's snarl.

"No, but I have a business to run, and when she upsets my guests enough for them to say they're never coming back as long as she's alive, I . . . I . . . I could kill her!"

This poor checkout desk was hearing some grisly threats, I thought.

The desk does not have ears.

Or, rather, the same threat over and over and over again. These women were all ones I liked and respected. To hear them threatening murder–even though I knew they weren't serious about it–was disconcerting. I hated listening to it. But that perverse side of me *did* listen. "Who did she offend this time?"

"What do you mean 'this time'?"

"This is installment number five, or six. I've lost count. So far Easton has ticked off Ida, Sally, Sharon, Glaze, Dee, and now you." Six. I was right. Wasn't all this confiding supposed to be–well–confidential? I *would* make a lousy counselor. Of course, as long as I was divulging, I might as well enjoy it. "Every one of you has threatened to murder the poor woman."

"Poor woman? Poor woman indeed! She's a boa constrictor. She's a scorpion. She's . . . she's . . . she's absolutely the most infuriating female I've ever known." I handed her the tissue box. "Why can't she behave herself?"

That is a good question.

"Why can't she keep her hands to herself?"

I do not know. Her hands are soft and beautiful, but she does not like me.

Melissa wrapped her arms around Marmalade and buried her face in the soft fur. Her sobbing gradually slowed down. Marmalade made a superb psychologist, and she could never divulge a confidence.

I could if you would listen.

I WAS TIRED of being the official Recipient of Complaints. It was wearing awfully thin. As I wound up the final chores and closed the library, I felt an urge to get away. To go somewhere where nobody knew me. Well, maybe Glenda. She'd been one of my dearest friends for such a long time. And she'd never met Easton. Or rather, Easton had never met Glenda's husband. So maybe the two of us could go get a bed and breakfast place somewhere and just chill out for a day, spend the night, and come back refreshed the next day. I needed time to talk or do nothing. Time for somebody other than me to make me a cup of tea. Time to forget about the chores waiting to be done. Time with no phone to answer. Sounded like a grand plan.

Naturally, when I called Glenda, she had a place in mind without even thinking about it. "I'm free next weekend," she said. "There's a quiet little retreat center over near Sautee. They make a great breakfast, too. Let's leave on Friday after you get through with work, stay two nights, and be back on Sunday."

"I don't want to be gone that long," I told her. "How about leaving early Saturday morning? Bob always spends most of Saturday goofing off in his workshop anyway. That way, we'll have all day Saturday and half a day or so on Sunday."

"Sounds good to me. You tell your guy. I'll tell my guy. I'll make the reservations, and I'll see you next week. You pick me up–we're headed out of the valley."

I looked at the calendar. November second. Sounded like an auspicious day.

". . . AND WE WANT to go next weekend."

Bob listened to me, frowned, and shook his head. This was turning out worse than I had anticipated. "Why," he asked, "do you need to go on a vacation without me?"

Or me?

"It isn't a vacation exactly."

He stopped massaging my left foot. "Sure sounds like it."

"It's a getaway–a retreat."

"Wasn't our honeymoon enough of a getaway for you?"

I missed you both.

The fact that it had been marred by a murder seemed to have slipped his mind. "Bob." I reached across Marmalade and stretched my hand along the back of the sofa so I could touch his shoulder. "Honey, you know I love you very much. What you don't seem to understand is that I have to have some time to myself. To regenerate."

"But why without me? And why, if you need time alone, do you want to take Glenda with you? That's not alone." He shook his head again. "And you have plenty of time alone during the day."

She is not alone. I am with her.

He didn't get it. Men got so much of their fulfillment from their wives. But for most of us women, time spent at home was *not* time alone. It was time spent with chores–cooking and laundry and shopping and straightening. For most women it was time juggled with a job, or with children or grandchildren. It was time spent at the beck and call of the telephone. It was time listening to the never-ending complaints in the library. It was time that wasn't just for *me.*

I tried once more. "Honey, I have to fill up my own pitcher. I can't keep giving and giving if I have nothing left to give with. Glenda is one of my dearest friends. You're one of my dearest friends, too, but you don't know how to talk girl talk."

He looked at me over the rim of his glasses and muttered, "I should hope not."

"Well, girl talk is just exactly what I need. And I need it away from this constant round of . . ." Of what? ". . . of everyday life." I needed to get away from this incessant rain, or rather from the depression I felt as a result of it. I also needed to be away from my daughter, but I wasn't willing to put that into words. I needed to talk with Glenda–long talks and a quiet evening, even if it was only for a day and a half.

Who will feed me if you are gone?

Bob watched Marmalade hop down onto my lap and nuzzle at my chin. "I suppose you want me to feed the cat . . ."

The cat?

". . . while you're gone." The way he said it, it wasn't a question. Marmalade echoed him with her yowl.

"Honey, I don't need to get away from you." Well, maybe from the chores he generated, but I wasn't going to say that out loud. "I need to fill my own pitcher."

"You said that already."

"Then it bears repeating."

"Well, I can't say I understand this," he said. "I can't even say I like it. But I suppose you know what you need. So, I suppose you can go."

Of *course* I could. Did he think I was asking his *permission?* I decided not to press the point. Too much. "I'm glad you agree with me," I said.

Chapter 27

Saturday, October 26th

BOB TOOK A step backwards and bumped into his desk. Three minutes ago his office had seemed plenty big enough. Now it felt minuscule. Why, he wondered, had he ever agreed to work on a Saturday?

Marmalade unwound herself from Bob's desk chair and hopped across the telephone to face the woman with the fiery hair.

She is a bother.

"You need something?" Bob echoed. "What do you mean?"

Easton advanced two more steps and touched the third button of his uniform shirt. "I need me a kiss," she rumbled. "And I need it fast."

Marmalade levitated from the desk to Bob's shoulder and, in one swift movement, swiped her tongue along Easton's cheek.

"Yuch! Cat slobber!"

I do not slobber.

They watched Easton retreat to the door. Bob reached up to scratch Marmy's white chest. "Thanks, little one," he whispered, without moving his lips.

You are welcome.

"You got your kiss, Easton," he said aloud as she turned the doorknob. "Hope you're satisfied now."

I will not kiss you again.

"I'm awfully glad you came to work with me today, little one," Bob said as soon as the door closed. "That woman gives me the willies."

What is a willie?

"AS YOU WELL know, Biscuit," Clara Martin's unwelcome voice purred at me through the kitchen phone, like a diesel engine idling on a cold morning, "I'm not one to gossip, but I thought you'd want to hear about this from me and not find out about it on the street. That's right, isn't it?"

I took a moment to rub my right hand across my eyes. "What is it, Clara," I said. I hadn't made it a question. More like the acceptance of the inevitable, since she was going to tell me anyway, whether I asked or not.

"Your husband Bob . . ."

The only husband I have, I thought.

". . . was kissing Easton Hastings at the police station a few minutes ago."

I'm going to kill that woman, I thought, and I wasn't quite sure whether I meant Easton or Clara. Maybe both of them.

"Bob wouldn't do that, Clara," I said.

"Oh, yes he would," she crowed back at me. "I was walking past his office . . ."

Probably listening at his keyhole.

". . . and he told her he hoped she'd enjoyed her kiss. That's what he said. A direct quote."

I'd heard some of Clara's so-called direct quotes before. I was perfectly sure that he'd said something different. But how different?

"As I said," she went on, inexorable as the Egyptian army approaching the Red Sea. I hoped she'd drown, too. "As I said, you needed to know this before it became common knowledge."

If she was the only one who saw it happen, it wouldn't become common knowledge unless she told everybody else. I wondered how many other women were on her call list for this juicy tidbit.

I DECIDED TO give Bob time to explain before I accused him of anything. I was pretty sure that as soon as he came home, he'd tell me right off that she had accosted him and he'd beaten her off. Clara was just inventing things. She thrived on chaos.

"Boy, am I hungry," he said as he and Marmalade walked in the door.

We had a good time at the station. Softfoot scratched my head a lot.

He hung his wide-brimmed hat on its usual peg in the front hall, while Marmalade wove in and out between his legs. "What's for dinner?"

I would like some chicken.

Maybe he didn't want to startle me too much. Maybe he was waiting. Maybe I'd clobber him first, and then get around to Easton. And Clara. Instead, I asked, "Did you have a good day?"

"Sure did," he said. "Marmalade and I got a lot accomplished."

Yeah, I bet. "Anything I'd be interested in?"

He shook his head. One lock of hair fell forward over his eyebrow. "Nope," he said. He looked shaggy. And decidedly guilty. "Just the usual stuff."

Usual? Kissing women at work was usual?

"What's for dinner?" he asked again.

"Battery acid and sewer sludge." I never liked myself when I got vindictive, but this felt good.

That sounds bad.

"Whoa, Woman," he said. "What's gotten into you?"

I tried for maybe two seconds to be civil, but it wouldn't come out that way. "You come waltzing in after making out with Easton Hastings in your office and you think I won't know about it? How dare you! Clara told me all about it. How could you? That slut! You men are all alike!"

The trouble was, he looked genuinely surprised. And then he narrowed his eyes at me. "Bisque," he said in what I knew as his dangerous voice. He'd used it on me only once before, but that time I was sorely mistaken about something. "Bisque," he repeated, "are you honestly trying to tell me that you'd believe Clara Martin before you'd believe in me?"

When he put it that way, I felt the tiniest bit hesitant. And when he put his hands on my shoulders and pulled me close to him, I felt maybe I shouldn't cry into the front of his uniform shirt.

Once I settled down just a tad, he whispered, "Now, would you like to hear what really happened?" Of course, once he told me, I picked up Marmalade and took her into the kitchen for a treat of chicken.

Thank you.

"What?" Bob asked. "No battery acid?"

"Chicken soup," I told him. "It's good for healing."

Chapter 28

Sunday, October 27th

THE SIGNBOARD AT the Old Church had proclaimed all week that the sermon would be called *My Cup Runneth Over.* I was supposed to be feeling grateful, but I was mad at Radio Ralph. He'd predicted rain. And here it was raining. How dare he be right for a change? The rain and Radio Ralph and my sore knee made it hard to think gratitude. It had been too long since I'd been able to do any yard chores. This sitting and thinking was for the birds after awhile.

Birds? Where?

Luckily, though, I'd always been pretty good at entertaining myself. Marmalade and I had racked up an inordinate number of hours looking at the back yard from my kitchen window. I'd started paying more attention to individual trees out back. Before all this rain, I'd thought of them as *the trees.* Now I could run an internal catalog. The oaks, the beeches, the tulip poplars, the hickories, the sweetgums.

The bird feeder.

Two river birches, some pretty little sassafras trees, a few pines, some firs and several hollies.

The bird feeder.

Maybe my cup *was* running over, I thought. There were a couple of magnificent maples that had to be at least a hundred years old. I could imagine them welcoming all the little birds into their arms–well, their branches. I could see how they must have enjoyed the rain coursing through their hair and watering their roots. I could tell they liked having the raccoons and possums and squirrels chitter-chattering around them all day long. Marmalade must have agreed with me. She was purring contentedly and looking out the window, too.

The soft afternoon light reflected from the wet leaves on one exceptionally long maple branch that was at eye level, just on the other side of the back fence. I knew it was the breeze and the rain making that particular branch dance about, but I couldn't help thinking that the old maple tree was waving at me.

Before I could wave back, the phone startled me into reality. "Mother!"

How did Sally manage to invest one simple word with so much disdain? It was on the tip of my tongue to ask her what I did this time, but instead I took a breath and said a simple, "Hey, Sally."

"Sandra told me about this trip you planned."

That was fast. "To the retreat center?" I stalled for time.

"Why are you doing that?"

I moved the receiver a bit away from my ear. Sally's voice had always been loud, but today she was outdoing herself. "I thought a short retreat would be a nice idea," I told her. I felt no need to explain my conversation with Bob about filling my own pitcher.

"But that's almost when the baby's due!"

"I know, dear. You don't need to holler at me."

"You *can't* go out of town when my baby's due."

What difference would it make? You don't want me around anyway, I thought. You and that husband of yours have ganged up against me. This'll serve you right. The answers careening through my head were not appropriate. They weren't very nice, either. I restrained myself and settled on asking her, "Why not?"

"Why not? Why not!" Her voice ascended half an octave. "Because what if the baby comes while you're gone?"

"Well, dear, I'm sure you and Jason can handle that just fine. And I know he'll take lots of pictures, so it's not as if I'll miss anything. And you can call me. I won't be unreachable."

"But, what if it comes in the middle of the night?"

"That doesn't matter, Sally. You can call me anytime." I sounded distinctly syrupy. "Or, if you'd rather," I added, "you can wait until the next morning."

"Mother!" She was getting louder. Marmalade looked up at me briefly before she turned around and settled back onto my lap. "What if our car breaks down?"

"Don't you have a backup plan?"

"Of course I have a backup plan. We'll call Jason's parents."

"Good," I told her. "Then you don't need me for anything. So why do you want me to cancel my retreat?"

"Because you might miss the birth!" She was whining. I was going to miss the birth anyway, so what was the big deal? I hated whining, especially when I was doing it, too. "You're just trying to get back at me," she said, "because you're still mad."

"Sally, this has nothing to do with that."

Why is your face red?

"Yes it does," Sally declared in a tone that challenged me to deny it.

You are both hissing and spitting.

Come to think of it, I was still a teensy weensy bit upset with her.

"What's happened to you, Mom? Ever since you married Bob you're just not there for me anymore."

"Not there for you? What are you talking about? I call you all the time, even though all you do is lecture me about my clothes, and we've invited you for dinner any number of times, and you always say no."

"That's because all you ever serve is *soup!"*

"That's because all I ever *cook* is soup. Or bread," I added in the interest of truthfulness. And I did make the best brownies in the world–dark, almost fudgy. Yum. How did she ever end up such a good cook? It certainly wasn't because of my culinary example, . . .

You cook good chicken for me.

. . . but I'd be darned if I was going to admit any such thing. I glanced down at Marmalade, who was watching me with those big green eyes of hers. Piercing green. She looked so calm. What was she thinking about?

I am thinking I am glad I am a cat.

It made me take a very deep breath. "You're right, Sally. I'm not a good cook. I understand why you'd rather eat at Jason's mother's house. But you've declined every single invitation, ever since you married that . . ." I bit my tongue and backtracked. "Since you married Jason," I said. Marmalade let out a yelp, and I smoothed down the fur that stood up along her back. "Well, come to think of it, you have gone out to lunch with me a couple of times." Not that I wanted to think about our last lunch together. Maybe the last one ever, if I had anything to say about it. "I'm surprised you even came to my wedding," I added, with more venom than I had intended.

"Sandra made me." Before I could register what she'd said, she went on. "Why did you hate Daddy so much?"

I almost dropped the phone. "What? What did you say?"

"You heard me. I want to know what he ever did to make you hate him so much."

"Sally, I didn't hate your father. We were happy together."

There was a long silence on the other end. "You said you were . . ." Her voice was uncharacteristically soft. In fact, I had to strain to hear her. ". . . you were glad he was dead."

"I never said that."

"Yes you did," she barked at me. "At his funeral. I heard you talking to Glenda."

Trying to dredge up a six-year-old conversation was like trying to find one chive in a field of wild onions. Sol, my husband of more than twenty years, had been horribly ill for one agonizing week before he said, "I love you, Biscuit McKee," and died as I sat beside him in the intensive care unit. I was stunned. I was in shock. I was ravaged with grief, and at the same time trying to hold myself together for our three children.

For weeks after his death I did my crying at night. I screamed silently into my pillow. Had I been wrong to try to hide my despair from the children? Did Sally think I was heartless because I couldn't show how my heart was broken? Glenda really was the only person I confided in. Glenda and my mom.

I thought back to the funeral, how they stood with me and the kids beside the grave. I remembered how, after the service while the kids were comforted by their friends, I had leaned into Glenda's hug and told her, "I'm glad. Glad he died . . ." I remembered rummaging for a tissue. Glenda handed me a wad of them. I remembered looking around for my children. Sandra and Scott, eighteen and sixteen years old at the time, were surrounded by a group of young people. Seventeen-year-old Sally was on the other side of the grave. Her back was turned to me, and she seemed to be listening to one of her friends. After I blew my nose, I finished my sentence. "I'm glad he died so quickly, so peacefully." Glenda held me until we had to turn away to thank the other people who had come to pay their last respects.

It was after the funeral that Sally seemed to draw away from me. I tried to help her deal with her grief, but I didn't know how to get through that wall she seemed to have built around herself.

AFTER SALLY HUNG up on me, I retrieved the blue-flowered box of tissues from the counter by the sink and poured myself another cup of tea. I knew she hadn't believed me. I knew she thought I was making it all up. The light faded as if a shroud had draped over the sun. The rain lashed the leaves in the woods out back. If I were a tree, I'd hate standing there day after day, year after year, letting any old bird fly in and poop on my hair. I'd hate putting up with rain and hail and wind. If I were a tree, I thought, Sally would buy the land I stood on, and she'd cut me down. . . .

I like trees. I like you.

. . . I put my face in my hands and let out a sigh. Phooey, phooey, phooey. Even Marmalade licking my hands couldn't cheer me up.

Chapter 29

Monday, October 28th

AUNTIE BLUE CALLED on Monday just as I finished the dishes.

"I unpacked the last box and got everything put away. Ohhh, I'm finally feeling like I'm settled in," she told me with a self-satisfied purr.

"Congratulations. It took you only a couple of weeks." I tried to keep from sounding too whiny. "I've been in this house since April, and I still have boxes that aren't unpacked."

"Oh, don't worry. You'll get to them as soon as your knee feels better."

Fat chance, I thought. "Sure," I said. "Now that you're all unpacked, do you want to drive up to the nursing home with Glaze and me tomorrow and pick up Grandma? It's supposed to quit raining. Mom'll meet us there."

"Lordy, a visit would be a good idea. I haven't seen your grandma but one time since I moved back into town."

"Every other week," I told her, "we all go out. Now that you and Glaze are here, we'll have a regular party."

"A girl's day out," she said.

Except for Grandpa, I thought, but he never said much, so it was almost like girl talk time. "Usually we drive back to Mom's house and eat there," I told her.

"No, no, no," she interrupted. "Let's have lunch here. It'll be a sweet gathering–my first in the new house. And Mama would probably enjoy sitting out back by the swimming pool for a little bit."

"Are the suds gone yet?"

"Well, mostly. In all this rain, they didn't have much of a chance."

I thought briefly of lecturing her about the detrimental effects of a box of soap flakes pouring into the water table, but decided to be tactful.

"We'll swing by between 10:30 and 11:00, okay?"

"Sure thing, darling. I'll be ready and waiting."

This would be a lot more fun than usual. Not that I didn't enjoy seeing my mom, but the lunches with Grandma and Grandpa did get a bit tedious at times, with Grandma off in la-la land and Grandpa complaining about everything under the sun. Sometimes I'd see Mom looking at her parents with a funny expression that I never could quite read. It must be hard to watch your parents gradually falling apart. I had no idea how I was going to cope with that when it was my turn to do the watching. Mom was still bright as could be at seventy-two, and Dad was chipper and funny and sweet. He'd slowed down a little because of the heavy arthritis in his hands, but his spirits were still way up there. I figured they'd both be going strong into their nineties. I hoped so, at least.

Chapter 30

Tuesday, October 29th

I COULDN'T UNDERSTAND why Auntie Blue had been so quiet all the way from Happy Days to her house. She and Glaze were both in my back seat. I'd kind of thought that one of them would ride with Mom and Grandpa.

When we got to the house, Auntie Blue hopped out of the car first. "Gotta get the front door open," she said, and walked right past Mom's car, not even stopping to open the car door for Grandpa. What on earth was going on? She wasn't usually grumpy.

Lunch was a quiet affair, but Grandma and Grandpa didn't seem to notice anything unusual. I caught Glaze looking over at Auntie Blue several times, raising her eyebrows. Mom tried hard to keep a conversation going, but Glaze and Blue weren't cooperating. Finally, she said, "Let's walk out back and see the yard, shall we? Blue, we want the grand tour." We got Grandma out of her chair, and I started pushing Grandpa's wheelchair out the back door. Grandma, though, insisted on walking behind it, pushing it and also using it as a walker. It was kind of cute, until she said, "You know, he doesn't need this thing. He just uses it to get sympathy."

Grandpa acted like he hadn't heard her, but he must have.

She was using her loud voice for a change, and his hearing aid had new batteries.

Glaze and Blue stopped along the cement walkway while Auntie Blue pointed out a little patch of zinnias. They looked perky in the early afternoon sunlight. I glanced around the yard. Auntie Blue would need some help fixing this place up. The previous owners had been zinnia freaks. Maybe they weren't gardeners–*obviously* they weren't gardeners!–and simply didn't know what else to plant. Of course, zinnias are fairly forgiving. I envisioned some multi-layered shrubs, varying heights to give depth and interest up against the privacy fence. Maybe some annuals at the base of the shrubs. I didn't care much for annuals myself–too much fussing around with all the deadheading and such–but Auntie Blue liked cut flowers in the house, so she'd need something other than zinnias to keep her company.

"I thought I'd start a rose garden," she was saying as I walked back to join them. Mom stood off to one side with her face raised and her eyes closed, just soaking up the sun.

"Where will you put it?" I asked. "Maybe here by the foundation?"

"No." She gestured toward the other side of the pool. "I was thinking out there at the end of the yard."

Glaze and I turned and saw Grandma pushing Grandpa's wheelchair farther along the path. We started to stroll after her. Then she gave the chair a shove that propelled it into the swimming pool.

"Grandma!" I grabbed her arm as gently as I could, considering how fast I had run toward her, and turned her back toward my sister and aunt. "Grandpa!" I yelled, "I'm coming!" I really should have taken one of those Red Cross lifesaving courses, I thought, as I jumped into the water. I should have kicked off my shoes first. Then my tennis shoes hit the bottom. That would have been hard on bare toes.

Grandpa stood in the four-foot deep water, glaring back at the knot of women by the poolside. He didn't even look at me.

Somehow he had fallen free of his chair and managed to right himself before I could reach him. His sparse hair dripped down his forehead. He coughed out some water, clenched his jaw, and started swearing. I'd never heard Grandpa swear before. I spit out the mouthful of water I'd splashed into my face. Never jump into a pool with your mouth open.

Mom was still frozen where she'd been standing. Glaze looked at Auntie Blue. Auntie Blue looked at Glaze. Grandma looked at both of them. She turned back toward the pool and said in a surprisingly lucid voice, "I knew all along what you were doing with those girls, you old fool. You had no right." All three of them pivoted and walked into the house. Auntie Blue on the left, Glaze on the right, and Grandma in the middle. Mom looked at me, shook her head, and followed behind.

Grandpa could have been killed, and they were walking into the house? Had I missed something? My surprise was matched only by the shock I felt as they turned their backs. Grandma's voice echoed through my head. "I knew all along what you were doing." I turned back and looked at Grandpa. Had I been blind my entire life? Had I been too wrapped up in my own concerns to see what was in front of me? Now that poem Glaze had read began to make some sense. Would I even have been able to handle it if they'd confided in me? Images from childhood flooded back. He's had challenges . . . you keep your sister right with you . . . that spanking I'd gotten because I let Grandpa do the babysitting . . . I don't like the games he plays . . . Ma's tight hand on my shoulder when I wanted to see the tool shed. Dammit! Why hadn't they *told* me? I could have dealt with it if I'd had the information. Did Glaze hate me because I hadn't protected her? Did she hate me because Mom had protected *me*? Would we ever be able to talk about this?

For now, though, I had a dripping wet grandfather to dry off before I could return him to Happy Days, and a dripping wet me to dry off before I could drive him there. How does forgiveness begin? Maybe it didn't. Not yet, at least. I was reeling with the knowledge that all four of those women had linked themselves against me. No, not against me. Against him.

I had to get him out of the pool. His teeth were beginning to chatter, even in the warm water, and his lips were turning blue. I made a conscious effort to relax my jaw, and reached for my grandfather's hand. He seemed to deflate, somehow, and he let me lead him to the stairs. Forgiveness didn't mean that what happened was okay. Forgiveness meant I wouldn't let it ruin my life. I wasn't ready to forgive yet, but I could at least act in a civilized manner.

GRANDPA SHUFFLED SLOWLY and painfully up the walkway, leaning on me for support. When we walked into the living room, the four women sat facing each other across the coffee table, two on chairs and two on the couch. Grandma was back in her dementia mode, talking about a dress she used to wear to church, but nobody listened to her. Not that she seemed to notice.

"Would any of you like to help me get Grandpa dried off?" I asked. "Auntie Blue, could we borrow some clothes?"

For just a moment I thought she wasn't going to answer me, but then she switched into hostess mode, rather like I'd done in the swimming pool. Acting civilized. "You can throw all this wet stuff in the dryer. I'll get a couple of robes for the two of you to wear." She bustled back toward the bedroom and I maneuvered Grandpa behind her down the hallway. It turned out he was a lot more capable of taking care of himself than we'd given him credit for. Maybe those male orderlies at Happy Days wouldn't take any pity-party guff from him. He slouched into the bathroom. I kept asking him through the closed door if he was okay, and he kept grunting what sounded like an affirmative. I undressed quickly while he was in there, and donned a green robe long before he finished. When he came out, enveloped in the puffy blue robe Auntie Blue had thrown at him, he seemed shrunken almost beyond recognition. Maybe it was just the huge bathrobe.

I sat him down in the wing chair, slipped a pair of borrowed socks onto his gnarled feet and covered him with the blanket that was draped over the end of the bed. "Stay here," I told him, trying to keep my voice neutral. I could have won an Oscar for that performance. His clothes lay on the bathroom floor where he had dropped them. I picked up everything except for his shoes, of course, and walked down the hall to the laundry room. Dryers are all the same. Stick stuff in, close the door, push a button or two, walk away.

Hindsight is so simple, I thought. How could I have been so blind?

NEEDLESS TO SAY, the trip back to Happy Days was quiet. We'd left the wheelchair in the pool. Auntie Blue said that Uncle Mark would get it out and dry it off. I volunteered to come back and pick it up, but she said, "No. Thank you. He can deliver it back to the nursing home." Her simple refusal felt like a slap in the face. I couldn't help it that I'd been safe.

They all three declined to ride with me. I loaded Grandpa in the back seat, strapped Grandma into her seatbelt in the front, and drove silently. Grandma muttered to herself. Grandpa didn't say a word.

Carla Blake, the young and ever-helpful activities director bustled out as I drove up. She pushed a wheelchair ahead of her. "Your mother called and said you'd need some help. She said the wheelchair had a jammed wheel. I told her she should have sent it on back here. That's what our maintenance department is for." She extracted Grandpa while I helped Grandma stand and get her balance. "Goodness," she went on, "these things always need some repair work, but your sweet mother said they had somebody at home who could work on it."

Yeah, I thought. Starting with a hair-dryer on the seat and back.

She eyed Grandpa's wrinkled pants. "Lordy! I'm going to have to talk to our laundry people. Those pants look like you slept in them."

"Don't do that." I didn't want anyone to get in trouble. "We had a little accident." She'd probably think he'd peed in his pants, but at that point I didn't care what she thought. "So we washed his clothes and dried them."

Grandpa raised an emaciated fist and shook it at Grandma. "Crazy old woman pushed me in the swimming pool. I 'bout drowned."

Miss Blake lifted his slipper-encased feet onto the footrest and took the brakes off. She patted Grandpa's arm. "Lordy, you do say the most outrageous things, Mr. Martelson."

MARMALADE MET ME at the front door.

Smellsweet is here.

I saw Glaze's purse on the drop leaf table, so it didn't surprise me when she walked out of the kitchen. "We need to talk," she said.

She already had the water boiling. I spent a few minutes gathering my courage and making tea. The two activities seemed to go together. When I set the teapot on the table, she reached out and laid her hand on my forearm. "You can look at me," she said. "I'm not dirty."

"Glaze, how could you think that? That's not how I feel about this. I had no idea any of that stuff was happening."

"You should have known."

"I was just a little kid. What did you expect me to do? How could I know about that? Nobody ever told me!"

Why are you shouting?

"And I was even littler and you were my big sister, and you were supposed to keep me safe, not make me go in there to that

. . ." Glaze moved her spoon from the right side of her mug to the left side. "That place," she said. Her voice, normally low and smooth, was up half an octave. She sounded like a little girl.

She sounds like a kitten.

Marmalade hopped out of my lap and slithered underneath Glaze's arm and nuzzled her orange head against my sister's jaw. "I thought I was over the hurt," she said. "I've worked on this so hard. I've seen therapists. I've read books." Her voice started inching back down into her normal range. "I even joined a discussion group for women who survived abuse. I thought it was all taken care of. I've been doing okay." She rocked Marmalade back and forth, almost like a teddy bear.

A bear?

"You didn't tell us he was going to be a part of the lunch group. You only said Grandma."

That's why lunch was so quiet, I thought.

"When Grandma pushed him in the pool, it felt kind of good to stand there and do nothing. And then you started running to save him, to save . . . him. . . . I just got so angry all over again. Not angry at him. I've dealt with that. Angry at you. For not protecting me." Her voice ran down and she kept rocking.

Our tea was getting cold. I should have put the bright yellow tea cozy over the pot. I was no good at taking care of anything. My daughter resented me. My sister hated me. My cat had abandoned me. "I don't know what to say," I said. "I don't know how to apologize enough. I don't know how to ask for forgiveness for something that you'd probably never be able to forgive. And I wouldn't blame you one bit if you never talked to me again. I'm . . . I'm so sorry." My words sounded incredibly weak.

Glaze raised her head from Marmalade's fur. She pushed the blue-flowered box toward me. "You need a tissue, Sis."

It was a start.

Chapter 31

Thursday, October 31st

AT TWO IN the morning–I knew it was two because I looked at the clock–Marmalade walked across my face. Something felt oddly wrong. She didn't seem too distraught, just a bunch of gentle meows, . . .

L*ook out the window.*

. . . so I didn't worry particularly, but I couldn't quite place what it was that felt funny. Maybe it was just the dream I'd been having. Something about a heavy door slamming. Bob was snoring gently beside me, my middle of the night symphony. I was about ready to give up and go back to sleep, but Marmy placed one soft paw directly on my right eyelid. Was she hungry?

We can go outside now.

I was thirsty anyway, so I slipped my legs over the side of the bed and used their leverage to swing me upright slowly. It had been a long time since I'd enjoyed hopping up in the middle of the night, if I ever did. I thought about the times I'd dragged myself out of bed to nurse Sandra. Worth it when I got there and could hold her and feed her. But then I had to burp her and change her and burp her again and finally put her back into her crib. Good grief, how did young mothers ever manage? I was exhausted just remembering it. And it was even harder with

Sally because she wouldn't nurse, and I had to put her on a bottle when she was just a couple of months old. Then I had to detour to the kitchen, warm the bottle, and go through all that routine, plus the burping and changing. Maybe I was a lousy mother, after all. Or did everybody resent the lack of sleep? I read once that the human body could never be acclimated to sleep deprivation. No wonder women went bananas sometimes.

I would not know about that. I am smart enough to take naps when I need them.

Bob kept snoring. Phooey on him. "All right, Marmy," I muttered back toward her purr. "I'm coming." Donning my fuzzy blue bathrobe–I love bathrobes; I must have five of them–I shuffled out of the bedroom and headed toward the stairs, but Marmalade skipped into the sewing room and hopped onto the wide windowsill. She seemed intent on something, probably a dog walking by, or another cat. It took me a moment to register that my front yard had changed completely. The dogwood tree was down. I hadn't heard any thunder. *That* was what was disturbing. I'd become so used to the sound of rain at night, weeks of it, and now it wasn't raining. Good. I was glad I'd figured that out. And the sound of the tree falling must have been the door in my dream. The branches were still trembling from the fall. I hoped there weren't any baby birds in the nests. Nonsense. This was October. Halloween in fact. Birds didn't lay eggs this time of year.

The birds sleep in the tree. We could go outside and look.

Well, there was nothing I could do about it now. The top of the tree reached the middle of the road. I could see it outlined against the wan light from Paul Welsh's front porch, filtering through the *Ligustrum* hedge that surrounded his lot.

"Let's go back to bed, Marmalade."

I would like to go outside.

She must have agreed with me, because she was purring gently, . . .

Mouse droppings!

. . . and sneezing. I was back in bed before I remembered that I forgot to get a glass of water.

"BISCUIT, HONEY." BOB'S silky voice cut softly through my dreams. Gentler dreams this time. "I have to go outside, and I didn't want the chain saw to startle you awake."

"Oh? You're cutting up the dogwood?"

"How did you know about that?"

"Marmalade told me." He raised an eyebrow at that, so I explained. "She walked across my nose last night and led me to the window."

"Smart cat." He tousled Marmy's head where it peeked from under the comforter.

Of course.

"I'll be up in a minute and come out to help with hauling branches."

"Don't worry about it. Every man on the street will be there as soon as I start up the chainsaw."

"Well, then, I'll get some coffee going." It used to bother me to think that there was *men's work* and *women's work.* But now I didn't get so bent out of shape over it. Most men were delighted to chop things up and haul them around. I tended to do such jobs only if they needed doing, but was perfectly happy to let my husband, and the other men on Beechnut Lane, have their fun this early Thursday morning. And I'd fill them with coffee afterwards. After all, they'd be helping us with our tree.

WHEN MARMALADE AND I moseyed outside ten or fifteen minutes later, there was a clutch of men looking like a bunch of broody hens, clucking around the base of the tree where the entire root ball had tilted up and out of the ground. These rains had left the ground so soggy the tree hadn't been able to hold on. I hoped we didn't lose any more trees like that.

I've known people with shallow root systems like that, I thought. People who breezed along through life without ever developing any particular strength of purpose. Sometimes they ran over the feelings of family members or alienated friends. Then, when they needed their strong roots to hold them up, they had no support at all, internally or externally. Clara was like that. For all she was so proud of her heritage, for all the branches on that family tree, I didn't think her roots went very deep at all. Was *shallow-mindedness* synonymous with *shallow-rootedness*?

Speaking of Clara, I could see her up the way in front of Matthew's house, surrounded by a bevy of town women. Easton was there, with her hair afire in the morning sunlight. She was talking to her sister, Louise, and gesturing toward the group of men. I could imagine what she was saying.

I walked up behind Bob. "Isn't your chain saw working?"

He shook his head and turned around. I didn't see the joking, buoyant face that Bob usually had when he was with his buddies. Matthew looked equally solemn. Paul's face was white. "We found my grandfather," he said, and pointed toward the tree roots.

It didn't look much like anyone's grandfather to me. Just a whole bunch of bones that may have formed a recognizable skeleton at one time, but now had been shifted and dispersed by the tree as it fell. Down in the hole, there was a skull. I felt like Hamlet. One large twisted root on the tree ball wound its way around a big brownish-white bone. I thought I recognized it as a femur. It was hard to mistake anything that big, with that knobby projection on the side.

"See?" Paul said. "Grandpa always walked with a limp because his leg had been broken. When he was a kid, he fell out of a tree, and then when he was grown up, there was a tractor accident. Same leg each time. The left one."

There were mutters from the various men. I knew most of them. One of them in particular watched the women up the street. Probably looking at Easton. She sure did stand out in a group. Doggone her hide. I recognized him from the library. Reebok. The happy young man who was named for an antelope. Ah well, as Sharon so pointedly reminded me, I was named for a pot. While I mused about names, Lyle, the handyman with the unfortunate ears, suffered a minor sneezing fit. He didn't look happy at all. He was supposed to repair the reference section shelves the next day. I hoped he wasn't getting sick.

I looked back at the bone being held, almost like a trophy, by the tree roots. How could you tell whether a bone was from the right leg or the left leg? Not that it mattered. Instead of a long, clean line, this bone had a distinct angle in the middle of it. Not very pronounced, but enough to tell that the bone had healed the wrong way. I wondered if the doctor had been drunk. Was there even a doctor available, or had a home made splint caused such damage? Paul must have heard me thinking.

"When he was a kid, there wasn't a doctor in town. Folks just made do with what they had on hand. They fed him some whiskey and set his leg while they had him stretched out on the kitchen table. My folks said he hobbled around for months with a couple of planks lashed to his leg and a pair of homemade crutches to hold him up."

I shivered even though the morning sun was bright and fairly warm. There was going to be a lot to talk about at the Halloween party that evening. While the men rigged an impromptu duct tape barrier around the base of the tree, Marmy and I walked up the sidewalk to join the women.

"See that guy over there?" I heard Easton trying to whisper to her sister. Her voice was too loud, though, and carried through the whole knot of women. "Would you look at the way his ears stick out?"

"It's not nice to make fun of what people look like, Easton."

Clara shook her head and turned to me. "What's going on?"

The story would be around town within minutes, so I wasn't divulging anything confidential. "They found some bones underneath the tree. Bob's roping off the area. He'll have to call in the medical examiner. They look like they're human–the bones, I mean."

Over Clara's shoulder I saw Easton grimace. I was surprised to see she had some sort of humane feelings. That was a nasty thought, Biscuit McKee, I told myself. Shame on me.

The men wouldn't cut up the tree anytime soon. Most of them stayed clustered where they were, but a few of them wandered up the street and joined the women. I noticed several of them glancing Easton's way. She began to circulate. If it hadn't been so infuriating, it would have been funny to watch the pathetic way she had of brushing accidentally against the men and then stopping to talk with them, one at a time. She really made the rounds.

Roger Johnson approached me. "Too bad about Mr. Welsh," he said.

"I'm surprised to see you here, Roger. Thursday's your garbage route."

"Yeah. But my truck had a problem. Carl's working on it. He swears he'll have it ready tomorrow." Roger looked around, but his eyes didn't seem to be focusing. Looked to me like he was going over his schedule in his head. I was right. "I'll have to pick up your garbage early tomorrow since I'll still have to do the grocery store run. Hope that's okay with you."

We hadn't put our trash out by the curb yet, so it hardly mattered to me. "Tomorrow will be fine, Roger. But you might want to call everyone on your route and let them know." He was a grownup. Why was I giving him instructions on how to run his business? He didn't seem to take offense, though.

"Won't need to," he said. "Most of them are right here. I'll just walk around and tell them all."

We went on speaking in soft tones–it didn't seem appropriate to talk loudly while there was a dead body nearby–until Easton stopped in front of us. Ignoring me completely, she said, "I know a secret about you."

Roger blushed. "A secret? I don't have any secrets."

That line was overworked. She'd already used it on both Ralph and Carl, and probably every man here in the crowd on Beechnut Lane.

"Of course you do. And I know you're the one who keeps the sign going at the church."

"Shucks." He was saying *shucks*? "That's not a secret."

"You're just too cute for your own good. I know a real secret about you."

Roger looked distinctly uncomfortable and I was tired of being treated like a doorstop. "Easton, I think your sister wants you." I nudged her arm and pointed up the sidewalk. Luckily Louise happened to look in our direction right about then. She nodded at us and Easton wandered up the way.

"How did she know about me? Do you think she meant my songs?"

"For heaven's sake, Roger. Your songs aren't a secret. Anybody walking past your house can hear them." Not that anybody would want to. They sounded like caterwauling to me. He couldn't carry a tune in a bucket with a lid on it. "And she's been using that line on half the men in town." He looked like he didn't want to hear that, but I was fed up with the men who fell for her phony angle.

Easton stood near her sister for a moment and turned to look back at the tree. Then she looked across the street where Paul's old house stood behind its enormous hedge of glossy privet. It was hard not to look at her, with that hair of hers like a red halo around her head. Quite a few people, mostly men, seemed to be keeping an eye on her as well. She grabbed Louise's arm and pulled her away, looking back once toward the fallen tree. I watched as they walked up the street. Good riddance. Why did Louise put up with her?

Glaze walked up, nodded at Roger, and pulled me aside. "That's where the dowsing rods clicked together," she muttered quietly.

"Oh good grief! Quit imagining things!"

"Well, it's just a comment."

"It's ridiculous, and you know it." The last thing I wanted was a police investigation in my own front yard. Maybe if I grumped at my sister, I could make it go away.

That does not make sense.

That didn't make a bit of sense. The man had disappeared forty years ago, and now he showed up buried in my front yard. Glaze followed me as I walked back down to the group of men that were still milling around. I told them they could come in for coffee if they needed a break. Bones, tree, duct tape. There wasn't a chance they'd leave the excitement. Glaze tugged at my arm. "Biscuit, look," she said.

I leaned across the duct tape next to her and peered into the hole. The disarranged skeleton looked sad. I could see a recognizable hand on the downhill side of the hole. Out of curiosity, I leaned over farther and saw another one bunched up about a foot and a half away from the first one. "I see it, Glaze," I said. "Let's go back inside."

"No, you don't understand." She pointed off to the other side of the hole. I stared at what she'd found. Glaze motioned to Bob as he came out of the house. He must have been calling the medical examiner. It would take more than an hour for him to get here. But you didn't fiddle around with bones. Especially not now with what Glaze had just seen. When Bob walked closer to us, Glaze asked him, "Why are there three hands?"

"That's why I just called the medical examiner and the GBI." He put a gentle hand on my shoulder. "I think you're going to lose one of your flower beds," he said.

I'll have to call Glenda and cancel our retreat, I thought. Doggone it. First my flower beds and then my vacation.

Chapter 32

SAM WAS TIRED of the subject. They'd been talking about it in hushed tones off and on all day. Now, just minutes before they had to leave for the Halloween party, Easton brought it up again. She crossed her arms in front of her and looked up at Sam who leaned against the doorframe watching her. "I just don't know, Sam," she said. "I can't remember for sure, but all of a sudden it looked so familiar. Of course, I was only five or six. I'm pretty sure it happened right there. I think I may have been hiding under that big hedge across the street."

Sam nodded. "There are a lot of hedges in town."

"I know."

"Do you remember anything at all about the guy? What he looked like?"

"No." She paused and her face went slack, so Sam knew she was really thinking, not just pretending to think. "I don't *think* so, but there was something different about him. I just can't remember what it was. All I remember was seeing him dig that hole, and then I ran away."

"Did he see you? You've always had that mop of red hair down your back."

"How would I know if he saw me? I was running for my life. I was terrified. I thought he was the boogeyman." Easton faced the mirror, but Sam didn't think she was looking at herself. More like she was looking inside. "I knew all the shortcuts," she went on. "He never could have caught me."

"Well, he didn't catch you. That's the important thing." Sam thought for a moment and added, "You need to tell Bob about this."

"But there's nothing to tell. I saw somebody I can't identify digging a hole, but I'm not sure it was that one. I ran away. How would it help to tell that?"

"Easton. There was a dead body in that hole. You have to tell Bob. Tell him at the party tonight. He's a good man. He'll listen to you."

Easton shook herself. "I'll think about it," she said. "Speaking of the party, do you like my pirate costume?"

"You already know what I think. You're just changing the subject."

Easton stood up and fiddled with the sash around her waist. "My voice is so low anyway, I can lower it another notch and spend the whole party saying 'avast me hearties!' and 'walk the plank!'"

"Avast me hearties? What on earth does that mean anyway?" Sam fingered Easton's plywood broadsword.

She tossed her head, sending her hair into a gyration of red flame, and leaned against the dressing table. "I don't know, but it sounds good, don't you think? Nobody in a million years will guess it's me."

Sam couldn't see Easton wanting to remain anonymous. Usually she expected to be the center of attention. She had a way about her that had been dangerous from the time she was eight or nine, but Sam had never figured out how to curb her need to latch onto people, particularly men. It had already caused her a heap of trouble. Sam had bailed her out a couple of times before she ran off with that scumbag. I don't know how to do tough love, Sam thought. Of course, keeping her from getting lambasted by those irate wives she left in her wake frequently meant leaving town, finding a new town, a new job, a new apartment. Maybe Easton should have paid for her mistakes, faced the wives, explained to the children of the families she'd broken up. But they were both used to running away. Sam had never run away from Easton, though. There was too much obligation. That was the only word for it.

How she ever had talked Sam into going to the town Halloween party dressed up as *Easton Hastings*, Sam would never know. The vibrant wig, as gorgeous as Easton's own hair, was itchy. The flyaway hair tickled. And the purple pants and bright yellow blouse, even though they fit, didn't sit well. Sam pulled down on the crotch. "These things are too tight. It's a good thing you didn't try to talk me into wearing one of those dresses of yours."

"Silly! You wouldn't have been able to fill them out where they need filling."

Sam had to admit she was right about that. "Why'd you bring this wig? We didn't know about the costume party before we came."

"I keep it around for bad-hair days. Nobody can tell the difference." Easton fussed some more with her hair, trying to tame it into a pony-tail of some sort. "Here," she directed, "help me with this. Put it in a French braid or something so I can get the bandana around it."

"I should have been a hairdresser." Sam's stepmother never would take care of Easton's hair; their father didn't care. So years ago Sam had stepped in as surrogate mother, substitute father, sister and brother, aunt and uncle, whatever was needed. Sam played all the family roles just for Easton.

The braiding gave Sam time to think. All Easton had going for her was her hair and her singing. Her face was unmemorable to say the least. She would be truly anonymous once the hair was covered, as long as she kept her mouth shut and her hands to herself. Not much chance of that though.

Sam had inherited the Cherokee facial planes. Easton just had the hair. Sam had a bright mind. Easton, sad to say–and Sam never said it out loud–was flighty, and tended to be more frustrating than a cat that peed outside the litter box. But she was family, and you didn't desert family just because they had no sense of boundaries whatsoever. Maybe she got it from Rupert, Sam thought. Darker thoughts tried to surface, but Sam didn't want to go there. Sam didn't want to think about coming home as a kid to a house that Easton had run from an hour before. Sam didn't want to remember searching Martinsville for a disappearing sister. Sam wouldn't think about drying Easton's tears after cornering her behind the old Millicent mansion or in the grocery store parking lot or under a hedge or between gravestones in the Old Church's cemetery. And Sam wouldn't think about remembering farther back, being five and running to hide in the caves. Sam understood. Oh yes. But now wasn't the time to think about it.

Once the French braid hugged Easton's hair to her head, she folded an enormous red bandana into a triangle and bound it over her forehead, tying it in back. All the glory of her hair was extinguished, but she didn't seem to notice that in her delight over the wide black eye patch she adjusted until it sat just so. "Can't see a thing with this on," she said. "You're going to have to guide me up the library steps."

Sam was assaulted with memories and ghost-like images that wouldn't go away. Sam needed a long walk before the Halloween party, a chance to lay some of the ghosts to rest before facing the friendly chaos of the town gathering. Even if only half the town showed up, the old mansion, big as it was, would be packed. Good thing it wasn't raining. Maybe people would loiter on the front steps and the garden paths out in back. That would help some.

"I'm going to circle the long way around. I need a walk to clear my head."

"Why? You haven't been drinking."

"That's not the only thing that muddies up a brain, baby sister."

"Quit calling me that. I grew up a long time ago."

Sam watched Easton's reflection fiddle some more with the bandana, and settled for a neutral reply. "You look like a real pirate."

The smile was almost as bright as her hair. Maybe Easton had more going for her than Sam gave her credit for. She lifted the eye patch and tilted her head to one side. "You don't look at all like me, except for the wig. Nobody's going to be fooled."

"How about if I practice the way you walk on my way to the library?"

Easton's eyes flitted back and forth between Sam's reflection and her own. "Won't work. They'll know exactly who you are. I guess your costume wasn't such a good idea after all."

"Don't be ridiculous. Of course it was. I'll see you at the party."

"Don't forget, we've got a surprise cooked up."

"Can't wait to see what it is. And remember to talk to Bob."

"I don't want to. Not after . . . Can't you talk to him for me?"

Sam paused, doorknob in hand. "Not after *what?* What are you talking about?"

Easton moved the hairbrush to one side. "Nothing," she said.

Sam's voice lowered a few tones. "Easton."

"I . . . I just asked him for a kiss, that's all."

Sam's knuckles went white on the doorknob. "You what?"

Easton crossed her arms and raised her chin, then dropped her eyes. "It was just . . . friendly . . . sort of."

"I've seen your idea of *friendly*, little sister," Sam said, "and I don't like it one bit. You had no right. He's married, doggone you. He's married."

"So what? A little kiss can't hurt. Anyway, he wouldn't kiss me." She turned her face to one side. "Don't look at me like that."

"You have to chase everything in pants, don't you? Why can't you grow up and take some responsibility for what you're doing?"

"Don't yell at me. Please, Sam."

Sam took a long, deep breath. "You are going to talk to Bob tonight and apologize for your . . . actions." Sam practically spit out the word. "Then you tell him about the man you saw digging that grave. How old you were when it happened, and exactly what you saw. Everything you can remember." Another deep breath. "And keep your hands to yourself while you do it."

Easton took a good-sized breath herself. "Will you go with me?"

For just a moment, the shaft of light was there, along with the beginning of a question. But then the light was gone. "Not a chance," Sam said and turned back toward the door. "That's your job, little sister."

MY FEET HURT. Dressing as Little Bo Peep for the town Halloween party had been a mistake. These black-strapped Mary Janes were agony. I should have sat down, but then I wouldn't have been able to see the children's costume parade. All the Martinsville kids had homemade costumes, thank goodness. I cringed every time I saw those catalogs with the prefab costumes. Why would anybody want to look identical to anyone else? We had beautiful little princesses and five or six pirates of varying heights, ghosts and witches, three frogs and two gorillas, a giraffe, a ham sandwich, and even a cardboard telephone complete with numbered buttons. Except for my feet, I was thoroughly enjoying myself.

From my perch on the stair landing, I watched Little Red Riding Hood hand her basket to the Big Bad Wolf while she adjusted her red cloak. We should have put more fabric into Glaze's hood. It didn't cover her silver hair. Of course, from the look in the wolf's eyes, Tom didn't seem to mind one bit.

I saw a vampire, three ghosts, and a high-spirited reindeer with a red nose disappear out the front door, toward the relative quiet of the front porch. I envied them. I spotted my three Petunias–a witch, Mother Goose, and a yellow daisy. Mother Goose was signing people up for library cards. I'd seen her hand out at least five applications. Maybe this hadn't been such a bad idea after all. I was glad, though, that I'd opted out of being on the planning committee. Clara had horned her way in. Of course, she had done a lot of work on the invitation flyers. And she'd organized the set-up for the potluck. Still, I didn't like her.

Speaking of the devil, she and Hubbard wove their way through the throng. He was Henry the Eighth–leave it to Hubbard to insist on being a *king.* I wondered if Clara knew that Henry had killed off most of his wives. With his square face, he even *looked* like Henry. It was bizarre. I pictured Clara with her head on the block. Delightful image.

"Mother! What are you doing dressed like that? You don't know anything about sheep."

What did that have to do with anything? I was proud that I didn't retort in kind. Well, not too much in kind. "And you don't know that much about Indians."

"Jason does." Sally, dressed as an extremely pregnant Sacagawea–who *had* carried a child on the Lewis and Clark expedition–scanned the room. I saw a Pilgrim approaching. Whoops! Maybe Sally was supposed to be Pocahontas. Was Pocahontas ever pregnant?

My own fluffy sheep, sporting a pair of white wool socks as droopy ears, waylaid Sally's Pilgrim and motioned back toward the check-out desk where long folding tables sported a thick veneer of assorted potluck dishes.

The tallest pirate, who'd been flirting with every man in the room for the past hour, headed our way. Why she ever chose to cover up her one glory, I'd never know. She seemed to think that nobody recognized her, but she'd irritated every woman in the room by swatting the female behinds with her plywood sword, while grating out stupid piratical comments. And her arm-wrestling matches with the men, always ending in her losing but somehow entwined in her opponents' costumes, hadn't endeared her to a single female soul, either.

Sadie, the yellow daisy, stopped the pirate. They held a hurried consultation. Sadie took Easton's hand and led her to an impromptu stage set up just in front of the children's section. Sadie stepped up on it, with a boost from Easton. There was a microphone. Where had that come from? Sadie tapped the mike a couple of times and called for attention.

"I'm so happy all of you decided to join us for our little Halloween party," she said. "As you know, we wanted to introduce you to our fine library, if you haven't seen it before. Be sure you fill out an application for a library card. Every application will go in that big bowl, and we'll draw for door prizes later on."

A few people began moving toward the desk where Esther–Mother Goose–supervised a stack of forms.

"And if you already have a library card," Sadie continued, "fill out one of the little slips of paper . . ." Esther waved them in the air, ". . . and we'll have a separate drawing from those. But . . ."

Sadie paused and the crowd settled down. She's quite the showman, I thought. Didn't know she had it in her.

"We've planned a little surprise for you. Some of us decided we need an official town song."

Oh no, I thought. One of those cutesy ditties where the first letter of each line spells out Martinsville. I did a mental count. Twelve lines. I could handle that.

"One of our town residents," she went on, "is a talented composer. A couple of weeks ago I found out that I'm not the only one who likes his tunes." She nodded toward the front row and Easton joined her on stage. Easton? I could hear, sense, feel an undercurrent course through the room. About half testosterone and half estrogen.

Sadie reached into a pocket on the front of her daisy costume and pulled out her harmonica. "This song," she said, "is all about home and what it means. I hope you enjoy it.

Her harmonica lessons had certainly paid off. She played through a haunting melody. I recognized it. I'd heard Melissa humming it a few days before. Easton stepped closer to the mike and began the verse. Her speaking voice may have sounded like gravel. Her singing voice, though, was a luscious low contralto that filled the room with the plaintive lyric. It sounded nothing like Roger's off-key gurgling. But he sure could write a good tune.

The words, though. The words pulled me into Roger's love of his hometown. They told of the people, the caring, the families. The joyful recognition of deep, long-lasting friendships. They welcomed home the traveler who might have left for a time, but whose roots were here, here in this quiet town. It was the story of the prodigal son. As Easton sang it, it was the story of the prodigal daughter. Halfway through the third verse, she broke down. Sadie kept playing for a moment, then stopped. I watched Easton's tears and wondered what to do.

From the middle of the crowd, a high soprano voice took up the song. Ariel, dressed as Elvis, started threading her way toward the little stage. The parting of the Red Sea gave her a clear path. As she stepped up beside Easton, Sadie resumed playing.

Once it was over, after a moment of awed silence followed by thunderous applause, Sadie invited Roger to join them on stage. "I love . . . love this town," he stammered. He swiped back his tears and hugged each of the women on the stage. The longest hug was for little pear-shaped Sadie. He turned back to the mike. "Thank you for believing in me."

"What was that all about?" Sally jostled my elbow. "What did I miss?"

I didn't even know she'd been gone. "Where were you?"

"I had to go to the bathroom. I left while they were talking about door prizes. Did Roger win?"

I knew I couldn't explain the last few minutes to her. "No," I said. "They sang a song."

Easton stepped down from the stage. People, men and women alike, reached out to touch her arm. I heard murmurs of *thank you, thank you* that followed her to the bottom of the stairs. She still held her broadsword, but not like a weapon anymore. More like a cane. Sally must not have noticed the difference. She took a step forward. "If you so much as think about touching me with that ridiculous sword, I'll punch you in your eye patch." Was this my daughter speaking? "And if you hit my mother," she continued, "I'll poke out your other eye."

Easton backed up as if she'd been struck. "Sam's not here," she said to me. "I need help. I need Bob to help me go look for Sam."

Fat chance, I thought. I'm not letting you haul my husband out into the dark, especially not after that glorious singing. "I'm sure Sam's just late. He'll show up."

She sent me a quizzical glance before turning away to search the crowd. When Bob walked up with my glass of lemonade, he echoed my sentiment. "Sam always did like long walks," he said. "Don't you worry." Good for Bob. "Great singing, by the way," he added. I figured Sam had probably decided to skip the whole thing. And I hadn't seen Louise, the sister, all evening. Maybe she had on a really good costume. I looked around the room, but couldn't spot her. What a shame. Their little sister finally did something good, and they both missed it.

Part III
November

Chapter 33

Friday, November 1st

IF HIS TRUCK hadn't broken down, Roger would have made one garbage run yesterday in the sunshine and only one run today in the rain. No such luck. It was two long garbage runs today with thunder as his only companion. Thunder and wet garbage. And wind.

He slid the last of the heavy grocery store bins up the ramp. Even in the rain, the ramp worked pretty well, but was more slippery than Roger liked. He'd thought about installing non-slip treads, but then he wouldn't have been able to slide the big bins. Sliding was easier than lifting, and Roger, no heavyweight, knew his limitations. A foot or two before the end of the ramp, a particularly vicious blast of wind forced Roger to lean farther forward than he should have. His right foot slipped out from under him. He lunged against the bin, then lost control as it slid backwards. He scrambled to keep from being run over by the flyaway garbage container, lost the battle, and watched as it struck his steel-toed work boot, overbalanced, tipped, and spewed its contents across the grocery store parking lot, like a bloated dark blue cat coughing up a hairball on a gray bed-spread.

Once Roger righted himself and the garbage bin, he ran to retrieve as much of the paper and plastic as he could catch.

Luckily the wind plastered most of it up against the back wall of the store, and he peeled it off with wet hands that were going numb in the frigid blast. Then he set to work picking up deflated boxes, packing material, lettuce leaves, overripe bananas, and assorted broken crates. He paused over a pile of sodden red fur intertwined with a tangle of thin wire and some of the dead bananas. A stuffed toy? A bathroom rug? A mop? No, it was hair. An enormous doll's head of hair, but without the head. He stuffed it into the bin along with bunches of wadded-up plastic and Styrofoam, forced the lid back into place and clamped it down.

By the time he hefted the bin onto the bottom of the ramp, shoved the whole thing up and into the truck, took down the ramp and threaded it between the bins, he seriously doubted his sanity. Sure he was making good money, but his numb hands were saying, "Quit, quit, quit." He swore under his breath. "Don't be ridiculous," he told himself, since no one was around to listen. "They may have liked my song last night, but nobody offered to buy my CD." He slid behind the wheel and turned the key. "I might as well haul trash."

BOB HAD BEEN gone for hours. I wondered how much trouble it was to retrieve the body from the now-defunct town dock. This rain couldn't have helped the process. How awful to drown in a river that ordinarily was so mild.

I hadn't expected him home for lunch, but here it was 6:00 and he was still gone. And no phone calls, either. Dinner–the soup I so often made when I was doing the cooking–would hold on the stove. But I was more than a little bit hungry. In fact, my stomach grumbled with an insistence that was hard to ignore. I knew enough by this time about being a small-town cop's wife not to be too concerned, but couldn't help feeling a wave of pity for him, out in the downpour. And self-pity for me, sitting there waiting and wondering.

Mostly I wondered about what I was going to do with the mess in my front yard. They'd found two complete skeletons yesterday, which meant that the front flower bed was now a former flower bed. The medical examiner came roaring in within a few hours after Bob called for help. People took pictures and dug and lifted bones and bagged and labeled and sifted and packed all morning and half the afternoon. The yard was a disaster. And the poor Welsh family. They were sure it was Augustus with the bent leg bone, even if the officials said that nothing could be verified until after a thorough examination. I truly did hate to be picky where dead bodies were concerned, but in one short day I'd lost a tree and a flower bed and my retreat with Glenda. The rain had turned the whole mess into a quagmire of mud. It was depressing.

I stood up, pulled a blue-ringed bowl out of the cupboard, and ladled out a cup of rich soup. Cream of leek. Comfort food for yet another rainy day. I was so glad I didn't have to be out in the deluge. Glad, too, that I didn't have to look at a dead boater. The soup tasted divine. I sliced a thick slab of oatmeal bread and sat back down. As I debated whether or not to page Bob, the front door squeaked open. When had it started squeaking? That was all I needed. I hated squeaky doors. The wood must have swollen with all the humidity in the air. "I'm in here, honey," I called. There was no answer.

My feet, still sore from my Little Bo Peep shoes last night, objected to standing, so I simply waited, listening to him take off his raincoat, hang it on the hook by the door, and slip out of his wet shoes. I could even tell when he pulled off his squishy socks and donned his slippers. I hoped he hadn't dropped his socks on the wide hardwood floorboards. There was a rubber mat next to the door; hopefully he'd left them there. I'd agreed some time ago to a truce about socks on the floor, but when they were wet, they could do some damage. As he walked into the kitchen, though, I forgot all about wet socks and water spots on the hardwood. He looked like heck.

I pushed myself up from the table, but he motioned me back as he turned on the hot water in the sink. He spent an inordinate amount of time washing his hands. Then he lifted his big blue mug from the rack and poured himself some coffee. I watched him trudge across the floor. He was usually so light on his feet, surprising in such a tall man. Something was very wrong. I had no clue what it was, but I knew it must be awful.

"Did you identify the body?" It might have been someone he knew. That was the only thing I could think of that could have caused such a pinched blue-white pallor to his face.

"Yes," he said. The slow drawing out of that word sounded like what Grandma Martelson always referred to as a death knell. In this case, we already knew that someone had died. "Yes," he repeated.

I waited quite awhile for him to go on. Somehow the questions I had didn't seem appropriate in the face of his obvious anguish. Instead, I patted Marmalade and waited.

"It was," he said, and paused. "It was . . ."

I could hear my blood pounding through my ears. It sounded very loud.

"It was . . ." His voice failed. His hands were shaking. I reached out and laid my hand on his forearm.

"Someone we know?" I asked.

"Sam," he said. The boy he and Tom had gotten into all sorts of scrapes with when the three of them were kids. The one everyone had been telling us about. "I recognized . . . Sam has . . . had . . . an amazing face. Lots of cheek bones and heavy eyebrows." Just like his sister Louise, I thought. "There was no way to tell the exact cause of death," he went on. "That'll have to wait for the autopsy, . . ." He lifted his cup, but set it right back down. ". . . but Nathan said it looked like she'd been . . . strangled."

"She?" I blurted out. "I thought you said it was Sam?"

Bob's eyes were bleary and red-ringed. "Sam, yes," he said. "Samantha Hastings. Samantha Louise. She hated her middle name." He sank his head into his hands, and didn't say anything else.

"Her last name isn't Hastings," I told him. "It's Cronin. She's divorced."

Bob's face sort of flattens out when he's bewildered. "How would you know that, Woman?"

"Her library card," I said. It made perfect sense to me. What didn't make sense to me was why he hadn't told me that Sam was female. And why hadn't she told me she was Sam?

Bob shook his head. "If you met her, then you already knew she was Sam," he said.

"No. She said she didn't use her first name, and I told her just to put what she wanted to be called on the application. She put Louise."

Bob's face went slack and gray at the same time. I'd read about things like that, but this was the first time I ever saw it happen. His voice, when he managed to speak, was a study in agony. "Oh no," he said. "Please, God, no. She wouldn't . . ."

"Wouldn't what?"

He seemed to tune out, his eyes a little bit glazed, like he was focusing on some sort of internal movie. It took a moment for him to come back. He twisted his coffee mug around a couple of times. "It was silly, I guess," he said. "We were just kids."

It didn't seem appropriate to say anything, so I sipped some tea and watched him gather his thoughts. And wondered what was coming.

"We were maybe fourteen or fifteen." Oh dear. Did I want to hear this? "Tommy was sick one day," he went on, "and Sam and I took some lunch over to the caves . . ."

"SAM, DOGGONE YOU! Stop running so fast."

"Don't worry. I won't lose you." Sam giggled and turned around to face Bobby. "You've got the food." She kept walking backwards. Light from one of the vents in the ceiling of the cave lit her hair, brushed her nose, illumined Pepper's head briefly. Then it was Bobby's turn to walk through the beam. Bobby loved the cathedral-like quality of the caves, even though they scared him sometimes. Of course, he'd never admit that to Sam. He hardly even admitted it to himself. Maybe it was that light, he'd told himself later. Maybe the light was why he said, "Sam?"

"Yeah?"

"You think you're ever gonna marry me someday?" It was funny, Bobby thought, how quiet a cave could be when nobody's barely breathing.

"What kinda question is that?"

Bobby wasn't standing in the light anymore, and the question did sound a little silly now that he thought about it. "Oh, nothing," he said. "I was just kind of wondering."

Sam leaned down to pat Pepper's upturned head, then nudged a small stone over toward the lip of one of those deep holes. "Tell you what," she said. "If I ever decide I'm going to marry you, I'll start telling people to call me Louise."

"Louise? You hate that name!"

"Yeah. Well, I guess that settles that." She spun around and took off at a trot with Pepper right behind her. "I'm hungry. Let's see how fast we can get to our club house."

BOB'S COFFEE MUG must have been getting dizzy, he'd been turning it around for such a long time.

A cup cannot be dizzy.

I kept smoothing Marmalade's fur from the top of her head all the way along her spine.

Scratch there please.

She wiggled around, arching her back underneath my hand as Bob quit talking and turned his cup around one more time. "We never mentioned that day again," he said. "It was like it never happened. And then, a couple of years after that, right after she graduated from Keagan High, she left. Took Easton and left. Tom and I really missed her."

"At least you still had Tom," I said.

"Um-hmm." Around went the coffee mug another time or two. "I'd already started dating Sheila. Then I went to Nam. And then I came back and got married."

And divorced six years later, I thought, but I didn't say it out loud.

"Sam kind of got lost in the shuffle. I never thought she'd . . . remember." He looked around the kitchen. I couldn't tell if he was seeing it or something else. "I have to get back to the station," he said. "I just wanted to come home and . . ." He stood rather abruptly, reached across the table and pulled me up into an awkward hug as we both tried to get our feet untangled from the chair legs. "I love you, Woman," he said. There was just the tiniest bit of emphasis on the third word.

> "THIS IS WRRT, the voice of Keagan County, broadcasting from Garner Creek, Georgia, in the heart of the Metoochie River Valley."

Radio Ralph sounded particularly florid this evening. I reached for the radio to switch it off, but stopped when he said,

> "The Metoochie River claimed a sad victim this morning. Kayakers found the body of a woman tangled in the wreckage of the Martinsville town dock where it had jammed near the boulders that normally block the entrance to the Gorge. All those kayakers and canoeists have been whooping it up, taking advantage of how deep the Metoochie's been because of all this rain we've been having. I suppose finding a dead body might slow them down a bit. Now we don't know who the woman was, but someone close to the investigation said that the body may have been somebody who had a boating accident. Her kayak may have been washed farther downstream . . ."

Someone close to the investigation? He had to be kidding. Apparently the rumors were circulating. I wondered how long it would be before they got the story right.

Chapter 34

Saturday, November 2nd

MY SKIN FELT creepy, crawly. I stepped around Marmalade. She looked so calm, sitting in the middle of the living room floor while I paced back and forth around her from the fireplace to the couch to the office doorway and back around to the fireplace.

Somebody had buried those two men in my front yard forty years ago. I swallowed to try to keep down the bad taste that flooded my mouth. Somebody knew. I felt old. And then there was Sam. Bob still didn't know why anyone would have killed her. While he was investigating, I wrestled with a monster inside me, and I didn't know if I'd win. As soon as I found out that Sam was dead, my first thought–well, my second one, after I wondered why Bob hadn't told me she was a female–was that it was Easton who should have been murdered.

Setterlady likes dogs. And birds. She does not understand me, though.

That would have solved a lot of problems around town. But I didn't believe that, did I? Surely I wasn't as vindictive as that. I believed in communication. I believed in confronting problems and finding a win/win situation. But I was seeing a piece of me that I didn't like admitting to myself. Even after the song, even after seeing how vulnerable she looked on that stage, I still wanted to cut that hair of hers down to a stubble.

I am glad I am a cat. You like my hair.

I knew it was totally unkind of me, but I giggled at the thought that if Easton ever went to Sharon to have her hair trimmed, she was in for a big surprise. Sharon would be quite likely to let her scissors slip. The giggle didn't last long, though, once I remembered Bob's gray face. I turned on all the lights in the living room, including that glaring overhead light that has always bothered me. Someone put a big ugly light up there where it did no real good whatsoever and then we had to add lamps all around the room so we could read the newspaper or a book without going blind. Of course, right now that overhead light felt vaguely comforting, as if it could make the shadows go away.

The rain was still holding off, but the day had been cloudy. Bob was back at the station trying to find out where Louise . . . Samantha . . . Sam . . . I didn't know what to call her. But he needed to know where she'd been for the last number of years. And Easton was no help at all, or so he'd told me when he phoned an hour ago. I sincerely hoped he wasn't questioning her without witnesses present. He needed that deputy the town council had been talking about.

I consciously stopped gritting my teeth and turned on the radio to flip through the stations. Not many were available. Marmalade jumped up onto the table and watched me. I heard a brief section of a news report.

Find the songs. They are good to hear.

I didn't want to hear talking, particularly not about genocide. I wanted music, so I kept going on the dial until I heard the last few bars of "Moonlight Serenade."

I knew it was in there somewhere.

I hoped they'd keep playing other songs in that vein. Sure enough, here came the opening strains of "Dancing in the Dark."

Talk about old. . . . That was when the overhead light went out.

I whirled around as Bob encircled me with his arms. “Hey, Woman,” he said. “I didn’t mean to startle you.” He pulled me closer to him and began to sway slowly back and forth.

I waited a moment for my heart to stop racing. When did the front door stop squeaking? I needed that early warning sign. Squeaky doors are such a help. Adrenaline had its good points, I supposed, but on a dark night after a murder, and after all my dark thoughts, I didn’t need any more of it flooding my system.

The swaying turned into a definite Latin rhythm. I leaned back and took a good look at this man I had married half a year ago. “I didn’t know you could dance!”

He nuzzled his chin against the top of my ear and said, “You never asked me.”

Oh, well. I relaxed into the gentle rhythm and forgot about murder and blood for a few blissful moments, until Bob whispered in my ear, “And I didn’t know you *couldn’t* dance.”

I took my right foot off the top of his left foot. “You never asked me,” I said.

Chapter 35

Sunday, November 3rd

BOB CAME HOME from the station for lunch, and probably to get away from the thought of the murder even for a short while. Cops, I was finding out, don't have weekends. I suppose I should have let him have his peace, but I still couldn't understand why he hadn't told me that Sam wasn't a man. So I asked him.

"Of course she wasn't," he said. "Everybody knew that."

"Everybody did not." My poor communication skills were surfacing.

"Yes they did." He sounded incredibly weary. "The whole town knew her. The whole town knew us."

I didn't like the sound of that *us*. "Us?" I said.

"Yeah. Tommy and Sam and me. We were like a team. We always got in trouble together. I told you about the time we got lost." His voice began to tremble just a little. Surely he wasn't going to cry. But no, it was a laugh getting started. "When we were about thirteen or fourteen, there was a big Halloween party at school, and Sam talked us into going as Adam and Eve. And the snake. Tommy was the snake. You should have seen his costume. Sam made him a forked tongue out of yarn that she braided. We glued it to his upper lip."

I didn't want to interrupt, but I did want him to get to the Adam and Eve costumes. It didn't seem to me there was much leeway there.

He took a big bite of his sandwich and munched it for an inordinately long time. "Sam and I," he said, "wore these big long tee-shirts over our clothes. We'd sewed some green felt leaves on them. We didn't know what fig leaves looked like, so we traced oak leaves on the felt and cut them out. Sam wore a long black wig she borrowed from somebody in town."

It sounded kind of cute, I had to admit, especially now that I knew they were wearing clothes.

"The only trouble was that Leon Martin's wife—"

"Let me guess. He was the town chair and she was just like Clara, right?"

"Right." He went on with his story. "She and some of the more vociferous parents decided that what we'd done was not only risqué, but blasphemous as well. That's what they said. They hauled us into the principal's office and accused us of all sorts of things. We thought they were nuts, but we were too cowed to object, so we had to apologize and promise never to do anything like that again. In fact, they told us we could never wear costumes again." He cocked his head to one side and looked down at his uniform shirt. "Maybe that's why I like being a cop. The uniform. The costume."

He sounded so sad, I wanted to take him in my arms. But then he chuckled. "We got them back, though. Every Halloween after that, we thought up great costumes that we didn't make or wear. We just told all the other kids about them. It was funnier than heck."

"What sorts of costumes?"

"Things like threatening to dress up like Leon and Matilda."

"Her name was Matilda?"

"Uh-huh. I said I was going to shave my hair off so I'd look like Leon. And Samantha was going to pad her clothes so she'd be pudgy like Matilda. And Tom was going to lead us around all day on a dog chain." By this time Bob was laughing uncontrollably. The story lost quite a lot in translation, but I could imagine that fourteen-year-olds might have thought it was hilarious.

He sobered, though. "She was a good, good friend. And when I find out who killed her, I'm going to have a hard time staying professional."

I HAD A gut feeling that Bob wouldn't want me discussing the case, but after all, Elizabeth Hoskins used to live in the house, and I thought she had a right to know that we'd found two bodies in her front yard. She might even be able to give me an idea I could pass on to Bob.

I wandered over to the desk, moved Marmalade to one side, and picked up my address book. It was still warm where Marmalade had been sitting on it. I knew I'd put Elizabeth's number in there, but she wasn't under E. That page was full. So where would I have put her? H for house-owner? No. G for gardener? No. What a ridiculous way to keep an address book.

What is wrong?

Marmalade shoved her nose against my face with a loud meow. "I don't have time right now, Marmy." Oh, phooey. This infernal system of mine was making me grumpy. I reached out to pat her, but she did one of those slinky cat maneuvers where she pressed her spine down into a U-shape and slid out from under my hand. I must have hurt her feelings. Now I really felt like a cad. No wonder she didn't want me to pat her anymore. She gave me so much love and here I was ignoring her just because I was ticked off.

I'd be in a much better mood if I could find Elizabeth. Let's see. She loved Barley, her old dog. Maybe I put her under B for Barley's mom. I thumbed back a few pages and looked. Wrong again. Doggone it! Where was she? I started at the beginning.

Finally found her on the V page. V? How stupid! Why on earth had I put her there? Oh, of course. V for vegetable garden.

I picked up Marmalade. "Sorry, sweetie."

You could scratch my chin.

She nuzzled her head into my hand and wiggled it around until my fingers found that soft fur underneath her chin.

Thank you.

Patting a cat or a dog helps lower the blood pressure. It certainly seemed to be working on mine. I tucked Marmy under my arm and called Elizabeth.

"Of course I have time for a visit," she said, with a quavery laugh in her voice. "I just love visitors. Maybe you'll have a little glass of wine with me." She turned serious. "You know I'm not driving anymore."

"No, Elizabeth. I'm sorry I didn't know. Can I bring you anything? Stop by the store for you on the way up there?" I felt momentarily guilty for not having dropped by even once. But usually when I went to Happy Days, I was on the other side of the facility, visiting Grandma and Grandpa in the nursing home. That was no excuse. I should have been more attentive. Of course, I hadn't known that she was impaired in any way. When she sold us the house, she'd said she just didn't want a big old house to take care of after her husband (and her dog) died.

"No, dear. I don't need a thing," she said. "They take good care of us here. I have my little apartment, and I eat all my meals in the lovely dining room. It's such good food, too. Nothing I can't chew. I have a denture problem, you know."

That was more information than I wanted. If she'd stopped there, it wouldn't have been so bad, but she proceeded to regale me with a list of all her bowel movements for the last three days. Heaven help me if I ever get to the point where I think that's a valid topic of conversation. It was too late to get out of visiting her, though, since I'd already committed myself. "I'll be there in half an hour," I told her.

Marmalade didn't often want to ride in the car, but she accompanied me out to the Buick and hopped in when I opened the door. It was a partly cloudy day, so I knew she wouldn't get too hot, and I could always leave a window open for her. I moved her carrier from the back seat to the front. Closest thing to a seat belt for a cat.

Sometimes I enjoy riding.

Happy Days was set back from the main road along a winding drive lined with azaleas and dogwoods, with a healthy sprinkling of taller trees that gave glorious shade in the height of the summer. Now, with a lot of the leaves down, the road was dappled with pale sunlight and shadow. I passed the huge goldfish pond, more like a small lake, that insinuated itself beside the road and stretched off under the overhanging trees. Someone had plugged a tremendous amount of money into landscaping this place when it was a private estate five decades ago. Now that it was a private care facility, some of the finer points of floral decor were neglected, but the pond seemed to take care of itself year after year.

I left Marmalade in the car, went up to Elizabeth's room, and had to say yes when she asked if we could walk around the grounds. I hadn't seen her in months, and was surprised at how fragile she looked, as if some vital spark had gone out when she moved away from the Beechnut Lane house.

We rode down on the elevator and walked out past my Buick, so I opened the door for Marmalade. "You don't mind if Marmalade comes along with us, do you?"

"Of course not, she's a good dog."

Dog? I am not a dog.

That was my first hint that maybe Elizabeth wasn't as balanced as I'd thought she was. Maybe she was missing Barley, who was buried in my back yard near the tree line. As we walked slowly along the path toward the pond, Elizabeth chattered gaily about nothing in particular. I tuned out long enough to wonder if Glaze's dowsing abilities would extend to finding Barley's grave. I knew it was somewhere around the small dogwood tree in the back yard, but Barley died a year ago and it was a private funeral.

I know where it is. I sat on the fence and watched the burial.

I listened to tales about Perry, her late husband, and their honeymoon in Asheville, all the while wondering how I was going to broach the subject of the two bodies under the tree. At the far end of the pond, we sat down on one of the many convenient benches set along the pathway. "I have some sad news, Elizabeth. It's about the Beechnut Lane house."

"Yes?" She seemed very alert.

She is not alert. She still thinks I am a dog.

"The big old dogwood tree in the front yard uprooted in all the rain we've been having. I guess the roots weren't very deep." It took her a moment to answer. I watched a man in the distance begin to stroll down the path. He disappeared behind a tree trunk and then emerged on the other side as he rounded the pond.

"That was a lovely tree," she finally said. "I remember planting it. It grew so well those first few years."

"You planted it yourself?"

"Well of course I did. I planted everything in that yard."

Poor Elizabeth. I could imagine her kneeling right over those graves, not even knowing there were two dead people below her. "It must have been tiny when you planted it."

"Oh, it was just a baby. But I knew it would grow up big and strong. I'm sorry it had to die. What did you do with it?"

"We've cut it up for firewood. It seemed a shame to let good wood go to waste."

"Yes, it would be good for firewood."

"Elizabeth? I need to tell you something else."

"Yes, dear?"

"When the tree fell over, they found some bones underneath it."

"Oh that's nice." Nice? That's not what I would have called it. "What are you going to do with them?" she asked.

"The police had to take them. We think somebody was murdered and buried in your front yard."

"Oh." She was quiet for a long time. I didn't know what to say, so I didn't say anything. I wondered if she'd even understood me. A splash in the goldfish pond caught Marmalade's attention, and she wandered over that direction. I watched her pad across the asphalt walkway and hop onto the low brick wall that lined the edge of the pool. Clouds that had been hiding the sun all day blew apart, and sunlight glinted on the water, throwing ripples of light up the tree trunks beside the pond. Marmalade seemed to be watching the reflections. She leaped onto the tree trunk as if she wanted to catch the light. Then she did a fair imitation of a squirrel, hopping up to one of the lower branches and then climbing higher up the trunk. She constantly amazed me. I had no idea she could scale a tree.

I have many other talents.

As I watched, she stretched out along one of the branches, rather like a leopard, with all four paws hanging over the sides. I hoped she could get down by herself when it was time to go. The reflected sunlight played across her face as she closed her eyes, the picture of feline contentment.

"Did you find all of them?" Elizabeth's voice called me back to the bench.

"All of what?"

"The bodies."

"The bodies? What are you talking about?"

"We put four in the front yard," she said. "And four in the back yard," she added, "where the vegetables are. Oh, we were very respectful, you know. Lyle had dug all those deep garden beds for me, so it was easy for him to plant the bodies."

I felt a squirm coming on. "Elizabeth, do you know what you're saying?"

She arched an eyebrow at me. "Of course I do," she said.

The woman was insane. Insane. "Eight bodies?"

"Yes dear. It was about forty years ago. Lyle was in high school at the time."

Something clicked. How dense could I have been? "Are you telling me that Lyle killed all those salesmen?" I shuddered. He had seemed so pleasant, so ordinary, so sane when he came into the library.

"Oh don't be silly," Elizabeth said. "I did it myself. I got the idea from that play about the two old ladies who killed nice lonely old men. That's what I did with the first one. Mr. Welsh who lived across the street missed his wife so much. He dropped by to visit one evening, and the poor man was miserable. Well, Perry was out of town, and I was having myself a little glass of wine. I did that every now and then. It's healthy, they say." She nodded, as if agreeing with herself. "And I just happened to have some rat poison on hand so I offered him some wine and added the poison to it. I mixed in some other things, too. Just to be safe and to cover up the taste. It worked pretty quickly. I don't think he suffered too much."

Maybe she was senile. Maybe she'd made this up. I most definitely did not want to think I'd bought a house from a murderer. "So you killed Mr. Welsh?" I began, but she interrupted me.

"I don't like to use such words. I prefer to think of sending him on his way. And then I thought it would be quite helpful if I got rid of those obnoxious door-to-door salesmen running around this valley. How they ever found us way down here, I'll never know. I never got rid of anyone if he was wearing a wedding ring. He might have had a really sweet wife at home, and I'd hate to cause any anxiety to her."

What about the parents, brothers, sisters, friends, sweethearts of those men? What about their pain? Their anxiety. Their anguish. I wanted to throw up.

Her eyes went out of focus, as if she were back in her luscious garden on Beechnut Lane. "They make excellent fertilizer, don't you see?"

So much for all my theories about the value of compost. I didn't think I wanted to eat anymore of those veggies.

"And Lyle helped you?"

"He didn't like the idea at first. He was a bit upset with me. I think he said I couldn't just throw a body in the trash." She smoothed out a nonexistent wrinkle on her skirt. "Of course I wouldn't do that. That would have been disrespectful. That's why I needed his help. Those lovely flower beds he dug for me were perfect. Perry–that was my husband, you know." She sighed. "Perry would never have understood, but he traveled a lot himself. I had to hide the bodies somewhere. I certainly didn't want to claim them. So I had Lyle turn up the ground again after dark. The next day I always planted the loveliest flowers and shrubs I could think of. And that one tree, too. Right over Augustus."

She still wore her hair in Mamie Eisenhower bangs, straight out of the fifties. She patted at the rectangular fringe of hair that came precisely halfway down her forehead. "The police came by and asked me about those salesmen, you know. I was on my knees planting some shrubs the first time they stopped to ask me questions. I told them yes, I'd seen those salesmen. I even ordered some things from each of them. But what I didn't tell them was that I invited the men back to my house after dark. I told them my husband was out of town." Her voice took on a distinctly judgmental tone. "And they came back to visit me. Every one of them did. They were not nice men. But I didn't let them leave. That was all." A murderer passing judgment.

Her hypocrisy made me want to scream, but my throat was too tight to make a sound.

Elizabeth reached out a veined hand and patted my knee. “I’ve never told anyone about this. It’s something of a relief to be able to talk about it. It was quite an adventure, and I’ve never been able to share it. Thank you for being so understanding.”

Understanding? I was in shock. This sweet little lady that Bob and I had bought our house from was a serial murderer. “Why did you stop killing after seven?” I croaked.

“Eight, dear. You’re forgetting Mr. Welsh.” She shook her head. “Lyle quit high school and went away, and I didn’t have anyone to bury more bodies for me. It was most inconvenient. Perry never forgave him for quitting high school. You see, Perry didn’t have the advantage of a high school education. Education is very important.” She reached out to pat my knee again, but I shifted farther away from her on the little bench. It was all I could do to keep from jumping up and running. “Perry begged Lyle to come back to town,” she went on, “but Lyle wouldn’t. Perry wrote him out of his will. And I couldn’t think of anyone else who’d be willing to bury my bodies for me, so I had to quit.” She looked up as the man I’d seen earlier strolled by. “Hello, Mr. White. It’s a lovely day for a walk.”

“Yes it is. I heard you telling this young woman about all those bodies. You don’t get any ideas about starting up again.” He shook his finger at her in a playful way.

“I wouldn’t think of it,” she said. They sounded like they were flirting with each other.

When he walked on, I turned back to her. “I thought you said you hadn’t told anyone else about this.”

“Oh, Mr. White doesn’t count. He thinks I made it all up. We usually eat our meals together. He has denture problems, too.”

Marmalade let out a small meow, and I watched her back her way down the tree trunk. I wished I could back my way out of this situation. "I need to go now, Elizabeth." My good manners won out and I held out my hand to help her up.

"That's a lovely idea. I'm a bit tired. Before you leave, though, I'd love to offer you a little glass of wine. I keep some tucked away in my closet."

"That's alright, Elizabeth. I think I'll pass."

"Maybe next time," she said with perfect equanimity.

I DIDN'T WANT to go back to my house. My house where there were six more bodies to dig up. And I knew where. Glaze's dowsing rods had told us. Two more in the other flower bed in front and four in the vegetable garden. I was going to lose my veggies, dammit, all because some seriously warped woman thought she could get away with murder. I needed to tell Bob right away, but I didn't want to go to the station. Clara might have been there. She was always roaming around the town offices. I couldn't face Clara today. I didn't want to go home either.

Our house is safe. There are no bodies inside it.

Marmy meowed quietly beside me. I rolled down my window. Maybe some fresh air would make me think more clearly. Melissa. I'd go to Melissa's and call Bob from there. There wasn't much hurry, I supposed. Those bodies weren't going anywhere, and neither was Elizabeth. She was probably headed down to dinner now with Mr. White. In the dining room. With the bottle of poison. Snap out of it, Biscuit; you're getting delirious.

By the time I reached Martinsville, I'd settled down a bit. The shock was beginning to wear off, even though the horror of it was still there. There was no statute of limitations on murder. My phone call to Bob was going to put an eighty-year-old woman in prison. She'd probably landscape the place during her exercise periods.

First Street looked so blessedly ordinary. The gas station, the grocery store. Mr. Snelling sweeping off the sidewalk in front of his frame shop. I saw Miss Mary putting up a new sign in the window of her dance studio.

I had fully intended to turn right on Magnolia, the fastest way to *Azalea House*, but I saw Sadie's yellow Chevy meandering down the street. Bless her heart, it wasn't worth the worry to try to go uphill when Sadie was headed downhill. I'd never seen her run into anything, but her close calls were hair-raising. So I drove to the end of First Street and turned right onto Willow just in time to see Easton crossing the street with her arms full of cardboard boxes. Right in the middle of Willow Street she stumbled and dropped the whole stack. I pulled the car over to help—not that I particularly felt like helping her, but my good manners got the best of me. Anyway, she'd just lost her sister. I could feel sorry for her about that.

She beat me to it, though. By the time I turned off the engine and unbuckled my seat belt, Easton was stepping up on the curb in front of Rupert's old house. I suppose I ought to volunteer to help her pack things up, I thought. Maybe some other day. I reached for the key, but Marmalade rattled the door to her carrier. It was only a block up to Melissa's, and Sadie was nowhere in sight, so what could possibly happen? Still, cats are supposed to ride in carriers. Oh well. Against my better judgment, I opened the door and Marmalade slid into my lap.

I glanced over at Easton. She'd put the boxes down on the front porch. I watched her carry two of them inside. Once more, I reached for the key, but stopped when I saw Lyle Hoskins, still clothed in light brown. Was that the only color he owned? Maybe if he wore navy blue his ears wouldn't show up so much. That's ridiculous, Biscuit. I took another look at him. He was sneaking down the sidewalk. That was the only word for it. He crept from tree to tree, pausing behind each one. He seemed to be looking across the street, watching Easton pick up the last two boxes. She was, for once, oblivious of a man who had his eyes on her.

Marmalade climbed onto my left arm and put her front feet on the top of the steering wheel. She looked like a riverboat captain. Lyle looked up and down the street. I waved, but he didn't see me through the windshield. He strolled across the street, stopped by the curb and picked up a baseball bat some kid must have left lying there. Then he headed around the uphill side of the house. I didn't like the look of that. Didn't like it at all. "Where's Bob when I need him?" I slipped out of the front seat and shut the door quietly. Marmalade hopped out the window. When I heard Easton scream, I started running.

Charging through an open back door was probably not the smartest thing to do. So, whoever said I was smart? The first thing I did was run over to Easton where she lay sprawled against the kitchen cabinet. The second thing I did was swear at myself for being stupid when Lyle closed the door behind me.

"Don't look at me like that." His lip curled up on the side in a snarl. He motioned me to back away from Easton's body. I was pretty sure she was dead, but it was hard to tell. The baseball bat in his hand had blood on it. She was face down, so I couldn't see how much damage he'd done.

I backed up a couple of steps. The door was too far away. If I could distract him, keep him talking, I might make it. But that wouldn't help Easton. If he hadn't killed her yet, he would just as soon as I ran for it. I couldn't risk that. "I don't understand," I said in the most reasonable tone I could manage. "Why did you kill her?"

That was the wrong topic of conversation. He clenched his teeth and his hands at the same time. At least he wasn't snarling. That was an improvement. "I didn't kill her," he said. He wasn't yelling, but I almost wished he had been. Maybe someone would hear and come to the rescue. His ears had turned a bright red. A sure sign of high blood pressure, I thought. "I didn't know I was killing Sam."

Sam? I was talking about Easton. He killed Sam?"I thought I was killing this one, the redhead. She told me she knew my secret."

I thought it might not be diplomatic to tell him that Easton hadn't known anything about him. He wasn't finished, though.

"I knew somebody saw me that night. I heard someone running away, but I couldn't find where they went. It must have been her."

I was truly curious now. "You thought she saw you?" It sounded neutral enough. Maybe he'd explain himself.

"She told me she knew, so she must have seen me burying Mr. Welsh."

Maybe Easton hadn't been teasing him. Maybe she really had seen something. "Why did you keep burying bodies, if you thought you'd been seen?" It didn't occur to him to ask how I knew that. What was I supposed to say–your sweet little old murdering mother told me, sonny?

"Nothing happened after that first one. Nobody told on me, and I couldn't let Mama get arrested. I just couldn't. It would have killed her to be locked up."

I forgot about caution. I forgot where I was. All I could see was Bob's anguish as he told me about Sam. "So you hid all her murders, and then you killed Sam, and now you're trying to kill Easton?"

His head snapped back and he lunged toward me. "I protected Mama!" he roared. "And I'm the one who got her to stop. I quit high school and left town so she couldn't do it any more. I gave up my education to save her. I gave up my inheritance. I was the good one. I didn't kill those men."

"Maybe not, but you killed Sam."

Uh-oh. He stopped cold and looked at me. His hands tightened on the baseball bat as his face crumpled up. "I didn't know," he said. “I didn’t know it was a wig until it came off her head when I dumped her in the river. I thought she’d go downstream, the current was so strong. I didn’t know what to do with the wig, so I took it behind the grocery store and stuffed it in one of the garbage bins along with the wire.”

Easton moved. I tried to keep my eyes away from her so he wouldn’t turn around. It didn’t work. He saw my face and pivoted. The bat was halfway up when I jumped on his back. I hadn’t known I was going to do it until I was there in mid-air, clinging to the back of a madman who was trying to brain Easton and me both. He spun around and crashed into the wall. My shoulder cushioned the blow for him. Nice of me.

I read somewhere that the easiest way to disable an attacker was to dig your fingernails into his eyeballs. That was just jolly. I hung on for all I was worth. There was no way I’d let go to try to find his eyes. In all the furor, he stumbled over Easton, she let out a yelp, he righted himself, with me still holding on for dear life and screaming my head off.

Easton managed to get to her knees and crawl toward the front room, leaving me to fend for myself. By the time Bob burst into the room, Lyle and I must have looked like the Marx Brothers in one of their slapstick routines.

Bob waved his gun around–he hated that thing–and shouted louder than I’d ever heard him holler. And Lyle simply stopped. I slithered to the ground, and it was over.

That’s when Easton stumbled back into the room and faked a fainting spell. She managed to land rather softly and very provocatively, with her hair spread out around her. I had to admit she looked lovely, even with the blood all down the side of her head. Bob gave her a disgusted look as he slapped some handcuffs on Lyle and started the Miranda routine. Bob didn’t even know, yet, that Lyle had killed Sam. Would he have to give him *another* Miranda warning about that? For a cop’s wife, there was a lot I didn't know.

Marmalade, who had run into the room along with Bob, . . .

I brought him here.

. . . sidled over toward Easton and licked her gently. What a sweet cat.

Thank you.

"Ugh! Cat slobber!"

I already told you, I do not slobber.

The End

Not quite.

Resource List for *Blue as Blue Jeans*

Composting:
Mother Earth News (my favorite magazine)
www.motherearthnews.com

Ecological responsibility:
The Nature Conservancy
www.nature.org

Depression / Bipolar Disorder:

Depression and Bipolar Support Alliance

www.dbsalliance.org

1-800-826-3632

National Institutes of Mental Health (for a depression self-check list)

www.nimh.hih.gov

1-866-615-6464

Suicide Prevention:

1-800-SUICIDE (1-800-784-2433) or

1-800-273-TALK (1-800-273-8255)

www.suicide.org

This website provides links to other suicide prevention sites.

Suicide is never the answer.
Getting help is the answer.

Animal Communication & Ethical Treatment of Animals

There are many fine organizations out there. There are simply two that I regularly support through contributions. I donate a portion of all my book sales to these two organizations, as well as to libraries and local animal shelters wherever I sign books.

The Gorilla Foundation

www.koko.org

The Humane Society of the United States

www.hsus.org

American Red Cross Blood Donation 1-800-GIVELIFE

Please donate blood as often as possible.

Childhood Sexual Abuse Prevention:

Rape Abuse and Incest National Network

RAINN is both a hotline and a referral service to direct you to an approved local resource

1-800 656-HOPE (1-800-656-4673)

www.RAINN.org

Prevent Child Abuse America

1-800-CHILDREN (1-800-244-5373)

www.preventchildabuse.org